THE
SORBONNE AFFAIR

ALSO BY MARK PRYOR

A Hugo Marston Novel

THE
SORBONNE
AFFAIR

MARK PRYOR

SEVENTH STREET BOOKS®
AN IMPRINT OF PROMETHEUS BOOKS
59 JOHN GLENN DRIVE • AMHERST, NY 14228
www.seventhstreetbooks.com

Published 2017 by Seventh Street Books®, an imprint of Prometheus Books

Cover image © Shutterstock
Cover design by Nicole Sommer-Lecht
Cover design © Prometheus Books

Inquiries should be addressed to
Seventh Street Books
59 John Glenn Drive
Amherst, New York 14228
VOICE: 716–691–0133
FAX: 716–691–0137
WWW.SEVENTHSTREETBOOKS.COM

21 20 19 18 17   5 4 3 2 1

Names: Pryor, Mark, 1967- author.
Title: The Sorbonne affair : a Hugo Marston novel / by Mark Pryor.
Description: Amherst, NY : Seventh Street Books, an imprint of Prometheus Books,
   2017. | Series: Hugo Marston ; book seven
Identifiers: LCCN 2017012785 (print) | LCCN 2017018405 (ebook) |
   ISBN 9781633882621 (ebook) | ISBN 9781633882614 (paperback)
Subjects: LCSH: Americans—France—Paris—Fiction. | Murder—Investigation—
   Fiction. | GSAFD: Mystery fiction. | Suspense fiction.
Classification: LCC PS3616.R976 (ebook) | LCC PS3616.R976 S67 2017 (print) |
   DDC 813/.6—dc23
LC record available at https://lccn.loc.gov/2017012785

Printed in the United States of America

*To Ann Collette, with my eternal gratitude for your guidance,
immense appreciation for your belief in me,
and deep admiration for your enthusiasm and honesty.*

CHAPTER ONE

The funeral was held in a small sixteenth-century church, ninety minutes east of Paris. The chapel sat on a hill between two villages, Saint-Jean-de-Vieux and Etange, giving its few regular congregants a beautiful view of the surrounding vineyards. Its small cemetery bristled with headstones, some new but most tilted with age, a hundred years old or more, and while the lush, one-acre space was fuller than the priest and the gravedigger would have liked, both found it hard to say no to grieving families.

This had been Isabelle Severin's church in her final years, and in his mind Father Henri Izner had on several occasions compared the lady with the church. Both were old and beautiful, small but robust, and both instilled in him a sense of awe and tranquility that were hard to explain. His Sunday talks with the aging movie star, sitting in the pews or slowly wandering the graveyard, were the highlight of his week.

The actress, a legend in America but a recluse in her later years, had met with Henri and his cousin, Marcella Harshbarger, the woman who ran the pricey but protective retirement home where Severin had lived out her life. In that meeting, Severin had been adamant that no fuss be made at her death. No media, no celebrities, no grand funeral. Her few friends at the home, Henri and Marcella, of course, and that was it.

Her remains were to be buried in Henri's churchyard, an event that both Henri Izner and Madame Severin considered an honor. They'd smiled at that delightful congruence just two weeks ago before she'd really started to go downhill. Smiled and held hands for a moment.

"I used to enjoy the attention," she'd told him, in her perfect, proper French. "Now, I like to be left alone."

"I understand," Henri told her. "You have my utmost discretion."

"Good, because if not," her eyes twinkled as she smiled, "I shall come back and haunt you."

Unfortunately for Henri, and through no fault of his own, word of Madame Severin's death escaped a day or so before the funeral, and the little church had been packed for the service, the heavy wooden doors staying open so the forty or so people who couldn't find a seat could nevertheless feel as if they were a part of the ceremony.

Thank the Good Lord this news didn't get out any earlier, he'd thought to himself numerous times that day. His phone just about rang itself off the hook all last night and all morning, but he'd had a good reason to ignore it: this was probably the most important funeral he would ever conduct.

He recognized maybe fifteen of the eighty or so people who'd shown up, and, now that the service and burial were over, most of the strangers avoided eye contact with him, as if he would chastise them for paying their respects to the lovely old woman. If, in fact, that was what they were doing; he'd seen more cell phones recording the event than he had tears.

A breeze picked up and rustled the branches of the young oak he stood beneath, a dozen yards from Severin's grave. He watched as the gravedigger, Alexandre Dupuis, gently shoveled wet earth onto the coffin, the heavy thumps quieting as Alexandre slowly covered the old lady's final resting place in a thickening blanket of soil.

Henri turned as a woman placed her hand on his arm. She was blond and in her early fifties, he guessed, slight and once pretty but now overly made-up.

"*Bonjour,*" she said, in an accent that was clearly American and made him wish he spoke better English.

"*Bonjour, madame,*" Henri said.

"*Vous avez faîtes très bien avec le service de funéraille,*" she said, and Henri guessed she was thanking him for the funeral service. Guessed, too, that she'd had a liquid something or other to fortify her for the event.

"*Merci, mon plaîsir,*" he said.

"*Je cherche quelqu'un.*" She leaned in as if looking for someone was a secret, and his suspicion about her drinking was confirmed by the sweetness of her breath. "*Il s'appelle Hugo Marston.*"

Henri furrowed his brow. The name meant something, rang a bell. One of the few phone calls he'd answered last night, maybe? Or one of the forty or so people he'd met briefly earlier in the day? An American name . . . *Ah yes*!

Henri looked over the woman's shoulder at the tall, handsome man who stood talking to an attractive woman, maybe his wife. Definitely close friends. Henri liked to do that, read people's body language; it was a way to understand them. In his line of work, understanding humanity was a mission, but priests were like lawyers—people told them what they thought they needed to know, sometimes the truth but not necessarily the whole truth.

"*Il est là,*" Henri said. *He's right there.*

"*Merci,*" the woman said, turning on one high heel and making remarkably steady progress through the heavy grass toward the man who'd introduced himself to Henri before the funeral. He'd not seemed like the others, there for the occasion, to gawp and take pictures. His handshake had been firm and his condolences genuine. His French was good, too, which made for a nice change.

But none of that had stopped Monsignor Henri Izner from wondering why the head of security at the American Embassy was at Isabelle Severin's funeral.

Hugo and Claudia had left Paris early, ducking into the car as the June rainstorm clattered against the hood and windshield. Hugo gripped the wheel against the wind that rocked the black SUV as they sped northeast along E50, toward the little Catholic church where Isabelle Severin was to be buried.

The storm blew itself out less than an hour after they'd left Paris, the sky clearing in a matter of minutes as a weak sun gathered its strength and dried the road ahead. The wind died, too, and for the last half hour Hugo turned off the motorway and they drove with the windows down, winding along the smaller roads, enjoying the breeze and the smell of fresh, wet earth and grass all around them.

Hugo had researched the name of the priest at the little church, not for any reason but because it was a habit, to know whom he was meeting beforehand. He didn't find much about Monsignor Henri Izner, wasn't looking to, but the couple of photos online showed a young but kind face. There was a small article in a local newspaper about Isabelle Severin converting to Catholicism in her last year, and attending the church. Izner's photograph appeared in the article, and he was glad to read that the young man and the old woman had become friends. The countryside of eastern France was a far cry from the glamor of Hollywood in the 1950s, he'd thought, but she was in the Champagne region, so maybe not so far after all.

He was talking to Claudia after the service as the other funeral attendees wandered away to their cars, when a blond woman in her fifties approached. She looked familiar to him, but Hugo couldn't quite place her.

"Hugo Marston?" she asked.

"Yes, ma'am," Hugo nodded.

"I'm Helen Hancock, the author."

Like there's only one author in the world, Hugo thought, but didn't say. "Nice to meet you," he said, extending a hand.

"We met before, about a year ago. Some event at the embassy, don't you remember?"

"Yes, of course," he said. A vague memory of her laughing with his boss, Ambassador J. Bradford Taylor, floated through his mind. "Sorry, it took me a second, I meet a lot of people in my job."

"I'm sure. Head of security, right?"

"That's right," he said. "Did you know Madame Severin?"

"Just by reputation, which of course was stellar. In every sense of the word. Did you?"

"A little," Hugo said. "Our paths crossed not long ago, only briefly, but she was a remarkable woman." He turned to Claudia. "Please, forgive my manners. This is Claudia Roux, normally a journalist but here today as a friend of mine."

"My pleasure," Claudia said warmly. "I've read several of your books; count me as a fan."

Hancock's face brightened immediately. "Oh really? How wonderful to hear. Do you have a favorite?"

Hugo glanced at Claudia, having assumed she was just being kind when she said she'd read Hancock's books. Apparently not.

"I know you've written many and I've just read a handful," Claudia said. "But I truly enjoyed *Under the Loving Tree*. I think it was the first time you moved toward suspense, maybe that's why, but I devoured that book in one weekend."

Hancock smiled broadly, and her pink lipstick glistened in the sun. "Well, aren't you an angel. Thank you so much."

"You're very welcome. Do you have a new book coming out soon?"

"Actually, yes. In about two months. It's called *The Palomino Painting*. Romance, of course, but with some more of that suspense thrown in—I hope you'll like it."

"I'm sure I will," Claudia said. "I may even get this guy to read it."

Hancock turned her gaze back to Hugo. "Not a romance reader? I don't know why men are so scared of showing their softer side."

Hugo smiled. "I'm more one for the classics, with maybe a few spy thrillers thrown into the mix."

"Typical man," Hancock said, rolling her eyes.

"Maybe I'll branch out," Hugo said. "Your new one will be published here in France?"

Hancock's smile faded. "Well, I sure hope so. The others have been, but my French publisher is being a little sticky with this one."

"Sticky?" Hugo asked.

"It's complicated, to do with the contract terms. They like to stay with what we had in the past, but in every other market a successful author is able to negotiate better terms." Hancock grimaced. "My publisher isn't quite so accommodating."

"Ah, well," Hugo said, sensing some discomfort in their conversation, "I'm sure you'll figure it out."

"Yes." Hancock's voice tailed off, and then she looked up at Hugo. "Can I talk to you for a moment? In private."

Hugo glanced at Claudia, who smiled and said, "I'll wait by the car. Maybe find us a place to eat, so take your time."

Helen Hancock watched her leave, then she turned back to Hugo. "I think someone's . . . stalking me."

"Stalking? What makes you say that?"

"I'm in France to teach a class and do some research for my next book; part of it is set in Paris. And ever since I got here, I feel like someone's been watching me."

"Someone in particular?"

"No, not really." She spoke slowly as if trying to picture someone. "It probably sounds silly, but it's more of a feeling."

"I'm a big believer in trusting your senses," Hugo said. "So don't feel bad about that, at all. Are you traveling alone?"

"Yes, staying at the Sorbonne Hotel on Rue des Écoles. Do you know it?"

Hugo did. It was one of those large and expensive hotels that pretended it wasn't part of a chain, along the lines of the Ritz or the Four Seasons, and pretended quite convincingly. "I've never stayed there, but I do know it. A great reputation."

"I stay there every time I come; they know me now so it's very welcoming. Almost a coming home."

"Any problems there?"

Her eyes slid away, as if she was thinking about lying. "That's why I've hesitated to say anything to anyone. They've always been so good to me. I don't want to complain or get anyone in trouble, especially when I can't really say that anything's happened."

"Fair enough," Hugo said.

She sighed. "I feel kind of stupid telling you. But I also feel better, getting it off my chest."

"Good. And if anything specific happens, be sure to tell the police.

At the very least, the hotel manager if it happens there." He dug into his coat pocket and handed her a business card. "And since you're an American citizen, I get to keep an eye on you, too."

Her eyes widened, then she smiled and her voice was flirtatious. "Well, now, don't say it like that or I'll start to hope something *does* happen."

She held up the card and tucked it into her blouse pocket, then took his hand for a little longer than was necessary before thanking him and turning toward the path leading out of the churchyard. Hugo watched her go, unsure if the wiggle in her hips was for him, or a result of those high heels and the whisky on her breath.

CHAPTER TWO

Hugo and Claudia found a small roadside restaurant just outside Meaux, fifty kilometers east of Paris. They took the minor roads, in no hurry to return to the hustle and bustle of the city, enjoying the wide, open skies and the clean, fresh air.

The restaurant itself was almost empty; they were the last ones to arrive for lunch, and they sat at a sturdy wooden table, seated by a rosy-cheeked hostess who also turned out to be their waitress and sommelier.

"Just a half bottle of the Bordeaux," Claudia said in French.

"*Oui, madame. Et pour monsieur?*"

Hugo and Claudia laughed. "*Non*," she said, "we'll share the half bottle, we're driving."

Their hostess tutted as if they'd actually ordered two bottles each before driving, and barreled off toward the kitchen.

The dining area was small, it might once have been someone's living room, Hugo thought. The low ceiling was crisscrossed by thick beams, and the furniture was old and solid, but comfortable too, and the food turned out to be what Claudia called, "good, country cooking." His stew was a little heavy for a warm June day, and she could have eaten her French onion soup with a fork, but garlic and butter made everything delicious, and they lingered.

"So can you tell me what Madame Hancock wanted?" Claudia asked.

"Have you really read her books?"

15

"Of course. Ten years ago, she was huge over here. Bigger here than in America, I'd say."

"Bestselling author, eh?"

"Most definitely."

"Romance?"

"You have something against a good romance novel?"

Hugo shrugged. "I've never read a good one."

"I'd guess you've never read one at all."

"Does *Romeo and Juliet* count?"

"These days they all have happy endings," Claudia said. "So no."

"That right? I'll pick one of them up."

"Nice deflection, by the way. You going to tell me what she wanted?"

"She thought someone might be . . ." *What? She'd said "stalking," but . . .* "Watching her."

"How?"

"She wasn't sure. It was more of a feeling than anything she could really explain."

"Huh. Paranoia?"

"Maybe. If she lives in an imaginary world, I'm sure she occasionally sees things that don't exist. Writers are supposed to be a little off-kilter, aren't they?"

"I'm a writer," Claudia reminded him.

"I meant novelists. But shouldn't she be seeing comely maidens and muscle-bound millionaires?"

"That doesn't sound very threatening." Claudia smiled at him. "Maybe she just wanted your number."

"Well, you can't blame her for that." Hugo signaled for the check. "What else do you know about her?"

"Not a lot. Bestselling novelist, used to be quite the socialite but has dropped off the radar a little."

"Of her own volition?"

"No idea. Probably."

Hugo's phone buzzed in his pocket, but he ignored it until it stopped. But five seconds later, it started up again, and Hugo knew it was either his best friend, Tom Green, or Ambassador Taylor. He shot Claudia an apologetic look and checked the display before answering.

"Tom, what's up?"

Tom and Hugo had been roommates at Quantico, fast friends from the day they met, even getting postings together when possible. They were like magnets, opposites that attracted each other. Tom's exit from the FBI had led him into the CIA, where his brashness and risk taking were more appreciated. He claimed to be retired but still took off from time to time on business he wouldn't even tell Hugo about, coming back days or weeks later to crash at Hugo's Paris apartment, where he'd made the second bedroom his own.

"You alone?"

"No, with Claudia. Late lunch."

"Yeah, well, I'm about to ruin your appetite."

Hugo straightened and Claudia gave him in inquiring look: *What?* He shrugged and listened as Tom continued.

"I want to talk about Rick Cofer."

"He got paroled, I know. We talked about this."

"I think he'll come for us," Tom said. "In fact, I'd bet on it."

"You'd bet on two squirrels fighting. We have no reason to think he'd come all the way out here and do something stupid."

"No reason?" Tom said, incredulous. "He has every reason in the world. And all the time in the world."

"Even if that's true, he's on parole. There's nothing he can do. He won't be allowed to leave the county without permission, let alone the state or country."

"Right," Tom said. "Because if there's one thing Mr. Cofer does, it's follow the law."

"And who's going to give him a passport?"

"He'll get one. You know he can."

"Alright, Tom, I get that you're upset by this—I am, too. But there's nothing we can do about it, and there's nothing he can do either."

Tom said nothing for a moment, and Hugo knew his friend was

deciding whether to blow up or hang up. "Fine," Tom said eventually. "*Bon appétit.*"

Hugo put away his phone and answered the quizzical look on Claudia's face. "You've asked me a few times about why I left the FBI. More specifically, how come Tom and I left at about the same time."

Claudia nodded and gave him a gentle smile. "Should I get out my tape recorder?"

Hugo grimaced. "No. For this story I need a blood oath of secrecy and silence until the day you die."

"That bad, eh?"

"Not really. Just trying to be dramatic."

"Right now it seems like you're trying to delay telling me a story."

"Yeah," Hugo conceded. "Kind of does, doesn't it?"

CHAPTER THREE

Fifteen years previously.

1600 hours, Houston, Texas.

Rick Cofer lay face down, mouth turned away from the weeds and dirt as his nostrils flared, dragging in air. His lips were drawn thin, but it was his eyes that Hugo concentrated on, black holes of hate and anger that bored into him and then swiveled and fixed on his partner, Tom Green, with even more intensity.

Every few seconds, Cofer's hands twitched, fingers opening and closing, pinned behind his back in Hugo's cuffs. The prisoner was six three and round in the belly, and Hugo would normally have considered using two pairs attached to each other to save the man some pain, to make breathing easier for him. But not with Cofer, not with what just happened. That sonofabitch was more than welcome to suffer the fate he'd brought on himself, be it the indignity of a face full of dirt or a cramping discomfort in his shoulders and arms.

Hugo looked up as the SWAT team surrounded the house, piling out of their armored vehicle like automatons, a fast-moving line of anonymous helmets, guns, and aggression. Twelve highly trained men looking for trouble but finding only Hugo and Tom standing over two bad guys; one dead, one alive and cursing, making threats and accusations with his mouth in the dust, telling a tale that no one cared to listen to, let alone believe.

The SWAT commander approached, wary but gun lowered. "Special Agents Marston and Green?"

"Yes." Hugo said. He and Tom showed their credentials, and the commander nodded.

"You're both Houston field office?"

"I'm with the BAU based up in DC, sent down to help with your robbery spree," Hugo nodded toward Tom. "But he is, yeah."

"I'm Sergeant Mo Siddiqui. You guys OK?"

"Yep, we're fine," Hugo said.

Siddiqui looked around. "So, this a planned op? We didn't know about it."

"Not planned, exactly," Hugo admitted. He shot Tom a look. "We had to wing this one."

"Happens," Siddiqui said. "We need to clear the house?"

"Yes, of course," said Hugo. "With the amount of noise we made, I'm pretty certain it's empty, but you should make sure."

"Ten-four." Siddiqui spoke into a microphone on his chest. "Make entry, sweep for suspects and victims." He looked at Hugo. "You want us to take this guy for you?"

Hugo glanced at Tom. His friend's jaw was set and he radiated anger, almost quivering with it. "Yeah," Hugo said. "Probably a good idea; we don't have a secure vehicle for him."

"Not a problem." He eyed the house. "Let me keep an eye on things here until the house is clear." He glanced at Cofer. "I'm sure he won't mind chewing the grass a little longer."

"Fuck you, pig," Cofer snarled.

"I'm not the one wallowing in mud, shit-head," Siddiqui said mildly. He moved closer to the house, a hand pressing his earpiece. "Ten-four." He turned to Hugo. "House is empty. Apart from his dead buddy, of course."

"Good, thanks," Hugo said. "Although technically that's not his buddy in there."

"What do you mean?"

"It's his brother," Hugo said. "His fraternal twin brother, to be precise."

Hugo turned and walked toward the black sedan that had just pulled up to the curb. His mouth was dry, but he tried to remain calm, and he ran the events of the day through his mind, getting everything straight.

A tall, thin black man in a dark-blue suit and sunglasses climbed out of the driver's side and walked toward Hugo. "Special Agent Marston."

"Yes, sir."

"You got them?"

"One in custody, one dead."

"How did that happen?" Ronald Fenwick was the new Special Agent in Charge, SAC, at the Houston field office. Three weeks and, according to pretty much everyone Hugo had spoken to, already making his mark—in some ways good and in some ways bad. One thing was certain: he was a man who stuck to the rule book and, as such, expected his agents to abide by policy and procedure to the letter, no exceptions. Not much of a problem for Hugo on this brief assignment, but less than ideal for his partner, Tom Green, who did his best to abide by the spirit of the bureau's policies but thought less of the specific rules and procedures.

"They're really just guidelines," Tom had once told Hugo, "General rules of warfare not designed to limit the field discretion of the agents."

Which pretty quickly put him squarely in Fenwick's bad graces, and soon after into the SAC's gunsights.

"Well, sir." Hugo cleared his throat and began. "We were set up outside the Bank of America on Bissonnet."

"Why that one?"

"I'd looked at the pattern. There were three banks I thought they might hit next, based on date, time, and location. We just got lucky."

"Fine," Fenwick said. "But I thought we hadn't identified any specific suspects."

"We hadn't. I had no idea it was them, which is why we had to wait. We watched twenty or so people go in and out of the bank before the twins arrived. They fit the profile, but I couldn't be sure it was them."

"Which is why you didn't call in backup?"

"Right, too soon. So, anyway, we were sitting there, watching. They arrived and went in." Hugo paused, choosing his next words carefully—some things Fenwick didn't need to know. Couldn't know, not yet at least. "We were about to go in for a closer look, figuring it might be them, so we got ready. Then we heard gunshots."

"Why did they start shooting? They haven't done that before."

"I'm not sure, sir. I honestly don't know what happened, why they started shooting." Hugo shrugged. "But they did."

"OK, I'll read your report on that later. Right now, I want to know why one of them ended up dead in this house."

"We got lucky. When they ran out of the bank, we followed, and even though they got a head start we caught up to them barely a block from here. As I was calling it in, they pulled into the driveway and ran into the house."

"Just two of them?"

"Right. Originally I was trying to get some local units to help, to pull them over. But as soon as they went to ground, I canceled the locals and just talked to FBI SWAT."

Fenwick nodded, grudgingly acknowledging that Hugo had done the right thing. "Then what?"

"I posted out front, Special Agent Green went around back. Watching brief, sir, that's all we were doing. Waiting for the guys with the body armor to flush them out, do their thing."

"So what went wrong?"

Hugo didn't like that his boss, and Tom's, was starting with the position that something had gone wrong, assuming that his men screwed something up. The most valued boss in law enforcement was the one whose first reaction to a bad situation was to back you up, look for the things you did right. Fenwick wasn't that. He was more interested in making sure any mistakes were hung around the necks of his subordinates, and if he had to do the hanging, so be it.

"Nothing went wrong," Hugo said, then he measured the terseness in his voice. "I heard shouts, then shots. I ran around the back to help and . . ."

"Saw Tom Green standing over a dead man?"

"A dead murderer," Hugo reminded him.

"We don't get to decide that; the courts do. And we're supposed to bring the bad guys in alive, unless you'd forgotten."

"We're also supposed to make sure they don't get away and kill more people," Hugo said, his jaw clenched. "And no one ever trained us to stand there and get shot."

"But you didn't see the actual shooting here?"

Hugo shook his head. "No, sir, I didn't."

"So you believe what Special Agent Green told you about what happened immediately beforehand? Taking his word?"

"Damn right," Hugo snapped. "You should try it."

Fenwick's face tightened. "Don't . . . Watch your attitude, Agent Marston."

"My attitude is fine. Sir."

"We'll see about that." Fenwick pointed to where Tom was talking to Mo Siddiqui. "Have Green come talk to me, will you?"

"It's not a closed crime scene, sir," Hugo said mildly, to disguise the sarcasm. "You're welcome to walk over there."

"Now, please, Agent Marston."

CHAPTER FOUR

O n Monday morning, Hugo got to the office just before eight to find a hot cup of coffee on his desk and the little red light on his telephone blinking.

"Bless you, Emma," he called through the open door to his secretary. He had no idea how she knew when he was arriving, but every morning she did. And that mug of hot coffee was a sign of her ruthlessly efficient regime, a matter of pride for her and pleasure for Hugo.

He pressed the Messages button on his phone, punched in his passcode, and picked up a pen to make a note of who'd called.

"Mr. Marston, this is Helen Hancock, the author. Please, I don't want you to think I'm crazy, but I think I found something in my hotel room. I think someone's spying on me. No, I'm sure of it, positive. I'm outside right now, it's Sunday evening and I don't dare call from the hotel phone. What if it's bugged? I'll call again Monday morning, I don't have your cell number. Please, I just want to know if you can help me."

Hugo took a sip of coffee, then dialed the number she left.

"Hello?"

"Ms. Hancock, this is Hugo Marston."

A sharp intake of breath. "Yes, of course. Are you in the office?"

"Yes, ma'am."

"Good. I'm in my room." She emphasized each word, making her message clear enough for a toddler to get it. "Can I call you in ten minutes?"

"Of course, I'll be right here. Whenever is convenient for you."

"Ten minutes it is," she said, before disconnecting.

Hugo got up from his desk and wandered out to talk to Emma.

"How's your morning?" he asked genially.

She raised a manicured eyebrow. "Fine. I got up at the same time as usual, ate the same yogurt breakfast as usual, walked the same path to work as usual, and here I am answering banal questions from my boss."

"As usual," Hugo finished for her, smiling.

"No," she wagged a finger. "He only does that when he wants me to do something and he's not sure whether or not it's outside my job description."

"You should have been a profiler."

"I *am* a profiler, I just don't get paid for it." Her voice softened. "What do you need me to do, Hugo?"

"I know you abhor gossip but are a literate and well-read person," he began. "This little task will therefore be pleasant."

She leaned forward. "I'm intrigued."

"Can you do a little digging and find out what you can on a writer named Helen Hancock?"

Both eyebrows went up this time. "*The* Helen Hancock?"

"You're familiar with her?"

"Well, of course," Emma said. "I have a friend who's in publishing here in Paris. I met Helen once at a party. And, of course, she's huge in the romance world, although she's not put a book out in a couple of years. And her last one kind of tanked, but that was because she went away from her usual formula, which has always been along the lines of a beautiful, strong, powerful woman suddenly finding herself . . ." Her voice tailed off and she colored slightly.

"Well, what do we have here?" Hugo said. "And I thought your reading consisted of the *Economist* and maybe a little Tolstoy or Dostoyevsky."

"Are you making fun of me, Hugo Marston?"

Hugo laughed. "Absolutely not. No. Never. I'm just mildly surprised—"

"That I like a little light reading?" Emma harrumphed. "I also enjoy fast food on occasion, you know, and I've even been known to watch soap operas and cartoons. And wear slippers during the day."

"Emma, you're ruining your superhero image, please, stop."

She bristled, but Hugo knew it was for show, like a grandmother trying to be strict with a child who was making her laugh.

"Go back into your office, Mr. Marston, if you please. I have work to do."

"Yes, ma'am, right away." Hugo backed away from her desk, hands up in surrender, and retreated into his office and behind his desk. He had time to turn his computer on and start reading the weekend's e-mails before Helen Hancock called, but only just. As it was, he'd read four of the waiting eleven when his phone rang.

"This is Hugo."

"Helen here. I'm at a café; it's safe to talk."

Glad to hear it's safe, Hugo thought, then chided himself for being uncharitable. *A writer is bound to be a little melodramatic.* "Has something happened, Ms. Hancock? Your message said something about being spied on."

"Please, call me Helen. And yes, most definitely. I found a camera, a hidden camera. At least, I think that's what it is; I'm pretty sure. It's in a painting over my desk. I think someone's trying to steal my work."

Hugo paused. "Is that a thing? I mean, forgive my ignorance, but do writers steal each other's work?"

"It may not be a writer. In fact, it probably isn't. It's probably a fan, or someone who thinks they can sell my work before it's published. Maybe someone who wants to turn it into fan fiction, I don't know. I really have no idea, but I don't like it one bit."

"Well, we can worry about the why later," Hugo said. "Let's make sure it is what you think it is, first. Have you told the police?"

"No. I'm not sure I should call them. I mean, I'm sure I can trust them to find out, do a good job, but there's the whole language barrier."

"You don't speak French?"

"Yes, of course I do. Some. Enough to get around. But I have no idea what the French for 'secret camera' is, that's for sure. And I don't fancy getting grilled by a French policeman who's more interested in protecting the reputation of one of his city's hotels than finding out what's going on."

"My experience has always been that the police here are very pro—"

"I'm sure your experience is valid, Mr. Marston." Her voice was curt. "However, the French have a reputation for the way they view women, and my experience has been more in line with that. You see, I'm treated as a woman at first, and then I get all the respect in the world when they find out I'm a writer. Until they realize I'm a romance writer, then it's back to square one."

"I'm sorry to hear that's been your experience," Hugo said, meaning it. "And, please, call me Hugo."

"Thank you, I will. But, Hugo, I don't plan on upsetting the hotel management, who've always been very good to me, by bringing in a bunch of uniformed police officers who will pat me on the head and tell me not to worry, that it's all a mistake."

"This is technically their jurisdiction, though," Hugo said. "If what you say turns out to be true, then there's nothing I can do about it alone."

"I'd assumed as much, and I understand that. However, I am sure you know someone at police headquarters who can look into this. Maybe let you on board, so to speak. At the very least, I'm hoping you know someone who doesn't have a bushy mustache and assume all women are hysterical every time they make a complaint like this."

"As a matter of fact," Hugo said, "I know someone who fits that description perfectly."

"You do?"

"Yes. Not only will she be discreet, but she knows a lot about spy technology, so let me give her a call and I'll get back to you."

"A woman?" Hancock asked, surprise in her voice. "I guess I figured all the senior officers in the French police were men."

"Funny you should say that," Hugo said. "Mostly true, but not entirely."

Hugo met Lieutenant Camille Lerens for lunch since it was a slow day for both, and they'd not caught up for a while. They sat outside in the shade of the café's awning, the tables around them slowly filling, and they were close enough to the door to smell the garlic and grilling meat, odors that to Hugo were almost sustenance all by themselves.

The waiter appeared with a bottle of water and two glasses, and, as he poured, Hugo held out the bread basket for Lerens.

"*Merci, non.* Cutting down on carbs," she said. "Help yourself."

"You know, I've wondered," Hugo said, "whether the hormones and surgery made a difference to your metabolism."

They didn't talk about it much. Lerens's transition from Christophe Lerens to Camille was a fact from her past, like her first kiss or favorite present from Santa. She was open to talking about it, but Hugo knew she'd had a hard time in the Bordeaux force before they'd accepted her for who she was, and before she'd transferred to Paris and made a name for herself. But the details, they'd never really discussed those. Hugo suspected that it was his own reticence rather than any reluctance on her part that had kept it out of their many conversations.

"Well, sometimes you get what you ask for." Lerens gave him a reassuring smile. *It's OK to talk about this.* "As a man, all that testosterone helped me keep fit. Now I have to cut back on bread and wine; it's very unfair."

Hugo patted his own waistline. "Not just a gender issue," he said. "I'm afraid that age will do that to you, too."

"You're not making me feel better, Hugo." Lerens scowled, and then broke into a smile. "We should work out together."

"Not a bad idea," Hugo conceded. "As long as you take it easy on me. I have ten years on you, at least."

"Think we could rope Tom into this?"

"Exercising? Not a chance. Though I'm sure he'd volunteer to eat our share of bread and drink all of our wine."

"He does that already," Lerens said. "How is he, anyway? It's been weeks since I heard from him."

"He was doing OK until recently. It's a long story, but a guy he and I nailed a few years back just got paroled from prison. A bad deal all around, and Tom's far from happy that the guy is out."

"They all get out sooner or later," Lerens said, with a typically Gallic shrug.

"Most of them. But when you rob a bunch of banks and kill people, you're not supposed to."

"So what makes this man so special that he's released?"

"Like I said, a long story. And not one for today." Hugo took a second piece of bread before realizing, but decided against putting it back. "A different tale for you today, one closer to home."

"Sounds exciting."

"It's either very exciting or absolutely nothing. Other than someone's paranoia taking over."

"Go on."

Hugo tapped the file he'd put on the table. "Do you know who Helen Hancock is?"

"The writer? Of course, she's huge over here."

"Have you read any of her books?"

"Most of them." Lerens smiled. "Oh, don't look so shocked. You and your literary aspirations; it'd be good for you to see what normal people read."

"That's not fair," Hugo said. "I read other things. Spy novels, for example."

"*Oui.* Let me guess, ones written in the 1960s by Graham Greene and John le Carré."

"And modern ones," Hugo said defensively. "Alan Furst. Philip Kerr, even."

"Congratulations, you're a true man of the people. Anyway, what about Helen Hancock?"

"She's here in Paris, doing research for her new novel and teaching a class. I met her at Isabelle Severin's funeral."

Lerens sat up straight. "You met her? What's she like?"

"Very nice," Hugo said. "But she thinks someone's spying on her."

"Are you serious? Who would be spying on her?"

"That's what she wants us to find out."

"Us?"

Hugo smiled. "She came to me because she's an American, and because she thinks the Paris police will, as she put it, pat her on the head and tell her not to worry."

Lerens nodded. "She's probably right. What makes her think she's being spied on?"

"She found a camera in her hotel room, or so she says."

"How intriguing."

"Like I said, that's what she thinks," Hugo said.

"What kind of hotel is she staying in?"

"The Sorbonne Hotel," Hugo said.

"Then I'd be shocked if there was a camera in there. You don't get much more reputable that that."

"You don't believe her?"

"I mean, it's possible . . . but not very likely. A place like that, it's like the Hôtel de Crillon or the Ritz. Reputation and service mean everything."

"I know. But a rogue employee could install one," Hugo said. "It wouldn't be hard to do these days."

"True enough. It should be easy to figure out, though. I mean, either it's a camera or it's not," Lerens said. "Let's have our lunch and then go take a look, shall we?"

CHAPTER FIVE

The lobby of the Sorbonne Hotel was a study in tranquility. The deep carpet muffled every footfall, and the oversized portraits of French aristocracy from years gone by seemed to whisper "*hush*" at all who passed through. Many of the grand Paris hotels had been refurbished in recent years, adding modern touches, opening the lobbies up to more light, and installing bright stone and marble surfaces to replace the wood paneling that the Sorbonne Hotel maintained.

Hugo liked the sense of calm the place instilled in him, the way the staff in their formal wear moved quietly about their business, no fuss, no hurry. He could see why a writer like Helen Hancock would come here; it was somewhere you could sit in a plush leather couch and watch the world pass by and not be bothered by overly anxious employees making sure you were alright every fifteen minutes.

Hancock met them by the elevators, her eyes scanning the dimly lit lobby in case, Hugo assumed, they were themselves being watched by a member of the hotel's staff. Hugo introduced her to Lieutenant Camille Lerens, discreet in civilian clothes, and as soon as the elevator doors closed on them, Lerens spoke.

"Hugo says you haven't touched it, is that right?"

Hancock nodded. "Right."

"How did you discover it?"

"Well, I have a niece who's ten. Her name's Nicola. She has this funny thing about hotel rooms, so whenever I travel I send her pictures of the room I'm staying in. I use my phone so I can text them to her."

"Makes sense," Hugo said.

"Yes, well, I didn't notice anything while I was taking the pictures a couple of days ago, but when I looked at them afterward, to choose which to send, I noticed a reflection."

"What do you mean, 'a reflection'?" Lerens asked.

"Of the flash. It was like a little burst of light coming from the corner of the framed picture in the wall above the desk. I thought that was odd, so I went and inspected the picture." The elevator doors opened, and they stepped out into the hallway. Hancock lowered her voice, as if someone might be listening. "That's when I found a little hole in the bottom corner of the picture itself. A hole with something in it, like a lens."

They stopped in the hallway to talk. "But you're sure that you didn't touch it in any way?" Lerens asked. "Like, move the picture to look?"

"Yes, I'm sure. I didn't touch it. I called the US Embassy and asked for the ambassador, to ask him what to do." Hugo and Lerens glanced at each other but didn't say anything. Hancock smiled. "That may seem a little extreme, but I know him. He's actually a fan of my books—that's how we met. I did a reading and book signing at the American Library and he came, introduced himself. Gave me his card and said if I ever needed anything . . ." She shrugged. "So I thought I'd take him up on it."

"He's a fan?" Hugo asked, highly amused but trying not to show it.

"It's not just sex-starved women who read my books, you know," she said, patting his arm. "Maybe you should try one; you might like it."

Lerens cleared her throat. "Back to the task at hand, maybe?"

"Right, sorry," Hancock continued. "Anyway, he wasn't in and when I explained the issue they put me through to the security division, or whatever you call it. They told me you'd be in on Monday, that you don't work weekends, and even if you did you were going to a funeral out of the city. I guessed which one and . . . *Voilà.*"

"*Bien,*" Lerens said. "Now, when we go in your room, don't say anything, in case it's recording. If they haven't realized by now that you have spotted it, it'd be good to keep them in the dark."

"Who is *they*, I wonder," Hugo mused.

"Can you trace who put the camera there?" Hancock asked. "I mean, if that's what it is."

"It's complicated, but the basic answer is 'possibly,'" Lerens said. "We'll just have a look for now, surreptitiously if we can. You said it's in the lower corner of the painting over the desk?"

"Yes," Hancock said. "It looks like it would capture the desk but could also get more of the room, including part of the bed and the bathroom doorway."

"*Alors*," Lerens said. "We'll just look for now, no talking and no touching."

They walked in silence to Hancock's room. When they got there, her keycard unlocked the door with a gentle clunk, and they filed in behind the writer.

The door opened onto a spacious one-room suite. In front of them was a sizeable white sofa, which was flanked by a pair of matching chintz armchairs, heavy and plush. These faced to their left, where a large, antique desk sat against the wall. Hugo's eyes automatically went to the oversized landscape that was hung above the desk, a swirl of color and movement that would make perfect cover for a small hole and a spy camera. Hugo glanced to his right, taking in the rest of the suite. A king-size four-poster bed with a canopy dominated most of it but left enough space for an armoire and matching bedside tables. *Mahogany or maybe teak*, Hugo thought. An expensive, classy room that would probably cost most people a week's salary for a single night.

They walked casually behind and around the far end of the sofa, then angled left toward the picture. To Hugo's right, floor-to-ceiling windows filled the room with light, and he paused for a moment to look out over Rue des Écoles before joining Lerens and Hancock, who stood with their backs against the wall on which the picture was mounted. Lerens was closest to the painting, and she bent to inspect it, trying to keep her head out of any filming that may be happening.

After a moment, she angled her cell phone toward the painting to inconspicuously take pictures of the tiny hole and maybe the camera itself. Although they remained in the camera's blind spot while investigating, there was simply no way to know whether their entry had been captured or, if it had been, whether the person who'd installed it was watching.

Is it motion-activated? Hugo wondered. *Monitored full-time? Surely not that . . .* Eventually Lerens moved out of the way and Hugo took a turn.

The hole was unmistakable. It was about the size of a thumbtack and had been carefully cut into a darker part of the painting for disguise. Hugo wasn't positive, but it did indeed look like something sat just beneath the cutout. He resisted the urge to lift the painting and check behind it, instead turning his head to look at the room from that angle, to see what a camera might see. Hancock was right: it would likely capture the desktop and most of the bed. Possibly the bathroom doorway, too.

He straightened and indicated with a nod that he'd seen enough. With Lerens in the lead, they retraced their path, walking quietly back behind the sofa and out the door. When they were in the long, quiet hallway, Hancock spoke up.

"Well?" she said. "I was right—it's a camera, isn't it?"

"I think it might be," Lerens said. "Impressive disguise, though, I'll give it that."

"So what now?" Hugo asked.

"My guess is, there's some equipment taped to the back of the painting, a transmitter that's sending the images, and possibly sound too, to a receiver." Lerens pursed her lips in thought. "Typically, these things have a fairly short range, maybe half an acre."

"So whoever put it there is in the hotel," Hugo said.

"Most likely," Lerens agreed. "Another guest or an employee, but my money would be on the latter."

"Why?" Hancock asked.

"Obviously I don't know what specific equipment they're using. But did you see any wires coming out of the painting to a socket?"

Hugo and Hancock shook their heads.

"Me neither," Lerens continued. "Which means it's battery oper-
ated. If my memory serves, the batteries on things like this last anywhere from fifteen to twenty-four hours, which means that if someone's
intent on capturing a lot of footage of Madame Hancock, they'd need
to change out the battery pack."

"Which an employee could do much easier than a guest could,"
Hugo said.

"So what do we do now?" Hancock asked. "I can't stay in that
room anymore. I don't even like being in there now."

"I'll need to get authorization to run a bug sweeper through the
room," Lerens said. "I'll need permission from the hotel manager as
well as my superiors."

"Wait, does that mean an official investigation or report?" Hancock
asked. Her eyes were wide with worry.

"Yes, I'd have to document everything," Lerens said. "Is that a
problem?"

"It might be." Hancock frowned. "If it becomes official, you'll need
copies of any video as evidence. I don't know what's on there, my work,
my notes. Maybe even . . . you know, me. Asleep or changing. I don't
want copies of that in anyone's hands."

"I can promise you," Lerens said reassuringly, "that anything we
kept would be held under lock and key."

"You can't promise me there'll be no leaks, though, can you?"
Hancock asked sharply.

"I suppose . . . not," Lerens conceded. "Do you have any other
ideas, though?"

"I do," Hugo said, and they both turned to look at him. "We need
the room swept, right? By someone who knows what he's doing and
can be discreet."

Lerens smiled. "Not so sure about the discreet part, but yes, that's
a great idea."

"What's a great idea?" Hancock looked back and forth between
them. "What are you talking about?"

"Not *what*," Hugo said. "But *who*. His name is Tom Green, and he's a former FBI agent, as well as my best friend. And snooping around a hotel room for hidden surveillance gear is his idea of heaven."

"Especially if you don't lock up the minibar," Lerens added.

"And if you're here when he does it," Hugo added, "he may try to seduce you. Fair warning."

"Well, now," Hancock said, a small smile playing on her lips. "We writers have to do our research somehow. Don't we?"

CHAPTER SIX

Hugo was stretched out on the sofa when Tom let himself into the apartment just after seven that evening. Hugo put his book down on the coffee table beside him and sat up. "I was wondering where you'd got to."

"Your author friend had some good whisky; seemed rude to say no," Tom said. "You reading again?"

"Can't seem to help myself. Apart from the whisky, how was your little adventure?"

"Great fun. Never been in that hotel before, but it's definitely my style."

"Meaning?"

"Chock-full of rich women."

"Helen Hancock included."

"But of course," Tom said, dropping into an armchair opposite Hugo. "Nice lady, quite apart from the whisky. So nice, in fact, that someone did indeed decide to bug her room."

"So she was right. Was it just a camera?"

"Nope, sight and sound. Pinhole camera that also records. Or, to be more precise, transmits pictures and sound."

"You didn't remove it, right?"

"You told me to leave it," Tom said. "You know I always do as you say."

"As long as you did this time."

"I did, so quit your fussing."

"How do those cameras work, exactly?" Hugo asked. "No call for those in my current job, and I'm guessing the technology's changed since we were at the bureau."

"Just a little. It's pretty simple, though. The camera can be left on or it can be remotely switched on and off, according to the operator's preferences. It will transmit the images and sound to an SD card. For that kind of device, it'd probably be thirty-two gigs at the most."

"How long do they record for?" Hugo asked. "Like, how much could they have captured?"

"Depends what they're using. Estimate ten minutes per gigabyte if it's a 1080p, which is the high-def version we use for evidence gathering and surveillance. Maybe fifteen minutes per gigabyte at 720p resolution. Still high-def and a high-quality recording."

"How—?"

"Hush, I'm still talking. Now, the user would likely have to change out that memory card because once it's full, the camera would stop recording." He snapped his fingers as a thought struck him. "No, not necessarily. He could set it to loop record and use just the one memory card."

"But wouldn't that mean basically taping over what was recorded before?"

"It would. So, if I'm spying on someone, I'm stocking up on memory cards and switching them out. You had a question?"

"I did," Hugo said. "How good is the picture quality likely to be? I'm thinking about what Helen Hancock said, about someone stealing her work. Good enough to do that?"

"Definitely. I just swept the painting and detected, mind you; didn't see the device myself. But a 1080 high-def resolution would allow someone to read her worst cursive, and most definitely any typed pages left lying on the desk."

"Good to know. It just seems odd that someone would try to steal her writing," Hugo said. "She mentioned a couple of reasons but none of them very convincing. To me, anyway."

"No clue."

"Me neither. . . . I need to ask her more about that. So can you trace the signal? I mean, find out who's picking it up?"

"Yes and no," Tom said. "It's not like a string, where I can just follow it to the end user. But it has to be someone fairly close, in the building most likely."

"Yeah, Camille said within half an acre."

"Give or take, yes. That doesn't narrow it down much in a busy hotel like that, though." Tom stood. "I need a drink, you want some wine?"

"Sure, red please. So how the hell do we find who's doing this?"

"Well, I can tell you that whoever it is, if we figure that out, they will have evidence on their computer or phone. Every camera has a unique ID number associated with it, which will be captured and displayed on whatever device they use to watch the footage."

"Kind of like a fingerprint," Hugo suggested. He took a full wine glass from Tom, who sat back down opposite him. "Thanks."

"You're welcome. And precisely. The problem we have now, though, is how to find whose finger it belongs to."

"I have two ideas," Hugo said, taking a sip.

"Of course you do." Tom rolled his eyes. "And I have three ideas, great ones. But you go first."

Hugo smiled. "Well, to begin with, I would like to know whether the hotel's electronic keycards leave behind any kind of trail."

"Keycards?"

"For the hotel-room doors."

"Ah, like when Helen's door was opened, how many times, and by whom?"

"Right. That kind of technology changes fast; it certainly has since our bureau days, so I'm not really clear on how it all works. You?"

"Not really," Tom said. He gulped down some wine and wiped his mouth with the back of his hand. "I'm more of a steal-your-card kind of guy. Which is to say, I'm the one going in and out of hotel rooms, not so much the one trying to find out who went in."

"But don't you need to know, for countermeasures? To avoid being caught?"

"Like I said, stealing someone's keycard is always the way to go. What was your second bright idea?"

"Well, Camille said that since there are no wires coming out from the painting, any camera will be battery powered."

"Right," Tom said. "And that battery will need to be replaced once every twenty-four hours. Something like that." His eyes lit up. "I see where you're going with this. We set up our own camera and record whoever is switching out the battery."

"Exactly," Hugo said.

"So, which approach do you want to take? Both at the same time?"

"No," Hugo said. "To find out about the keycards, we'll need the cooperation of the hotel management. And that could tip someone off."

"Good point," Tom said. "Which means we're staging our first spying op together, Hugo. How cute is that?"

"I prefer to think of it as regular surveillance, and we did that plenty while at the bureau," Hugo said. "But feel free to get sentimental on me, I don't mind in the least."

"Killjoy."

"You know it. Anyway, we'll have to put in our own camera without being spotted. We'll need to assume that whoever our bad guy is, he's watching every time there's movement in the room."

"Should be easy enough."

"If you say so," Hugo said. "By the way, did you sweep the whole room or just the painting?"

"Painting only," Tom said. "No way to do all of that room without it being caught on camera."

"Good point. But that means there might be more than one camera in there," Hugo said.

"Oh, crap." Tom suddenly looked worried. "I'm getting as rusty as you. I didn't think about that."

"Well, nothing we can do about it now. If there is, when our suspect changes the one battery, he'll change any others in there, which we will be able to see. And that question will be answered."

The following morning, Tuesday, Hugo checked in with his boss, Ambassador J. Bradford Taylor. As a former CIA agent, and one of the smartest people Hugo knew, he thought maybe the ambassador would know why someone might try to steal Helen Hancock's work.

"Pretty cool we get to help out Helen Hancock, eh?" Taylor said, sitting forward behind his huge desk. He was the definition of ordinary-looking, perfect for spy work but not great for imposing himself on large furniture. Of average height and with no distinguishing features apart from a balding pate, he looked like he was one of the moving men, not a representative of the most powerful nation on Earth.

"Why do people keep fangirling over her?" Hugo asked. "I mean, I've heard of her before now, but it's not like she's Harper Lee or Maya Angelou."

"You're a book snob, Hugo. You always have been." Taylor shook his head. "That woman has brought delight to millions of readers for many years and deserves all the credit and recognition she gets. And quite possibly a little respect from people like you."

"She seems real nice," Hugo said. "And I'm sure her books are wonderful; they just don't happen to be my cup of tea."

"Which you'd know because you've tried them, right?"

"Then I'll rephrase. Her genre isn't my cup of tea."

"Then you need to branch out." Taylor snorted with a little laugh. "It's not like you have too much romance in your life, now is it?"

"Very amusing, boss," Hugo said. "Thanks for pointing that out, but I'll have you know things are going great with Claudia."

"Right, sure. So what's this business about a spy camera?"

"I wish I knew. There's definitely one in the painting; Tom swept it yesterday and detected a transmitter."

"He swept the room or just the painting?"

"The latter. He was worried that someone would be watching and see him do the rest of the room, which would screw up our plan to catch whoever it is."

"What plan is that?" Taylor asked.

"To plant our own camera and catch the suspect in the act."

"I like it. You have the hotel's permission?"

"That's one of the reasons I'm here. To pick your brain as to why someone might do this, but also to get your help smoothing things over with the hotel."

"The police can do that better than I can."

"Hancock doesn't want the police formally involved."

"Why the hell not?"

"Because if this guy has recordings of her, those will be copied and taken into evidence, and she doesn't want potentially embarrassing things leaked onto the Internet."

"Embarrassing like what? She have bad handwriting or something?"

Hugo smiled. "No idea. But that camera, depending on its lens, is likely to have captured her dressing and undressing. It picks up not only the desk, but also part of the bed and the bathroom. She knows the police will try to keep everything secure, but think about it—one cop who needs some money, he could easily sell a couple of minutes of one of the world's top romance writers in the buff in her fancy hotel room. Or just post it for free for jollies."

Taylor suddenly seemed more concerned. "I don't know, Hugo. I appreciate your consideration for her privacy, but this could make some people very upset. The hotel, the Paris police . . ." His voice trailed off.

"The police know. I have them in the loop," Hugo said.

"Your friend, Lieutenant Lerens?"

"Yes."

"Who you, no doubt, also asked to be discreet and not act officially, or write any kind of report."

"Well, true," Hugo conceded. "But the police know at least."

"So you want to run a secret operation to catch a criminal without the police's official blessing, and I'm supposed to get the hotel management to agree to that."

"Yep." Hugo nodded. "That's pretty much it."

"They won't do it." Taylor shook his head. "Think about it from their perspective. What if their guests found out? That kind of hotel, with their wealthy private and business patrons—no way. It'd be a public-relations nightmare."

Hugo tried to hide his irritation. "And you know that without asking them."

"Yes. Hugo, we put guests of the embassy up at that hotel. We can't just call over there and book a few rooms, then set up a sting operation."

"I don't see why you can't let them make that call."

"Again, think about it from their perspective—"

"I am," Hugo snapped. "Look, if one of their employees is doing this, do you think they'd rather have the police involved, and by extension make it public, or have us go in there under the radar?"

"And what if you nab someone? Are you guys going to rough him up a little and then leave it at that? No, you're going to have him arrested, at least you damn well ought to." Taylor shook his head again, emphatically. "Either way, the police are getting involved. Now that you've established that someone's bugging the place, there's no way to keep a lid on this." He sat back. "I'm sorry, Hugo, but that's just the way it is."

Hugo and Taylor locked eyes for a second, both breaking away when their phones pinged simultaneously. A group text message, which usually came from the on-duty security officer and more often than not meant an emergency or some kind of alert.

Both men checked their phones, and Hugo was the first to speak. "Well, I guess that moots the police issue."

Hugo looked back at the text from his subordinate, Regional Security Officer Ryan Pierce: *Body found at Sorbonne Hotel. Maybe an American. Want me to go down there?*

Hugo tapped on Pierce's name and waited while his colleague's phone rang. He answered straightaway.

"Hey, chief. All quiet if you want me to cover that for you."

"No, I'll go, thanks," Hugo said. "I'm with the ambassador, so let me put you on speaker." He looked at the display and pressed the button. "There, you're on. What do we know?"

"Not a lot. We just got a call five minutes ago from our liaison at the prefecture. One of the guests stumbled over a body in the stairwell. For some reason they think the victim is an American, so they let us know right away."

"Is it a man or a woman?" Hugo asked.

"I don't know, boss. I did ask for whatever details they have, but they didn't give me any more than I told you. Not even why they think it's an American."

"Very helpful," Taylor muttered.

"OK, thanks, Ryan," Hugo said. "Can you stay put in the office and be available for me?"

"Of course."

"Great, I'll be in touch." Hugo disconnected and looked at Taylor. "Well, field trip to the hotel for me. Let's just hope it's not our favorite romance writer."

"No kidding," Taylor said, his forehead creased with concern. "This isn't good. Not good at all. I mean, if they were looking at a public-relations nightmare before, this will take the cake. Whether it's Ms. Hancock or not."

Hugo stood. "I'll let you know as soon as I get down there, but while I'm on my way, say a prayer that it's not her. I may not be a fan of her books, but the world needs more writers, not fewer."

CHAPTER SEVEN

The body was still in the stairwell when Hugo got to the hotel. The police were obviously trying to keep a low profile out of respect for the hotel's reputation, but the tension in the large lobby was palpable. Four or five uniformed officers lingered, looking uncomfortable, awaiting orders that they no doubt hoped would take them out of there to do some actual police work.

Hugo showed his credentials to the clerk behind the desk and said that he was expected.

"Third floor, *monsieur*," the woman said. "The stairs will be to your left when you exit the elevator."

Hugo thanked her and moved to the elevator bank. As he waited, he heard a familiar voice behind him, a soft Scottish brogue.

"Mr. Marston, nice to see you again, sir."

Hugo turned to find a bald policeman in uniform smiling at him.

"Paul Jameson," Hugo said, shaking his hand. "You're still working with Camille?"

"Yes, sir, I sure am. Best detective on the force, why wouldn't I be?"

Hugo had met Jameson on a previous case and had been impressed by his intelligence and attention to detail. The fact that he was a happy Scotsman in a *flic*'s uniform appealed to Hugo's sense of humor, too. Like Hugo himself, Jameson was a fish learning to swim in new and occasionally dangerous waters.

"So what do we have? Your office passed on almost no details."

"That doesn't surprise me. As you can imagine, the hotel's putting all kinds of pressure on us to keep mum. I mean, people will find out, but later is better than sooner for them."

"But they're cooperating with the investigation?"

The elevator dinged and its door opened. Jameson gestured for Hugo to go in first. "Yes, as far as I know. Lieutenant Lerens wouldn't stand for any less, I can tell you that."

"Very true." Hugo pressed the button for the third floor and gave Jameson a wry smile. "Are you intentionally deflecting and not giving me details?"

"Yes, sir," Jameson replied, with a smile of his own. "Orders. You know how it is."

"Just tell me this. Is the victim Helen Hancock?"

"The author?" Jameson looked surprised. "No, sir. It's an American all right, but not her. Since it's you, I can probably just tell you . . ."

"I can wait twenty seconds," Hugo said. "Can't have the only Englishman on the Paris police force getting in trouble."

"I'm Scott—" Jameson shook his head, a wry smile on his face. "Right, got it. You know that."

Hugo smiled, and the elevator stopped with another *ding*. The door opened and Hugo waved an arm. "Here we are. After you."

They turned left and walked to the end of the hallway, where a uniformed *flic* guarded the door to the staircase. Voices drifted up to them through the open doorway, and Hugo recognized Camille Lerens's among them. The officer took his name down on the crime-scene log and stepped aside.

"Go ahead, sir," Jameson said. "The crime-scene people have come and gone, so you don't have to worry. It's on the next landing down. Sorry, *he's* on the next landing."

Hugo nodded, stepped through the door, and looked down one flight of stairs at the three police officers who were standing over the body of a man. Hugo started slowly down the stairs, waving a hand at Lerens when she looked up and saw him. He didn't recognize the other two officers, but they moved apart to let him stand next to Lerens on the step just above the landing.

The body of a man lay spread-eagle on the floor, face up. Blood smeared the area around him, including the wall of the stairwell, which was painted with red, half-formed handprints and finger trails. Black dust covered various parts of the white stairwell, the only evidence that a careful crime-scene team had been and gone. Hugo looked down and studied the man's face. It was square and solid, with freckles to match his thick, sandy hair. He could have been quite handsome, Hugo thought, or maybe not. Looks were hard thing to judge on a dead man.

He looked at Lerens. "*Qu'est-il arrivé?*" He gestured to the body with his hand. *What happened?*

"*Je ne suis pas sûr.*" Lerens. said. *I'm not sure.* "About all I know is who he is and how he died."

"Cause of death already? They usually make you wait for that."

"The knife wounds in the back plus the kitchen knife itself left on the stairs were a bit of a clue. Even our medical examiner at his grumpiest acknowledged that."

"Doctor Sprengelmeyer?"

"That's the one," Lerens said.

"Then he acknowledged it informally, of course."

"Of course. You want to know who the victim is?"

"He works here at the hotel," Hugo said. "His name is Andrew Baxter, and he's an American citizen. He has a gambling problem. Rather, he *had* a gambling problem."

Lerens grinned and the two uniformed officers stared at Hugo, then exchanged confused glances. "You should probably explain that," she said.

"I got his name from the crime-scene log, I've told you guys before—you should use an ID number instead of a name for that. He's an American, because you called us here, of course."

"And the gambling problem?" Lerens asked.

"From the dirt on his fingers and the pair of dice on his necklace. I saw him the other day in a bellhop suit in the lobby. So he's working two jobs here, some kind of cleaning or maintenance job as well as carrying bags. Given the dice, I presume the two jobs are to pay for his gambling habit."

"Very nice," Lerens said. "I can confirm his name, and it's on the crime-scene log because it *is* confirmed. He stays at the hotel—they have some rooms converted for employees, almost a dormitory. Anyway, we have his passport. Andrew Baxter from California. Been here four months, and you're right about the double shifts. Hard worker, the manager tells me."

"Did Dr. Sprengelmeyer suggest a time of death?"

"Reluctantly. Sometime within the last three hours."

"And how many stab wounds?" Hugo asked. "Mind if I look?"

"Four. And go right ahead." She turned and spoke to one of the officers, the one still wearing blue surgical gloves. "Turn him over, please."

The officer did so and Hugo knelt to inspect the wounds. Lerens handed him a pair of gloves, and when he'd snapped them on Hugo probed with fingertips at the deep cuts in Baxter's back. He tried to assess the angle and depth without damaging any of the already-slashed flesh.

"One of these must have pierced his heart," he said, looking around.

"Right, otherwise there'd be more blood."

"Precisely. And he died quickly, because he didn't go up or even fall down the stairs," Hugo said, turning to look around him. "But not before he grabbed at the wall, so the first blow didn't kill him right away."

"That tell us anything about his killer?" one of the cops asked.

"Maybe." Hugo stood and peeled off the gloves.

"Drop them on the floor, we'll clean up later," Lerens said. "Any questions?"

"I think you know the first one," Hugo said.

"Let's talk upstairs." She turned to the policemen. "Wait here, please, until the medical examiner's people come to take him. You know the drill."

Both men stood to attention and murmured acquiescence, an impressive show of respect. In the company of other officers, other people really, Hugo had often found himself protective of Lerens, but the more time he spent with her, the more he was coming to realize that she was accepted by the men and women of the Paris police, most anyway, for who she was. And he well knew that she didn't need his protection, either; she could take care of any problems herself, but it was a mark of his respect and a measure of their friendship that he felt that way, so he didn't chide himself for it.

Once in the hallway, they walked side by side toward the elevator. Hugo's phone buzzed and he read the incoming text from Ambassador Taylor—which was just a question mark. He replied, typing, "Not HH, American hotel employee."

"You want to know if this guy has any connection to Helen Hancock?" Lerens said.

"Other than the hotel connection, yes."

"None that we've found yet. We can go talk to her right now, if you like."

"We could if her room weren't bugged," Hugo said.

"*Merde*, that's right." Lerens paused. "Well, now we have to do this officially, Hugo; no more Tom sneaking around in the shadows. We need to move her into a new room and start an official investigation into that."

"Let's just see if the two things are related," Hugo said.

"*Non*, absolutely not. Maybe we won't find a connection now, but if we get deep into this murder investigation and discover there is one, that won't look good. At all."

"Fine. But let's talk to her briefly now to establish an alibi. You know as well as I do that the sooner we do that, the better. We can talk in the hallway; it won't take a moment."

"I prefer to do my interviews at the police station." Lerens frowned. "But I would like to check where she was at the time of the murder, and you're right that we should do that soon."

Hugo nodded and continued down the hallway, not waiting for her to change her mind. At the elevator, he pushed the up button and the doors opened immediately. Lerens followed him in and twenty seconds later they were in front of Hancock's door.

Hugo knocked. Nothing.

He knocked again, and after a moment a weak voice came from inside. "Who is it?"

"Ms. Hancock, it's Hugo Marston from the embassy."

"Wait a minute, please."

Hugo and Lerens swapped concerned glances but didn't say anything, waiting until Hancock opened the door. When she did, Hugo was surprised by her appearance. She wore a white flannel robe wrapped tightly around her, and her face was pale and free of makeup.

"I hope this is important," she said, turning and leaving the door open as she walked back into her suite.

"Ms. Hancock." Hugo indicated with his head that he wanted to talk outside the room, not inside.

She sighed and shuffled toward him, picking up a room key from a side table as she went and dropping it into a robe pocket. She closed the door behind her and turned, a frown on her face.

"What is it?" she asked.

"Are you feeling all right?" Hugo asked.

"I'm fine. Resting."

"You're sure? You look . . . a little under the weather." Hugo kept his voice soft, so she'd know it was genuine concern driving his questions. He wondered whether she'd taken some medication, a strong painkiller or maybe an antidepressant, because this wasn't the peppy, alert woman Hugo had talked to before.

Hancock looked at him in surprise, then smiled. "This is going in a book."

"What is?" Hugo asked.

"You show up here and get all concerned for my welfare because I'm not made-up and I'm acting a little dopey."

"Well, it is midmorning," Hugo pointed out. "So I was just—"

"Oh, for goodness' sake." She waved a hand to silence him. "I'm not wearing makeup and I'm floppy like a noodle because I just had a facial, a mani-pedi, and then a ninety-minute hot-rock massage. Seriously, you try that and tell me how you are afterward."

"Ah, that does explain it," Hugo said, feeling a little sheepish.

"Well, we won't take up any more of your time. Those services were here in the hotel?"

"Of course. I just got back to my room. What did you need from me?"

"Nothing," Hugo said. "It's not important right now; you can go back to relaxing."

"I wish I could," she said. "Unfortunately, I have a dozen e-mails to respond to, from fans and bloggers."

"Always working, eh?"

"It's not just the stories that need constant attention. If I don't write back to a reader within a few days, well, it feels rude to me. Although they always seem very grateful, even if I leave it for a week."

"We'll let you go then. . . . Oh," Hugo said, "do try and stay out of sight of that camera."

"I put flowers in front of it."

"Excuse me?" Lerens said.

"I ordered a tall vase of flowers and put them in front of where the camera is. They may be able to hear me while I watch television or hum while I write, but they can't see anything." She held up an admonishing finger. "And before you tell me I've tipped them off, I don't care. I'm not going to continue to act like I don't know about it and be careful with everything I do in there. So I don't care if they think I know, because I do."

"That's fine," Hugo said.

"Have you decided what to do about it?" she asked.

"Pretty much. Can we come by a little later and talk again?" Hugo glanced at Lerens. "We're kind of in the middle of an emergency right now."

"Oh, really? Anything I need to know about?"

"No, it's not related to this," Hugo assured her. "You'll probably find out about it soon enough anyway, and, if not, we'll fill you in later."

"Now I'm curious," she said.

"Well, we have to run. Thanks for your time; we'll call before we come by. Make sure you're available."

"I'm going out to lunch, but otherwise I'll be writing or napping," she said. "Either way, feel free to interrupt."

Hugo followed Lerens down the hallway to the elevator bank, where they stopped to talk.

"'Unrelated,' eh?" Lerens said. "Why does that seem so unlikely to me?"

"Me too, but it's certainly possible, isn't it?"

"*Bien sûr*," she said. *Of course.*

"Especially since she seems to have an alibi."

"I'll have Jameson check the spa to make sure she was there for that whole time period. If so, and if Sprengelmeyer is right about the time of death, then she most certainly does."

"Exactly." Hugo clapped her lightly on the shoulder. "Which means you guys now have *two* mysteries to solve."

CHAPTER EIGHT

Hugo decided to walk with Lerens to the hotel's spa to confirm for themselves that Helen Hancock was indeed at the spa for almost four hours. She'd arrived fifteen minutes early for her appointment, sitting in a robe in a comfy chair and reading over some pages of her manuscript, the receptionist said. At least, she'd assumed it was her manuscript. "After all, she's a famous writer—what else would it be?"

That question answered, Hugo left Lerens to organize her investigations and stepped out of the hotel to stroll down Rue des Écoles, deep in thought. Early on in murder inquiries there was a temptation to try to figure out who did what and why, to want to catch the killer as quickly as possible. All well and good, Hugo knew, but his first task was always to gather information, not to point fingers. He's seen good cops, and agents, decide too soon who the bad guy was and subsequently fail to investigate other aspects of their cases. Confirmation bias, but of a particularly pernicious nature—because at one end there was a dead person, and at the other, someone risked losing their freedom.

Facts before findings, Hugo's mentor had told him, *not the other way around*. Hugo had followed this advice all his career and to his knowledge had never arrested, let alone seen convicted, an innocent man. His mind flicked past this case to an image of Rick Cofer, and he shook his head. *Not that convicting the right guy necessarily guaranteed justice.*

A rumble from his stomach guided him into a nearby boulangerie, and he stood inside the door for a moment to savor the sights and smells of the fresh breads and other baked delights. He selected a vegetarian brie and tomato sandwich, the baguette bread crisp and crumbly in his fingers, and he took a bite as he left the bakery and ambled slowly back toward the hotel.

Ten minutes later, as he dropped the sandwich wrapper into a trash can, his phone rang.

"*Claudia, bonjour*," he said.

"*Salut*, handsome."

"I just ate lunch, if you're calling to take me out."

"What is that word you Americans use?" she asked, then answered her own question. "Ah, yes, I think it is *moocher*."

"A fine word," Hugo said. "But a little harsh."

"I'm joking, silly. Anyway, this is an official call. Newspaper business."

"How interesting. What can I do for you?"

"A little bird told me an American employee at the Sorbonne Hotel was murdered today. Is that right?"

"You don't cover the crime beat now, do you?"

"As you well know, I cover whatever story is worth writing. And stop avoiding the question."

"Shouldn't you be asking the police?"

"I did. They told me Camille Lerens was in charge, and she's not answering my calls. Even if she did, she'd give me the party line, which would involve a lot of words but no information."

Hugo smiled. "'Can't say much until the cause of death is confirmed,' 'looking into all angles,' 'will issue a press release in due course.'"

"Precisely. And since she's involved, and the dead guy was American, I knew you'd have your nose stuck into things."

"Delightfully put."

She laughed gently. "Well, I am a writer. Speaking of which, isn't Helen Hancock staying at that hotel, too?"

"I believe she might be," Hugo said. "No connection, though, if that's what you're hoping."

"How can you be so sure? Especially this soon."

Hugo paused. "Fair enough. So far there's no evidence of a connection; how's that?"

"Not much better. Come on, Hugo, give me a little something I can use."

"Now who's mooching?"

"Not me, I'll make it worth your while for sure." She softened her voice. "Maybe tonight if the information is good enough."

Hugo's smile broadened. "I think I should get paid in advance."

"Hugo—"

His phone buzzed. "Let me call you right back. Camille's trying to reach me."

"Fine, but you better. *Ciao* for now, sexy."

Hugo clicked over to Lerens. "Any news?"

"You could say that. Where are you?"

"About thirty steps from the hotel."

"Good. Take the elevator to the top floor. I'll be waiting."

When the elevator doors opened, Hugo stepped out and looked to his right. Camille Lerens and Paul Jameson, carrying a black bag, stood outside an open door, talking in quiet voices. They both looked over at Hugo and waited for him to join them.

"Found something interesting?" Hugo asked.

"Understatement," Jameson replied. He turned to Lerens. "I'll get right to it." He nodded to Hugo and started down the hallway toward the elevator.

"Where's he going?"

"I'll tell you in a moment," Lerens said. "First, I have something to show you."

Hugo followed her through the open door into a large hotel room that had been converted into a sleeping space for four people. A single bed was tucked into each corner, a shoulder-height metal locker beside each one. The rest of the space was taken up by armchairs of various sizes, none of them matching.

"Sleeping quarters for some of the staff," Lerens said. "There's a kitchenette down the hallway, bathrooms too."

"Very cozy." He nodded to one of the beds. "That's Andrew Baxter's, I assume."

"Correct," Lerens said, but she cocked her head as if to ask how he knew.

"Oh, too easy. Each bed has storage for private items, those lockers. The other three are padlocked shut, only that one has no padlock. I assume you already removed it, searched his locker, and found something interesting."

"Correct again, Sherlock." She turned and walked to Baxter's locker, and Hugo followed her. She opened its door and moved aside so Hugo could look inside himself. "Forensics and the photographer are done; put these on and touch whatever you want." She handed him a pair of blue surgical gloves. "I wanted you to have a look before I bagged it all for evidence."

The locker had three shelves in the top half, leaving the bottom open for larger items. Baxter had used this lower space for shoes and to hang a heavy winter coat made of wool, one that had seen better days. On the top shelf, Hugo saw several books, and he took them out. The first was a winner's guide to online gambling, or so the title proclaimed.

"Looks like you were right about his hobby," Lerens said.

Hugo nodded and looked at the other two books, both novels. And both by Helen Hancock. He took out his phone and photographed the front covers, then inspected them more closely.

"These don't look like he's read them. Pristine covers, no grubby pages. I'm not sure he's even opened them."

"And never will."

"You're not thinking this is enough to bring our favorite writer into the investigation, are you?" Hugo asked.

"Not by itself, no. But we found more than just the books."

Hugo looked into the locker, running his mind over what was there and, more important, what wasn't. "His laptop," Hugo said.

"You're good at this," Lerens said with a smile.

"Been doing it a few years now. This empty shelf and the lack of any laptop or tablet tell me you already took it and went to work on it." He smiled. "And Paul Jameson was carrying a computer bag when he left."

"I took a quick look myself. Not even password protected."

"No?" Hugo rapped his knuckles against the metal of the locker. "Maybe not too surprising; it's not like anyone's busting into this thing easily."

"True."

"Which reminds me. How did you get into it?"

"The key. Paul Jameson found it under his bed."

"In what way?" Hugo asked. "Like he'd dropped it there, or like he'd put it there on purpose?"

"It was in a shoe." Lerens pointed to a pair on the floor beside the locker. "More like a slipper, I guess, but it was tucked into one of those. And no doubt you're about to ask me which one, left or right, for some reason."

"Nope," Hugo said. "I don't think that matters." He stooped and looked at the worn leather slippers, picking them up one before the other, inspecting the top and the sole of each. "I assume you checked inside them both? Given the odor, I'd prefer not to reach inside even with gloves on."

Lerens smiled. "We did. Rather, Paul did. I happen to agree with your assessment of them."

"Smart woman. Anyway, back to the computer. Find anything interesting on it?"

"I thought you'd never ask. 'Yes' is the short answer."

"And the long answer?"

"Is that we found evidence, well, proof really, that our friend Andrew Baxter was the one who set up the camera in Helen Hancock's room. Video clips of the room and also the software he used to record her. It's a probably a formality, but I have my people taking out the camera right now, and when they're done we'll match the camera itself with the unique ID number on his computer."

"Well, well," Hugo said, relieved that he needn't go through the hassle of setting up countersurveillance in Hancock's room. "How interesting. Any clue why Baxter would do something like that? Was it for the manuscript?"

"We didn't find any evidence of that on the computer. Just a bunch of downloads, no indication as to why he was doing it, or what he was after."

"Gamblers are often short of money," Hugo said. "Maybe he just hadn't got around to the blackmail request."

"Exactly what I was thinking."

"What else was on the hard drive?"

"Nothing," Lerens said.

"Nothing at all?"

"Well, I didn't look very hard," Lerens said. "When I saw that spy software, I gave it to Jameson to run over to our tech people. They'll scrub it and let me know what else is on there if it's at all relevant. I doubt there'll be much, as it's a fairly new computer, and it's possible he bought it specifically for this." She shook her head. "That's a lot of drive space. Who knows how long he'd have gone on recording if . . ."

"If someone hadn't hit his stop button," Hugo said.

Lerens grimaced. "That's one way to put it, if not the most delicate way."

"Well," Hugo said, "in my experience, murder is rarely a delicate business. What's your plan now?"

"I think it's time for a more formal interview of our celebrity guest, Helen Hancock."

"Agreed," Hugo said. "She's the only person who might have some clue why Baxter was recording her, and whether it's related to his sudden demise."

"Apart from the murderer, of course," Lerens said.

"Right. If it weren't for her cast-iron alibi, she'd be a decent suspect."

"I know. I asked Jameson to drop off the computer and then double-check that alibi, get a statement from her masseuse and whoever else saw her. We just took the receptionist's word, but I suppose it's possible Hancock excused herself to the restroom and . . ." Lerens shrugged. "Not very likely, but we need to be sure."

"Where are you interviewing Helen?"

"At headquarters," Lerens said. "We need this to be official, recorded and witnessed properly."

Hugo nodded. "Good. And as a representative of the United States, I should be present at the questioning of my fellow American."

"I think that's an excellent idea," Lerens said.

CHAPTER NINE

Hugo decided to sit next to Helen Hancock in the interview room. He caught Lerens's eye as he pulled the chair out, and she nodded almost imperceptibly. The writer may know more than she was saying, but she certainly wasn't a suspect in Baxter's death—Paul Jameson had spoken to the two people who'd provided her spa treatments, and both were positive she'd been with one or other of them the whole time, four solid hours. No bathroom breaks at all.

Hancock looked up at him as Hugo sat beside her, and he patted the back of her hand reassuringly.

"Don't worry, you're safe here," he said.

"Am I in trouble for something?"

"Not at all," Hugo said. "The police just have a few questions. I assume you heard about what happened this morning?"

"Just that someone died. Climbing the stairs or something. Was it a heart attack?"

"No," Hugo said and looked at Lerens. Her English was decent, but he knew she'd want to ask very specific questions, and in her own language. "Why don't you do this in French and I'll translate. Is that OK with both of you?" He looked back and forth between them, and both nodded. "Good. I'll save any questions I have until the end and try not to interrupt."

"*Bien*," Lerens began. "The man who died, I'm afraid he was murdered. Stabbed, to be precise."

Hugo translated and watched as Hancock's eyes widened.

"Murdered? Right there in the hotel? How awful! Why would someone do that? *Who* would do that?"

"That's what we're trying to find out," Lerens said after Hugo had relayed her statement. She pulled out a picture of Andrew Baxter that she'd found in his wallet. She folded it in half, cutting out the young woman he'd been standing next to, and slid it across the table. "Do you know this man?"

Hancock leaned over the picture and studied it. "He looks familiar. Does he work at the hotel?"

"I'm asking you that," Lerens said gently.

"Then, yes. I think I've seen him at the hotel. In the picture, he's dressed . . . differently, but I'm sure it's the same man. Is this who . . . ?"

"Who was killed, yes," Lerens said.

"Oh, how awful." Hancock dragged her gaze away from the picture and up to Lerens. "But I don't think I've ever spoken to him. Maybe a *bonjour* here and there, but nothing more than that."

"Actually, he's American."

"Oh, I didn't know that."

"No reason why you should," Lerens said. "Here's why I'm asking, why you're here. It seems that he was the one who put the spy camera in your room."

Hancock's mouth opened and closed, and she sat back in her chair. "Him? But why?"

"We're not sure yet. We found a computer that has downloads from the camera, and the ID on the software matches what we took from behind the picture. So when I say it *seems* he put the camera there, we're almost certain. At the very least, he was the one monitoring you."

"Do you mean someone else was involved, too?"

"That we don't know yet. Given that he's dead and you have a solid alibi, I'm betting so." Lerens held up a hand. "And before you ask me who, I don't know. That's what we're trying to find out."

Hancock visibly paled. "Am I . . . in danger?"

"We'd like you to change hotels," Lerens said. "Just as a precaution, until we know more."

The writer sat quietly for a moment. "But I've tried other hotels. The Sorbonne is the only one where I can get any writing done. It's quiet, the walls are thicker, and . . . just the atmosphere of the place, everything about it. I don't think I can work anywhere else."

"It'll just be for a few days. Maybe a week. Can you take some time off from writing for that long? Have a break for a week?"

"I don't know," Hancock said weakly. "I have deadlines. Expectations from my publisher."

"I'm sure they'd understand under the circumstances; and, if not, I'd be happy to talk to them." Lerens smiled. "Or get Hugo to."

Hancock nodded. "I'll call them. I think it'll be fine, but . . . I just want to think for an hour or two. It may seem silly to you, but this is my livelihood, it's how I define myself. Switching hotels, it's . . . a disruption. Do you really think I'm in danger?"

Lerens and Hugo exchanged glances, and Hugo finally spoke.

"Personally, I doubt it very much. From what we've gathered so far, it seems likely that whoever is involved in this wants something from you. It could be a copy of your work, maybe pictures of you undressed."

"Blackmail?" she asked.

"It's possible," Hugo went on. "Like Camille said, we're working on it. But I don't see how anyone benefits from doing you harm. And it's still possible that Baxter's murder has nothing to do with the spy camera in your room. We just don't know yet."

Hancock stared at the photo on the table. "I can't decide whether to feel sorry for him or be angry at him." She looked up at Hugo. "It's all just so insane, I can't believe this is happening."

"We'll get to the bottom of it," Hugo said.

"I know. At least, I hope you will," she said. She looked at the watch on her wrist. "Do you need me anymore? I'm supposed to be meeting with my writing group this evening, in less than an hour. Not that I have the energy or motivation for that."

Hugo thought for a moment. "Why don't you let me take you back to the Sorbonne, you can call your people and see about changing hotels. Then I'll go with Lieutenant Lerens and talk to your students, let them know a little about what's going on and why you can't meet. We should talk to them anyway."

Lerens understood and showed it with a nod. "A good idea. In the meantime, I'll get with Jameson, see what's he's found and have him stationed at the hotel with Madame Hancock, for her peace of mind."

When Hugo translated for her, Hancock turned to Lerens. "Thank you." Then her expression suddenly changed, from tiredness to worry. "You don't think any of my students . . ." Her voice tailed off.

"No reason in the world to think anything untoward about them," Hugo said. "But before I drop you off, you can tell me about each of them. I should know who I'm meeting."

Hugo let the folks at the American Library know that he was sitting in for Helen Hancock and, because he knew the staff, gave them enough details to raise some eyebrows but not enough so they could gossip too much. He'd asked one of the employees, Michelle Juneau, to have the three students wait in the main library when they arrived, and he'd see them one by one in the conference room.

The library had added several exhibits to the room since his last visit, or since he'd last paid attention, anyway. Instead of filling it with books, they'd put in a long, low, glass cabinet that contained a dozen or so artifacts related to books or writers. Hugo leaned forward to read the label under a pair of spectacles, which apparently had belonged to F. Scott Fitzgerald. Beside them was a handwritten note to the same author from his wife, Zelda, referencing a supper at the home of someone called Melissa Shearer, a name Hugo didn't recognize.

The next item in the case caught his eye, and he smiled as he read the printed card describing the object.

This dagger was owned by the late great actress Isabelle Severin. In her later years she used it as a letter opener but, if the stories are true, in the 1940s she used her movie-star status to aid the French Resistance in

WWII, and used this very dagger to kill an SS soldier and save a Resistance fighter. The dagger was left to the library by Madame Severin at her death. Please consult a librarian to see the rest of the Severin collection.

He checked his watch, then inspected the other items in the cabinet, stopping at the last one, which he recognized as a .44 Magnum. It was accompanied by a scatter of bullets lying artistically around it, and the display card read: *This gun belonged to Hunter Stockton Thompson, 1937–2005. Donated to the library by Lorne Kerlin, philanthropist and friend of Mr. Thompson.*

He turned when someone entered the room, expecting a nerdy writing student and immediately adjusting his expectations. Nerdy she was not. Wendy Pottgen looked like she would get along great with his kink-oriented friend, Merlyn. Pottgen had the bold lips and big eyes of a Marilyn Monroe and exuded a similar sexuality, but she packed her curves into tight white jeans and a shirt that looked like it was made of leather but probably wasn't. She sported a studded leather collar around her neck, and when Hugo stood to greet her, she squeezed his hand like she was trying to hurt him.

"Ms. Pottgen, I'm Hugo Marston," he began. "I'm sorry to—"

"Please, call me Buzzy. Everyone does." Full red lips smiled broadly, and her accent was southern and soft, almost sensual. "I hope everything's OK; you're sounding very official. Are you a cop or something?"

"No, I'm not. But there's been an incident at the hotel where Ms. Hancock is staying. She's fine and we're keeping an eye on her, but she's not able to attend."

She tilted her head. "You're sure you're not a cop?"

They sat down at the large conference table. "No, I'm the RSO at the US Embassy. Regional Security Officer, that is. It's my job to help Americans who need it and work with local law enforcement on cases involving Americans."

"Sounds important."

"Sometimes." Hugo smiled. "There's also a lot of babysitting involved."

Pottgen raised an eyebrow. "So is this important or babysitting?"

Smart woman. "As far as Ms. Hancock goes, that's undetermined as yet."

"You said she's OK, though."

"She is, yes. But I need to ask you a few questions, if you don't mind."

"Fire away, I'll help any way I can."

"Thanks." Hugo pulled a pen and notebook from his jacket pocket and flipped the latter open. "How long have you known her?"

"Helen? About a week. I applied for the tutorial online and was accepted."

"Where are you from?" he asked.

"Baton Rouge, born and raised. You can't tell from my accent that I'm a Louisiana girl?"

"I might have guessed," Hugo said with a smile. "Tell me about the tutorial, what exactly that is."

"Sure. So it's a new thing, but I think she plans to do it every year. It's a two-week course, two hours a day with Helen. It's pretty informal, but at the end of every session she gives us a writing exercise to complete for the next day."

"Do you find it helpful?"

"The exercise or the tutorial?"

"Both," Hugo said.

"Yes. I mean, look, I'm doing a masters in fine arts, creative writing, at New York University, but she's not really teaching what they teach there. She gives a more . . . personal perspective. She talks about the publishing process, agents, and editors. It's been very enlightening."

"And only three of you are taking this course?"

"Supposed to be four but one guy dropped out, I heard. So, yeah, now just three of us."

"Tell me about the other two."

She tilted her head again. "Are you asking me to snitch on my fellow writers?"

"Have they done anything wrong?"

"Not that I know of."

"Well then," Hugo said with a smile. "It's not snitching, is it?"

"Did you used to be a cop?" she asked.

"I used to be with the FBI, yes."

Pottgen sat back in her chair. "Wow. That's pretty hot."

"Thanks." Hugo cleared his throat. "Now then, your writing colleagues...?"

"Yeah, sorry. So, two dudes, both Americans. One is Ambrósio Silva. Super nice guy. I guess he used to play soccer, always going on about some team called Benfica. Anyway, we've become good friends. He's a real charmer, not in a sleazy way; he's just funny and cool to be around."

"He's Portuguese?"

Pottgen laughed. "Don't say that to him; he'll correct you real fast. His family is from the Azores."

"Good writer?"

"As far as I can tell. A huge fan of Helen's, which is a little odd to me, but when you go on a small course like this you hope desperately the other people will be cool. And fun. He is."

"Wait, why is it odd he'd be a fan of Helen's?"

She shrugged. "I don't know. I guess the type of books she writes. I mean, they're heavy on romance, light on sex, and only her recent couple of books have moved toward what I'd peg as 'guy material,' like suspense and murder."

"You don't think guys read romance?" Hugo pressed.

"Do you read it?"

"Fair point," he conceded. "So he gets on well with Helen."

"I don't think there's anyone in the world he wouldn't get on with. Like I said, a super nice guy."

"And the other person?"

"He's nice, too. Mike Rice. From Austin, Texas, I think."

"Really? That's my hometown," Hugo said.

"What a coincidence," she said. "Isn't that the city famous for being weird? Didn't have you pegged as a weirdo."

"You never can tell, can you?"

"Ain't that the truth. Anyway, Mike. Extremely not weird. Kinda quiet, has a dry sense of humor, and laps up everything Helen says. Takes notes nonstop, to the point where a couple of days ago she told him to put his pen down and actually listen. Engage in the discussion."

"He's a romance writer?"

"Unpublished, we all are. But yeah, he wants to be." She thought for a moment. "He seems more . . . business oriented than Ambrósio or me."

"What do you mean by that?"

"So I approach writing as an art that has a large measure of craft to it. In other words, for me, I am learning all I can about the craft of writing so I can express the things I want to say, tell the stories I want to tell. The ability to write well, which is what I mean by *craft*, is really just a mechanism to allow me to get the words out in the best way possible. Does that make sense?"

"I think so, yes."

"So, imagine a beautiful piece of music. If you give that to a man with a violin, he can make it sound good. But he's limited in what he can achieve. Give that same piece of music to an orchestra and it really comes alive, captures the emotion and magic that the composer dreamed it would have. The mechanics of writing, that word *craft* again, is the addition of instruments. The more I learn, the better I can play out my stories."

"A nice image," Hugo said. "I get what you're saying."

"OK, good. So that's why I'm here, why I'm doing my MFA. For Mike, it all seems a little less arts-oriented, more like he's looking for a formula to make himself a bestseller." She held up a hand. "And I don't mean that in a bad way; it's just a different approach. Businesslike, I guess."

"'No man but a blockhead ever wrote, except for money.'"

"Well, Helen disagrees with Samuel Johnson on that issue. She said the opposite, that if you write purely to make a buck, you're gonna be sorely disappointed, because most authors don't make much at all."

"She seems to."

Pottgen shrugged. "I guess."

"You guess? She's a bestseller all over the world."

"I know. I think she's having a hard time with the business side of things now, is all. That's why she's so adamant that we write because we're passionate about it, not because we want to get rich. Did you know that her first book was rejected by about thirty agents and almost all of the major publishing houses?"

"I didn't, no."

"Rejection is a big part of the game, she told us. Which is why we need to take refuge in the work itself."

"Sounds like sage advice."

Pottgen gave him that broad smile again. "I guess we'll see, won't we?"

"I suppose so." *If force of personality counts for anything, you'll be just fine*, Hugo thought. "Anything else that might help me?"

"I don't know. You haven't really said what you need help with."

"True, and forgive the coyness; it's by necessity not choice. Has Helen Hancock talked about run-ins with anyone? Sometimes famous authors have stalkers, or people who think they've been put in a book against their will. Anything like that?"

"Not that she's mentioned to me or the others, as far as I know."

"Do you know someone called Andrew Baxter?"

He studied her closely for a reaction but her face gave nothing away. "No, I don't think so. Who is that?"

"Someone from the hotel. Where are you all living, by the way?"

"I'm renting a studio apartment," Pottgen said. "The guys are sharing a place about two blocks from me, a one-bedroom. I gather Mike won the toss for the bedroom and Ambrósio has the couch, which he barely fits on."

"Big guy?"

"Six three and must be two-fifty. When he told me he used to play 'football,' I had assumed the American kind."

"Is he doing an MFA too?"

"We all are. A precondition to applying for the course."

"Makes sense. Well, thanks for your time." He slid a business card to her. "If you think of anything, call me. And would you ask Mr. Silva to step in here?"

"Sure thing." She stood and put out her hand, squeezing his hard again, her head tilted and a strand of brown hair falling over one eye. "You need anything else, just let me know."

As he sat in the quiet of the conference room, Hugo's phone buzzed in his pocket. When he answered, it was Lieutenant Lerens.

"Camille, you have some news?"

"Yes. Paul Jameson identified the store where the camera was purchased. Took him a lot of phone calls, but he did it."

"Excellent, tell him well done."

"You want to guess who bought it, or you want me to tell you?" Hugo smiled at the humor in her voice. "You know I like making you guess."

"Then I'll go with the disappointingly obvious answer. Andrew Baxter."

"Correct."

Hugo thought for a moment. "You know, I've visited a few of those stores and, as you might expect, they have great surveillance footage of everyone inside and out. Can you see if they do? Could be that someone's waiting in the car outside; we know there's another person involved."

"Because Baxter's dead?"

"Right. And assuming the spy camera and his murder are connected, which we should."

"I've been thinking about that. Maybe he just owed someone money, got himself killed that way. We don't know for sure that the surveillance and his murder are linked."

"That's possible," Hugo said. "But usually loan sharks rough you up a little first. They want their money, and killing the client puts a stop to any chance of that."

"Good point."

"We can look at both angles, but in the meantime can you have Paul get any footage they may have?"

"Will do. You being productive?"

"Moderately," Hugo said. "I'm talking to Hancock's students."

"Enjoy. Let me know if you come up with anything."

"Will do." Hugo looked up as the door to the conference room opened. Pottgen stuck her head into the room.

"Mike's in the restroom but will be right here. Ambrósio, apparently, didn't want to wait around. Took off about ten minutes ago."

"Do you know where to?"

"No clue, but when I see him I'll tell him to call you."

"Please do," said Hugo. "I'd appreciate that."

CHAPTER TEN

Hugo introduced himself and studied Michael Rice as they sat. In his midthirties, Hugo guessed, he looked like a rugby player acting the part of a writer. He was solidly built, with a square jaw and barrel chest, but didn't look to be carrying any fat on him. He wore a worn tweed jacket over a plain white shirt. His corduroy pants looked new, as did his small leather bag that might have contained a computer and, more likely, a few moleskin notebooks. He sat opposite Hugo and said nothing, just looked around a couple of times.

No nerves at all, Hugo thought, before saying, "You're probably wondering why I'm here instead of Helen Hancock."

"I am."

"There was an incident at the hotel. I can't really tell you anything more, but I've been tasked with letting you guys know and talking to you about her."

"Is she OK?"

"She's fine. Just some . . ." Hugo cast about for the right words, suddenly aware he was talking to a writer. "I guess you could say *weirdness* going on with her, but she's not hurt or anything like that."

"Glad to hear it; you being here had us worried."

Hugo nodded to show he understood. "So, let me ask you, did you meet her for the first time here, in Paris?"

"We talked a couple of times on the phone, as part of the final application process, but yes, I didn't meet her until I got here."

"You think she's a good teacher?"

Rice pursed his lips as he considered the question. "Yes, I'd say so."

"That's it?" Hugo pressed.

Rice shrugged. "I'll be honest, Mr. Marston. I am a fairly good writer. I'm also an extremely fast writer. I can put out a book in a month, two months at the most. There's a lot of money to be made by authors who are prolific and writing in the romance genre. I'm not here to learn how to become the next James Joyce or Ernest Hemingway. I want to know the tricks of the trade, and *her* trade specifically." He gave a wry smile. "In my limited experience, a lot of writers don't share that approach, don't approve of it."

"Does Helen Hancock?"

"She doesn't seem to mind. I mean, it's not like we've explicitly had that conversation, but I'd think it'd be obvious how I'm looking at things." He shrugged. "She's a pragmatist, too, you know. She knows as well as anyone that it's a business as well as a creative endeavor. Almost half of what we talk about is the publishing side, how editors and agents work, marketing and sales, that kind of thing."

"I see. In your dealings with her, have you come across anyone who might dislike her?"

"She's a famous author. I imagine they all have people who don't like them, probably people who *think* they know them but don't."

"Disgruntled fans, you mean."

"I guess. . . . But in her case specifically, I really don't know of anyone."

"And she gets on well with Ms. Pottgen and Mr. Silva?"

"Yes. We all get along fine." He leaned forward. "Can you tell me more of what this is about? If I'm supposed to be helping you with your inquiry, it'd be good to know what you're inquiring about."

"I'm not too sure myself," Hugo said. "Are you familiar with the Sorbonne Hotel?"

"In what way? I mean, I've heard of it, of course. Only been there a couple of times."

"On this trip?"

"Yes. Helen is staying there; she wanted us all to come over and have a drink together in the bar the first night we got to Paris."

"And the other time?"

"I met with her for tea. They do a fancy English spread, different types of tea, scones, cucumber sandwiches, that sort of thing."

"Did she do that for the others?"

Rice laughed gently. "What, invite them for tea and then make them pay?"

Hugo smiled in return. "As you said, it's a business as well as a creative endeavor. Do you know anyone who works there?"

"No."

"Does the name Andrew Baxter mean anything to you?"

"No. Who is he?"

"An employee there. OK, last question."

"Fire away."

"Do you know if it's common for writers to steal each other's work?"

"I've not been in the business long," Rice said. "But I doubt it. I assume you're referring to budding writers like me stealing from successful authors?"

"Well, that's one possibility, but I was wondering more generally if there was much to gain from it."

"I don't think so. Most people write on computers, so it'd be easy for someone to show when they wrote a passage, or an entire book. And, speaking of computers, they've made plagiarism much easier to uncover." He frowned in thought. "That said, there have been a few cases in recent years, and possibly some that weren't discovered. Is that what's going on with Helen?"

"No idea," Hugo said truthfully. "It's one of several possibilities." He took a card from his pocket and handed it to Rice. "If anything crosses your mind, something you feel I should know about, you'll give me a call?"

"Sure," Rice said, with another wry smile. "Not sure what that would be, but if I see it I'll let you know."

"Thanks. I gather Mr. Silva left the building."

"No, he's here. Went outside to take a phone call is all. Want me to send him in?"

"Please." They shook hands, and as Hugo watched Rice leave, he let his mind wander over the reasons that either he or Buzzy Pottgen might have to spy on Helen Hancock. He'd forgotten to ask Pottgen about writers stealing other writers' work, and he had hesitated before asking Rice, but if either one had put the spy camera in place, they'd know by now it'd been discovered.

Hugo had already searched on the Internet for examples of plagiarism in the fiction world, and he had come up with more than he'd expected. Some had been newcomers to the business stealing from older or more established writers, but some had also been well-known authors plucking entire passages from more obscure works. And Hugo knew, as Rice had indicated, that he was only reading about the ones who'd been caught.

But plagiarism didn't seem the most likely explanation for the spy camera. For Rice and Pottgen it would be hard to pull off unless they knew someone who worked at the hotel, and not just knew them but trusted them and could somehow get them to go along with it. A lover, maybe? But he'd confirmed with each one that they'd only been in Paris a week, hardly time to capture someone's heart to that degree, even if Pottgen did vibrate with sexuality. Rice, not so much.

They were also too obvious as suspects, not to mention the fact that they already had open access to Hancock. *No*, Hugo thought, *surely they have no need to go to such extremes, and they have too much to lose if caught.*

Which meant that if this was about stealing her work, it was someone at the hotel, someone who wasn't Andrew Baxter.

And if it wasn't about plagiarism, Hugo knew that blackmail was the most obvious motive.

Ambrósio Silva was, indeed, a big guy, but he carried his weight lightly and Hugo would've guessed him to be a former athlete if he hadn't already known. He was also a perfect fit for the word *affable*.

"Come in, Mr. Silva; please sit." Hugo put out a hand. "I'm Hugo Marston; I work at the US Embassy."

"So I gather, very cool." Silva settled into a chair. "What's going on?"

"I just had a few questions about your course instructor, Helen Hancock."

"Is she in trouble?"

"Not at all," Hugo reassured him. "But there's been an odd incident at the hotel where she's staying. I'm not at liberty to go into the details, but I'm helping the Paris police with their inquiries. Are you familiar with the hotel?"

"Sure, the Sorbonne. Very fancy. Too much so for my blood, but she's certainly earned it."

"How old are you, Mr. Silva?"

"Please, Ambrósio. I'm thirty-eight." He smiled, showing white teeth. "I've been told I look a little younger. I call it the 'Azorean discount.'"

"Lucky man. Well, I don't want to keep you longer than I need to, so can you tell me if you know a man by the name of Andrew Baxter?"

"The name doesn't ring a bell," Silva said. "Should I know him?"

"No, not necessarily. You said you've not spent much time at the Sorbonne Hotel."

"Right. A beer costs about thirty euros there, so unless someone else is paying I steer clear."

"And you've known Helen Hancock for how long?"

"I met her after applying for the course. We talked on the phone once or twice, then actually met for the first time here."

"You get on well?"

"Absolutely. A nice lady and I feel like I'm learning a lot."

"Have you ever been published?" Hugo asked.

"Not yet. I finished three novels that went nowhere, couldn't even get an agent, and that's when I decided to go the MFA route. Right now I'm halfway through my fourth novel, which is a lot better than the first three. At least I hope so."

"Is it romance?"

"It definitely has elements of romance, yes. Most of the MFA programs..." He searched for the right words. "Let's just say that they don't necessarily promote the various genres of writing. They are most proud when their graduates produce works of literary fiction, rather than mysteries, romance, or horror. Personally, I'm a big fan of Sherlock Holmes; read every single one of them. Brilliant solutions to ingenious mysteries. Agatha Christie, too."

"We have that in common, then."

"Glad to hear it. But not many instructors at the MFA programs would name them as favorites if you asked."

"Snobbery in the book world, imagine that," Hugo said with a smile.

"Your words, not mine. But yeah, you're not far wrong."

"So help me with this, then. If you're being steered toward literary fiction, why would you want to take this course?"

Silva smiled, then looked down as he spoke. "Appropriately, it comes down to three French words."

"Go on."

"Can you guess?" He looked at Hugo, waiting for the penny to drop. It did.

"Ah," Hugo said. "*Nom de plume*. You write literary fiction under your name, while at the same time producing genre works under a pen name."

"Precisely. Did you know that romance is the bestselling category of books? Beats everything hands down."

"I think I'd heard that."

"Right. So you can see why I'd want to invest in this course, learning from the best. The others might not be honest about the commercial side of this, but it's a reality. Well, Mike would 'fess up to it."

"He did already," Hugo said.

"Another reason to be here is that we all want Helen's name on our books. A cover blurb and endorsement from her could be a huge boost to our careers. And before all that, being here and working with Helen will help us get an agent, probably, and a publishing deal for our books."

"Makes perfect sense to me," Hugo said, handing Silva a business card. "Well, I don't really have any more questions right now, but if anything occurs to you that might be relevant, please give me a call."

As soon as he stepped outside the library, Hugo called Helen Hancock.

"Can you e-mail me a copy of the manuscript you're working on right now?" he asked.

"I never let anyone see a work in progress."

"It's not for my reading pleasure," Hugo said. "I want to set up a repeating search of the Internet to see if any parts of the book show up. To do that, I need to have the manuscript to sample."

"How do I know it won't get leaked somehow?"

"Helen, I'm trying to help you here. There are dozens of ways to establish what you wrote and when, so if someone does leak it or steal it from now on, we can easily prove whose work it is. And I give you my word, I'll do all I can to keep every word confidential."

"How much of a guarantee is that?" She sounded dubious.

"Look, when we run the searches, your name won't be associated with any of the content we look for. And I'll make sure one tech, and one only, does the work. After I've sworn him to secrecy."

"Are you making fun of me?"

"No, I'm trying to take your concerns seriously."

"Well. I'm not happy about this; it feels like another violation of my privacy."

Hugo's patience was running thin, and he heard the frustration in his own voice. "Helen, listen to me. I will do all I can to keep your work safe, but without it I have no idea why someone was filming you. I want to be able to confirm this angle or rule it out, and I can't do that unless I have the manuscript."

A long pause, then Hancock said, "Fine. I'll e-mail it to you. Just you and one other person are allowed to see it."

"Fine, thank—"

"And if you read it, please remember it's called a 'work in progress' for a reason; it's a long way from the finished, polished book."

"I don't even plan on reading it," Hugo said. "How about I wait until I can buy it?"

"Fine. OK, I'll trust you. Hold on a second." Hugo heard a clunk, then silence for a full minute before she came back on the line. "I used the e-mail address on the business card you gave me, is that right?"

"Perfect, thank you. I'll let you know the second we get any matches on a search, but I'm not expecting to."

"Well, I certainly hope not," she said. "But do let me know."

Hugo wandered along the busy Rue de l'Université, slower than the businesspeople en route to their next appointment and chattering on their phones, slower even than the tourists who drifted along in pairs and in packs, stopping in the middle of the sidewalk to point something out or take a photo. Hugo found it amusing, and occasionally irritating, how visitors to Paris would spend so much time recording the buildings and monuments of the city for later viewing, perversely oblivious to the swirl of Parisians all around them. For Hugo, it was the people slotted into this city that made it so beautiful, their talent for cooking, for drinking, for making art and writing books. And not just their talent but their passion for something greater than themselves, be that a Baudelaire poem, a performance at the Bataclan theater, or a perfectly fluffy cheese soufflé.

Not to mention they spoke the sexiest language on the planet, and had given him the opportunity to learn it. He smiled at that thought, and decided to put his skill to work. He dialed Lieutenant Lerens, who answered immediately.

"Camille, it's Hugo. Can I send you a document and ask you to assign a technician to see whether it's being plagiarized online?"

"Madame Hancock's new book?"

"The one she's writing here, yes."

"I can get two or three people to work on it; that way we'll know something more quickly."

"I told her we'd use just one person. And the same person all the time, if he or she runs multiple searches."

"Why?" Lerens caught herself. "Oh, she's afraid we'll steal or lose it, right?"

"Something like that, yes."

"Understood. I'll have a tech e-mail you directly so it doesn't even have to come through me."

"*Merci*," Hugo said. "Any news from you?"

"We have a little more on Baxter, but not a lot. It's more what we haven't found that's interesting. No cell phone and no laptop."

"Wait, we have—"

"Turns out the computer we found really does have nothing else on it, just the spy stuff. No e-mail, no Internet history, nothing. It looks like he bought it for one purpose only, which means I'd expect to find something else for his personal use. A tablet or laptop, certainly a cell phone."

"Maybe he was old-fashioned."

"Maybe, but I'm not betting on it."

"Which reminds me," Hugo said. "You're absolutely right that he'd have another device."

"What makes you say that?"

"If I'm right about him being a gambler, and working two jobs to pay for it, then he must have been doing it online."

"Good point. We'll keep looking, of course. And there are a couple of illegal gambling places near here; we're checking those out, too."

"Good, but I don't think this is about gambling. Too much of a coincidence. Did you go through all the footage from the camera yet?"

"Yes, and there's a lot of it. It looks like he activated it manually, as opposed to just leaving it running."

"Are you thinking it's for blackmail?"

"I would be, but she's not really doing anything. There aren't even any clips of her naked, so I can't imagine what he would blackmail her with."

"Maybe he's just a voyeur and got off on it," Hugo suggested.

"Then why choose her room specifically? She's attractive enough, but that hotel is always brimming with young and beautiful women. And who gets off on watching someone type on a computer?"

"Hey, it takes all sorts."

"It does, but I'm sure he targeted her specifically," Lerens said. "I just don't know why, or who else is in on this."

"I agree that she was targeted, and I'm guessing if we found out by whom, we'd have our killer."

"Hugo, let me call you back—I'm getting an incoming call from the hotel and should answer it."

"Sure, let me know if it's something important. Or even unimportant."

Lerens ended the call, and Hugo started the long walk through the Seventh Arrondissement back toward his apartment in the Sixth. He distracted himself en route, stopping to look in the windows of agencies selling apartments in the city, imagining what his permanent place might look like. The beamed-ceiling apartment in Rue de la Huchette, just a stone's throw from his favorite bookstore, Shakespeare and Company? Or maybe the modern place on Rue de Monceau, on the other side of the river and by the park of the same name. *No, too far from the action*, he thought, and sighed with pleasure at the idea that he might one day be able to make such a choice. With a little more lift in his step he started walking again, and he had just crossed Rue Malar when his phone rang. He checked the display and saw it was Lerens.

"Hi, Camille, what did they have to say?"

"*Salut* again, Hugo. Ready for this? They called to let me know that they found another spy camera."

CHAPTER ELEVEN

The next morning, Hugo walked the mile from his apartment to the Sorbonne Hotel, stepping out of his building onto a sidewalk that was wet from a light rain that had stopped an hour before, leaving the air smelling fresh and clean.

As he left Rue Jacob, Hugo passed a man and his son, maybe nine years old, sitting on a pink blanket against the stone wall of a bank. They didn't look homeless—both were clean and seemed well-fed, and in fact the man's large, round belly was his most distinguishing feature. His son thought so, too, because he kept poking it to make them both giggle, over and over, each attuned only to the other, laughing in their own world and seemingly oblivious to the passers-by who glanced down but ignored the paper cup at the edge of their blanket.

At the hotel, Camille Lerens was waiting in the lobby, talking to a woman in a blue business suit. She had dark, curly hair, and when she turned to look at Hugo, he saw large, dark eyes to match. Lerens introduced her as Jill Maxick, one of the senior hotel managers.

"She's got the device in her office," Lerens said. She smiled at Hugo. "I need to make a call, you go ahead and ask her all the questions I just did."

"Thanks, I will," Hugo said. He turned to Maxick, who was smiling.

"Lieutenant Lerens said you probably would, but I don't mind," she said in English. "Shall we go to my office?"

"Sure. So you're an American?"

They walked side by side around the end of the reception desk into a roomy and modern office. "Yes, but I've lived here for fourteen years. Please, sit."

"Lucky you," Hugo said, taking one of the chairs opposite her desk.

"Lucky is right. I started following Depeche Mode around when they went on tour back then. One of the band members fell for me, and me for him, and he brought me here."

"I was a fan back in the day. Which band member?"

"Ah, that would be telling," Maxick said with a wink. "And I don't kiss and tell. Anyway, he brought me here and I guess he left me here, too, not that I'm complaining now."

"It's a great place to live," Hugo agreed. "And you like working at the hotel?"

"As good as any job I've ever had. It's still work, don't get me wrong, but yes, I do."

"I'm not sure I'd be wild about dealing with rich and picky customers all day."

"Most of them are very nice, actually. The Americans and the Russians tend to be the worst, which may or may not surprise you."

"It would not," Hugo said with a smile. "So, to business. Let me first ask, who found the camera?" It sat in a plastic bag between them, and as he listened he picked it up and inspected it. It looked, to his inexpert eye, just like the one from Hancock's room.

"One of the maintenance men. I asked a couple of them to check every single room. You know, after finding out about the one in Ms. Hancock's room."

"Very sensible," Hugo said. "Whose room was it in?"

"The room was empty. Had been for two weeks; we'd remodeled the bathroom, which promptly sprung a leak and needed re-fixing." She pulled a face. "Lucky for us, we've not been at full capacity; otherwise we'd have needed that room."

"Were you about to use it?"

"Yes. It went back online, so to speak, yesterday. Leak fixed and everything in good shape. We had a guest scheduled today, so as you can imagine we're relieved to have found the camera."

"Have you checked all the rooms?"

"Yes, we finished that task last night. No others found."

"And who is the person checked into that room?"

"It's a couple. Italians in their fifties. They'll be here for five nights." She gave a wry smile. "Assuming they don't find out about the cameras."

"Well, if you've cleared the rooms now, you should be fine." Hugo wasn't sure what she'd told the French police about the dead man in the stairwell, and it wasn't his case, but he was curious about him. "Did you know Andrew Baxter well?"

"Yes, I did. I already told the lieutenant all of this but, if it helps, I don't mind repeating myself. He'd worked here two years, which is a fairly long time for hotel staff." She sighed. "He was quite a character. Fun, funny, and big into his sports. During the soccer season he'd take the train to London to watch his team play, Chelsea. I never understood it, but it was his passion."

"He have any other hobbies?" Hugo wanted to ask about Baxter's gambling but didn't know if Lerens had mentioned it to Maxick, or if she wanted it made public.

"You probably already know, but he did gamble a bit. And when I say a bit, I mean a lot."

"Did he owe money to anyone?"

"I have no idea. I knew he gambled, but we never talked about it."

"Was he addicted?" Hugo asked.

"I don't know that either, sorry."

"Does Lieutenant Lerens have the names of the people who shared his room?"

"Yes. Just two right now, and both speak English fluently. Lionel Colbert, who he's friends with, and Thomas Prehn, who he's not."

"I see. Did he have some problem with Prehn or they just don't get along?"

"The latter, I think. Partly it's because Tom's German, and not just in the sense that he's from there. He tends to exhibit a few of that country's stereotypical traits. Andy found him a little . . ." She shrugged. "I don't know. They just didn't see eye to eye, and rooming together probably didn't help."

"You couldn't put one of them somewhere else?"

Maxick frowned. "I could have, yes. But they're grown-ups, not children, and I have plenty of paying guests to worry about. I have neither the time nor energy to be mommy to boys who don't play well together."

"Fair enough." Hugo said, and stood. "One more question, do you guys have surveillance or security cameras in the hotel?"

"No," she said. "Our clientele isn't the kind that calls for those kinds of precautions, and I suspect they would be less than happy to be filmed in the hallways and more public spaces. One of the things we try to offer our guests is privacy." She grimaced. "And, yes, I'm well aware of the irony of that statement, given recent events."

They both turned as Camille Lerens tapped on the door frame and walked in. She looked at Maxick. "Could Monsieur Marston and I use your office to talk for a couple of minutes?"

"Sure thing." Maxick got up and shook Hugo's hand. "I hope you find out who killed Andy, and whoever's behind this crazy spying business." She paused. "Are they connected?"

"Good question," Hugo said. "We'll let you know when we figure it out."

Once she'd gone, Lerens signaled for Hugo to sit, and she did the same. "Maxick tell you anything useful?"

"Not really. Same stuff she told you, I'm sure."

"Well, I have Thomas Prehn waiting for us in his room, their room, I suppose."

"Good. What about this Colbert guy—anyone spoken to him?"

"Not yet," Lerens said, "but we have a call into him, waiting to hear back. I did look into keycard usage but it looks like whoever accessed Madame Hancock's room either was a maid or used a maid's key. And they don't have cameras in the hallways, so that's a dead end."

"I asked about that too."

"One interesting development," Lerens said. "Andrew Baxter's computer, the one we found with the spy software on it. Well, it had no fingerprints on it."

"None of *his* or . . . ?"

"None at all. Wiped completely clean."

Hugo sat back and thought for a moment. "You're right, that *is* very interesting." He sprang to his feet. "And on that note, should we head upstairs?"

Lerens nodded and rose, picking up the bag containing the camera. Hugo followed her out of the office and to the elevators, and three minutes later they were sitting opposite Thomas Prehn in the room he'd shared with Baxter and Colbert. He was a stocky man in his midthirties, with wavy black hair and watchful eyes. He was dressed in a white shirt tucked into jeans, as if he couldn't decide whether to be formal or casual today, and he perched on the edge of his bed as Hugo and Lerens pulled up chairs to face him. It was an uncomfortable, almost formal, setting and not the relaxed one Hugo would've preferred, but at least the man was on home turf.

Lerens placed a digital recorder on the floor between them and spoke in French, introducing everyone present for the recording, as well as the date and time. This was her investigation, so Hugo knew she would ask the questions. Plus, having Lerens take the lead allowed him to focus on their subject's nonverbal responses.

"Monsieur Prehn, let me start by making sure I am pronouncing your name correctly."

"You are," he said. Even though he replied in fluent French, Hugo immediately detected the staccato of his German accent. "It's like *prayn*, not *prenn*."

"Thank you. So, how long did you know Andrew Baxter?"

"I've been working here for almost a year, so ever since I got here."

"What do you do at the hotel?" Lerens asked.

"Reception. I sometimes double up as the concierge when needed, but mostly I'm at the desk."

"Did you two get on well?"

"Not especially, but I expect people have told you that already. To begin with we had troubles; he didn't seem to respect my space and he was very loud. Like all Americans, perhaps?"

"Not all," Hugo assured him. "Just like not all Germans are humorless."

"No matter. When you share a room, you have to be respectful of the others in that room." Prehn shrugged. "After a while, I think we got used to each other. He was working a lot and when he was off, it seemed like he was on his computer most of the time. And it helped when I bought some large headphones."

"When did you last see him?"

"The night before he was . . . found." Prehn shook his head. "He wasn't my favorite person in the world, but I can't believe this has happened."

"Do you know anyone who might have wanted to harm him?"

"No, no one. Even if he was loud and annoying sometimes, that was all. He wasn't a bad person."

"Did he have any hobbies?" Lerens asked.

"Just his computer games."

"What kind of games?"

"I don't know, never asked."

"Did Andrew know many of the guests? Like, for example, Helen Hancock?"

Prehn smiled. "Everyone knows Helen; she's been coming here for years and is," he paused, searching for the right word. "If the hotel had a personal treasure, she would be it. We all know her to say hello, but I don't think Andy knew her more than anyone else."

"What about his other friends. Girlfriends, boyfriends . . ."

"We didn't hang out together, so I don't really know," Prehn said. "You should ask Lionel; he was Andy's friend. Best friend, probably."

"We will," Lerens said. "Is there anything else you think we should know, about Andrew, or anything else that might be good for us to know?" Lerens smiled. "Sometimes we don't find stuff out because we don't ask the right questions, so if there's anything you can think of that might help . . ."

Prehn shook his head. "I don't think so."

Lerens handed him a business card. "If something occurs to you, please call me."

"I will." He watched as she leaned down and clicked off the recorder. "Do you think anyone else is in danger?" He cleared his throat nervously, and his eyes flicked between Hugo and Lerens. "I mean, was this a one-time thing, or should I worry that whoever did this could come back and do it again? You know. To me."

Hugo gave him a reassuring smile, and both he and Camille shook their heads. But, as Hugo well knew, someone with murder in their heart and blood on their hands was unlikely to stop killing until they were caught or their mission was complete.

And since we don't know what that mission is . . . Hugo kept the thought to himself, instead saying, "No, we have no reason to think that you're in any danger."

A text from Tom Green as they waited by the elevator reminded him that you could never really be too sure, and Hugo felt a chill run down his spine. He needed to find Andrew Baxter's killer, to bring justice to the dead man and to make sure people like Thomas Prehn were kept safe, but also so he could focus on the man who, quite possibly, would be heading his way. A man who'd already killed and whose heart, if Tom was right, was not only murderous but filled with a desire for vengeance.

CHAPTER TWELVE

Fifteen years previously.

1545 hours, Houston, Texas.

Hugo wiped the sweat from his brow with his left sleeve, then took a firm grip of his gun with both hands and edged toward the corner of the house. The deck wrapped all the way around, at least as far as Hugo could see, but it was old and its paint was mostly gone, burned off by the Houston sun or peeled away by the humidity that draped itself over the city day after day, summer after summer.

He took one more look at the front door, then stepped onto the deck and into the shade. The shouting had come from the back of the house, and Tom wasn't responding on the radio. Not to him or the dispatcher, which was a bad sign.

The shade felt good and Hugo strained to hear the sirens of either the local police or the FBI SWAT team that was supposed to be on its way. Nothing. He readjusted his grip, the sweat making his gun heavy and awkward in his hands, and edged closer to the corner of the house, conscious of every footfall, every creak in the boards beneath his boots.

Two shots rang out from the back of the house, and Hugo started forward. Speed took over from stealth, but he stopped at the corner of the house to confirm that the deck extended to the rear of the building, and that it was safe to access. His gun swept through the thick air in front of him, and he strode along the side of the house. He could see the large oak tree behind which Tom had been stationed.

A watching brief for both of them, they'd agreed, until the cavalry arrived.

At the next corner of the house, Hugo paused and dropped to one knee. Anyone watching for him would be aiming higher, so this little trick should give him a split-second advantage. *Should.* The two bank robbers inside the house were suddenly trigger-happy—they'd proved that much today—and Hugo wasn't taking anything for granted.

He tried Tom one more time on the radio but got nothing in return. He took a breath and swiveled around the corner, his body low and his gun high.

No one.

He rose to a crouch and moved forward, with his eyes sweeping the weed-tangled yard to his right, but with his gun staying pointed at the back door. When he got close to it, he called out.

"Tom. Can you hear me?"

"Yeah, in here. It's clear, but keep your gun handy because this motherfucker looks twitchy."

Hugo moved quickly to the doorway, and squinted into the dim room, making out a table and chairs to his left, a stove and fridge to his right. Tom stood in front of the fridge, his gun pointed at something or someone on the floor. A tumble of cardboard boxes blocked Hugo's view, so he stepped into the small kitchen and moved toward his friend. When he reached him, Hugo stopped and took in the scene.

One of the robbers lay on the floor, two bullet wounds in his chest. The man's eyes were open, his mouth slack, and he didn't appear to be breathing. The second man was, though, his chest heaving and his eyes fierce, furious, when he looked at Hugo. He was on his knees, about three feet behind the dead man, with his hands on his head and an expression of pure hatred on his face.

"What happened, Tom?" Hugo asked. He looked around the dusty room, and his nose wrinkled at the stale air.

"Have a guess," Tom growled.

"I'd rather not. You were supposed to be outside, waiting. Watching." He holstered his gun and unclipped a set of handcuffs. He turned to the kneeling man. "Hands behind your back. Try anything, and my friend here will gladly shoot you."

The man complied. "He murdered my fucking brother. Just came in here and shot him!"

"I doubt that," Hugo said. "Special Agent Green is an officer of the law and takes his oath to serve and protect very seriously."

"Bullshit, he fucking shot him—"

"Zip it," Hugo snapped. The oppressive heat in the room made the cuffs slick in his hands, but he finally got them on the subject. "You have any identification on you?"

"Yeah, a fucking library card."

"That right?" Hugo asked. He raised a boot and placed it between the man's shoulder blades, then shoved him face-first into the floor. "I'm shocked you can read." He went through the man's pockets but found nothing identifying him. Nothing at all, in fact. No ID and no guns. The latter confirmed Hugo's suspicion that the dead man was the one responsible for the three murders at the bank. "Just so you know, you're under arrest for bank robbery in accordance with statute eighteen, US Code section twenty-one thirteen. And when we're done with you, no doubt the state of Texas will charge you with capital murder."

"I didn't kill anyone. Your fucking partner did, though."

"So did your brother, in that bank. And under the law of parties, you are equally responsible."

The man jerked on the floor. "Bullshit. I didn't even know he had a gun."

Tom stepped forward. "Now that's a load of bullshit. You're as guilty as he is." Tom pointed his gun at the man's head. "And you deserve the same damn fate."

Hugo stepped over the prostrate man, getting between him and Tom. "Easy, partner."

"Yeah," the man said, "try to explain killing an unarmed man. You think I'm not gonna say something?"

Hugo glanced at Tom, a question in his eyes. *Unarmed?*

"He had a gun, fuckface," Tom snapped.

"Stay where you are," Hugo said to the man. "Or it'll be me who shoots you, and I won't care whether you're armed or not because I'm entitled to shoot a fleeing murderer and robbery suspect."

"I ain't going nowhere. You're fucking dead men, both of you."

"Naw," said Hugo, in his best Texas drawl and nodding toward the still form on the floor. "He is, though."

"Damn right," Tom said.

Hugo steered Tom to the doorway and kept his voice low. "This was a good shot?" he asked.

"He's dead, isn't he?"

"You know what I mean."

Tom ran a hand over his face. "I guess."

"Thing is, you shouldn't be in here. You shouldn't have come inside. Can you explain that?"

"It was quiet," Tom said. "I didn't see or hear any movement, I thought maybe they'd left."

"We were watching the house; that's not possible."

"Yeah, well. I came up close, still didn't hear anything. I opened the door and stuck my head in. Jackass number one came into the kitchen about a second later."

"With a gun in his hand?"

"Sure."

"Tom, for fuck's sake."

"What?" Tom demanded. "You know what he did, he shot and killed—"

"I know what he did," Hugo interrupted. He looked out across the backyard as the distant sound of sirens drifted in through the door. "You have maybe a minute to make sure all's well that ends well."

"That's easy enough." Tom drew his gun from his holster and turned toward the man prostrate and muttering on the floor.

Hugo put a hand on his arm. "No." Hugo felt a flash of panic that Tom might actually do this, put a bullet in a man who was in custody.

That panic turned into anger at the thought that his friend might already have crossed a line But, first things first—they had to get out of whatever mess they were in.

"Then what?" Tom demanded.

Hugo walked over to the dead man and looked down. "Where's the gun, Tom?"

"He must have put it back in his pocket. Or somewhere."

"After you shot him twice in the heart?"

"He's a tough one. Was."

Hugo knelt and patted the man's pockets, pausing when he felt a familiar bulge. "In his pocket all right."

"See?" the man on the floor said. "He fucking murdered him."

"Shut up," Hugo said mildly. "You have no cause to complain about anything." He walked over to Tom. "I think I need to check the front of the house, make sure it's secure."

"Why? What the hell are you talking about?" Tom asked.

"Just to make sure." Hugo put his face an inch from Tom's and fixed him with a serious look. When he spoke, his voice was barely a whisper. "So your position is that these men were trying to escape from the house when you commanded them to stop and the dead guy drew on you. I can't remember if you said you were inside or closer to the backyard."

Tom stared at him for a moment, then said, "Closer to outside."

"I thought you said that, yes. Inside would've been hard to explain, especially given . . . you know."

"Yeah," Tom nodded. "Go check the front. I got things back here, no worries. My mess and all that." He unclipped the cuffs on his belt and handed them to Hugo. "You should take these."

"Right, thanks. And, Tom, the other one. The one that's *alive* right now."

"Yeah, I know," Tom sighed. "He stays that way."

Hugo squeezed his friend's shoulder and strode quickly outside onto the deck. He turned right, toward the front of the house and away from the crime scene.

CHAPTER THIRTEEN

Hugo and Camille Lerens stepped out of the elevator and were almost flattened by Helen Hancock, who was red in the face and shouting over her shoulder at Jill Maxick. For her part, Maxick just stood and stared at her celebrity guest, mouth agape, wordless.

"What's going on?" Hugo asked.

Hancock sputtered, unable to find the words, and shoved her way past Hugo and Lerens into the elevator. As the doors closed, she pointed past them at the manager and shouted, "Ask her! Just ask her!"

When Hancock disappeared from view, Maxick's shoulders slumped.

"Follow me," she said. "I'll show you."

Hugo gave Lerens a look, but she just shrugged and started after Maxick. Hugo trailed behind them, all three gathering in the manager's office.

"Is Helen OK?" Hugo asked, impatient with Maxick's silence. She was fiddling with her computer, muttering under her breath, and Hugo was pretty sure he heard some curse words.

A moment later, she swiveled her laptop so the screen faced them.

"What are we looking at?" Lerens asked.

It took a second to register, but Hugo soon caught up. "It's one of your hotel rooms. From a spy camera?"

"Correct," Maxick said.

"A new camera?" Hugo asked.

"Just watch and see," she snapped.

After a few beats, a figure appeared on the screen. It was blurry at first, but then the camera focused and a naked man walked across the room to a woman lying on her front, sideways across the bed. She raised her head and Hugo clearly saw the face of Helen Hancock. And a lot more when she rolled onto her side, clad in a black bra and panties of a style, Hugo guessed, designed for effect rather than comfort.

The more you pay, the less you get, Claudia had once explained, and the romance writer had evidently paid a great deal for this set. Hugo watched as Hancock pushed herself to her knees and beckoned for the man to join her. He knelt on the bed and embraced her, kissing her as he deftly unhooked her bra.

Hugo glanced at the URL bar but didn't recognize the name of the website. He looked up at Jill Maxick. "This was posted online, I take it."

"Oh, yes."

"Where?"

"Everywhere you can think of. YouTube for a while, then Reddit, 4Chan, xHamster."

"And clearly she knows about it."

"Blames us. Which she probably should."

"How long does it go on for?" Lerens asked.

"About twenty minutes. As long as it takes to . . . Well, you can guess."

"And you get to see . . . everything?"

"Absolutely," Maxick said. "Including fur-lined handcuffs, two vibrators, and what looks like a leash but might not have been. It's quite a show."

"Do you know when it was posted?" Hugo asked.

"No, I didn't look." Maxick shrugged. "I don't know if you can tell somehow, but the first I heard about it was when Ms. Hancock came knocking down my door moments ago, right before you showed up. I gather a few of her fans, quite a few, saw it and let her know. I presume overnight."

"Who's the man in this little performance?" Lerens pointed at the screen, where Maxick had paused it. "Does she have a boyfriend or lover here in Paris?"

"I don't know who he is. I've never known her to have a male friend for dinner, much less a lover." Maxick shook her head. "But I feel like his face is familiar. I couldn't say how or why, though I can tell you he certainly doesn't work here."

"No," Hugo said. "He doesn't."

Maxick and Lerens both looked at him. "You know who he is?" Lerens said.

Hugo gave them his best enigmatic smile. "I do, indeed."

"Well?" Lerens put her hands on her hips and glared at him.

"He is an aspiring writer. A friend, student, and apparently lover of Helen Hancock."

"He's one of her students?" Maxick asked. "That's right! Now I remember, I've seen him here, they had tea together a week or so ago."

"His name is Ambrósio Silva. Nice fellow," Hugo said. "But I think we need to go talk to him again, because apparently he likes keeping secrets."

"Guys, come on." Silva sat at the small kitchen table at the apartment he shared with Mike Rice. Hugo and Camille Lerens sat across from him. They'd not yet told him about the online publication of his encounter with Hancock, just that they knew the two were sleeping together. "I couldn't tell you, surely you can see that?"

"Not really," said Hugo mildly. Lerens had suggested that he ask the questions since her English was good, but not perfect. It was her tape recorder, though, that sat on the table between them. "You knew we were investigating a murder at the hotel, right?"

"I read about it, of course."

"Then, given the choice between telling the truth and lying to officers conducting a murder inquiry, I'd have thought telling the whole truth was a given. But that's just me."

"No, look, I wasn't lying!" Silva looked genuinely upset. "I didn't lie, I just didn't . . . tell you. I couldn't, because she made me promise not to. I mean, it's not like I'd go around blabbing about it anyway, I'm not like that, but she thought it'd look really bad if she was caught sleeping with one of her students."

"She was right," Hugo said. "It does look bad, and by hiding that from us you just made it look a lot worse."

"I'm sorry, I really am. I know it wasn't for me to judge, but I promised her, and I figured it wasn't really relevant to anything, you know?"

"As you said, but that's not exactly your judgment to make."

"How did you find out?" Silva asked.

Hugo shifted in his seat. "Well, I'm surprised you've not heard from anyone else. Do you have e-mail, social media?"

"I do, but I haven't been online today. Every morning I put my phone in my suitcase until I've written two thousand words. And we don't have Internet in the apartment." His brow furrowed. "Wait, why would I have heard from anyone else about this? You're confusing me."

"Ms. Hancock no doubt told you," Hugo began, "about the spy camera found in her room."

"Yeah, she did. And she said I wasn't on it; you guys told her that."

"It seems someone selectively edited what we found and kept a few tidbits for themselves." Hugo paused to let it sink in. As Silva's eyes widened, Hugo went on. "There's a twenty-minute clip making the rounds online. In it, Ms. Hancock is wearing very little and eventually nothing. You start out naked and end up that way, and I hope to God your mother doesn't see what happens in the meantime."

Silva's face drained of color. "Us having sex? Online?"

"I'm afraid so."

"And you can see . . ." His voiced tailed off.

"I didn't watch it all," Hugo said. "But I gather there's absolutely nothing left to the imagination."

"Oh, my God." Silva sat back, shaking his head slowly from side to side. He looked up. "Does Helen know?"

"Some of her kind readers let her know first thing," Hugo said. "I imagine she's tried to call you."

Silva shook his head again. "She's going to be so humiliated. Poor thing, I can't believe someone would do this to her."

"To you, too," Lerens said.

Silva nodded, and smiled sheepishly. "Yeah, but it's a little different."

"How so?" Hugo asked.

"Well, for one thing, I'm not a famous author with worldwide name and face recognition," Silva said. "For another thing . . . and, look, don't get mad that I didn't tell you about this either, because I'm certain it's not relevant to anything." He took a deep breath. "I've always wanted to be a writer, but I dabbled in the other arts when my soccer career ended. Like acting. Let's just say that my screen name was Max Peter."

"How delightful," Hugo said, unable to hide his smile. "And I think we can forgive you for keeping that to yourself. I don't recall asking for your job history."

"Yeah, thanks. It's not something I'm especially proud of, although I got to travel and meet some interesting people. Five films was enough, though, and hopefully they won't haunt me forever. My point, though, was just that this doesn't amount to a great humiliation for me, depending on what's actually posted." He gave them a small smile. "To me the outrage is in not being paid for my performance."

"Well, when you take that all into account," Hugo said, "one might actually come to the conclusion that this is a good thing for you."

"I wouldn't say that," Silva began, then caught Hugo's meaning. "Now, wait just a moment. Are you suggesting I had something to do with this? Because if you are, there's no way!"

"Oh no," Hugo assured him. "I'm sorry, sometimes I think aloud when I'd be better off keeping my mouth well and truly shut. It's just that this raises your profile without doing it much harm. That's all I was thinking."

"I don't want my 'acting' confused with my writing," Silva said emphatically. "Remember, I'm in an MFA program—you think this looks good for me?"

"Does the school know about your filmography?" Hugo asked.

"No, they don't." Silva was getting testy, which was what Hugo wanted. "As far as I recall, it wasn't one of the questions on the application."

"I don't suppose it was."

"Have you talked to Helen about this? How is she?"

"Not yet," Hugo said. "We figured she'd need a little time to get over the shock, maybe talk to her publisher and figure a way to get as much of it off the Internet as possible."

"Poor woman," Silva said. "She's such a private person; this will be humiliating. You can see her naked, too?"

"Yes," Hugo said. "When we leave, you can hop online and see for yourself."

"I guess," Silva said sadly. "Been a while since I've seen myself naked on screen, and things are a little more wobbly than they used to be. Plus, I don't want to add clicks to something like that. This may sound odd to you, but everything in the porn world is totally consensual. Some stuff can seem pretty freaky, but behind the scenes everything is negotiated and worked out in advance. So this, doing it without us even knowing, it's sick, frankly."

"We agree on that," Hugo said.

"You think you can catch who did it? And about the guy who was killed there—did the same person do both?"

Lerens spoke up. "That's why we're here, Monsieur Silva. Since you know Ms. Hancock better than we thought, do you now have any ideas that might help us solve one or both of these crimes?"

"I said I was sorry." Silva frowned. "And no, I don't know of anyone who'd murder someone. It sure as hell wasn't me, I can promise you that."

"And you're sure you didn't know the victim, Andrew Baxter?" Hugo pressed.

"Positive. Never hung out with him, never even said a word to him. Nothing."

"What about your roommate, Michael Rice?" Lerens asked.

"What about him?" Silva shrugged. "Quiet guy, harmless, keeps to himself." He smiled. "Now I'm making him sound like a serial killer, which I'm pretty sure he isn't."

"How can you be so sure?" Hugo asked. "Do you know him well?"

"Never met him before coming here. And, yeah, you're right, maybe he is a serial killer, but I've not seen any of the bodies. Nor any packing tape, plastic bags, or sharp knives." Silva stood, and Hugo was again aware of the man's size. "I need a beer, you guys want anything?"

"On duty," Lerens said.

"Yeah, but this is Paris. Wine's allowed on duty, surely."

"Only after we've caught the killer," Lerens replied.

"And the bastard who posted that video," Silva added. "Although it's probably the same person, don't you think?"

"Could be," Hugo said. "Well, you have my card if anything else comes to mind. Thanks for your time."

Hugo and Lerens shook hands with Silva and walked down the front steps to the street. Once they were a few feet away from the apartment, Hugo turned to Lerens. "Did you get all that?"

"I think so. What do you think?"

"He seems genuine enough." Hugo shrugged and gave her a small smile. "But, then again, he used to be an actor, didn't he?"

CHAPTER FOURTEEN

Lerens bought Hugo a sandwich as they walked back to the hotel, stopping for a moment to answer her phone. When she hung up, she said, "Lionel Colbert is back. Apparently he drowned his sorrows last night and is a little worse for wear."

"He's at the hotel?"

"Sleeping it off. Jameson is there; he'll make sure Colbert doesn't leave again."

"Good." Hugo took a bite of his ham and Gruyère baguette as they started walking again. "I really don't think I can leave this city, Camille, I'm going to have to retire here."

"The food's too good?"

"Everything is too good. The food, the history, the architecture."

"The police force."

"Not bad," he said with a twinkle in his eye. "But back to food, I've heard that the street food is great back home in Austin nowadays, fancy food trucks serving more than just tacos. What you'd call *nouvelle cuisine*, perhaps."

"I think I'd like to see Texas. Does everyone have a horse and a gun?"

"These days, I think it's a pickup truck and a gun."

"How long since you've been back?" Lerens asked.

"Two years." Hugo pointed at his feet with his free hand. "Had to get my boots fixed."

"*Vraiment?* We have shoe repair in Paris."

"Oh, I know. But these aren't shoes."

"Do you miss it?"

"My mother used to tell me I was never a true Texan, whatever that means. Even as a kid I wanted to travel and see new places, and my parents encouraged it, even though they didn't really have the travel bug." He thought for a moment. "But I think maybe she was wrong, my mother. When I retire it probably *will* be in Austin, maybe a little ranch in the Hill Country just outside the city." He finished another bite of his sandwich. "That's assuming I can get food this good over there, of course. Otherwise, I'm staying."

"How about the FBI life, do you miss that?"

"It's a lot more paperwork than people imagine, although, yeah, it was fun, too. But I don't think I do miss it all that much. No, being in the Behavioral Analysis Unit for those years, I was neck-deep among the worst of the worst, and it's not healthy for anyone to be immersed in that for too long."

"Is that why you left? Sick of the death and destruction?"

Hugo thought about that old house in Houston, with the heat pressing in on him, a dead man on the ground and another one swearing vengeance.

"Kind of, yes. Close enough." Hugo took a last bite and dropped his sandwich bag in a trash can outside the hotel, then held the door for Lerens. In the moment it took for his eyes to adjust to the dim interior, he heard Wendy Pottgen's voice, urgent and angry. She was at the reception desk, talking to Jill Maxick, and Hugo hesitated for a second, unsure whether to hang back or intervene. Curiosity got the better of him, and he moved toward them, Lerens in tow.

"Everything all right?" he asked when he reached them.

"No, it most definitely is not," Pottgen said. "She won't let me see Helen. Talk to her even."

"I'm sorry," Maxick said calmly, "but she asked not to be disturbed. Gave us explicit instructions. She's a guest, and I intend to respect that request."

"Where was that respect when you put a spy camera in her room?" Pottgen snapped.

"Now hold on," Hugo said gently. "We don't know who put that there; best not to be accusing people."

Pottgen held up a hand. "No, you're right, and I don't mean to be losing my temper. But I paid a lot of money to come over here and learn from her. I appreciate what she's going through right now—I saw the video, so I really do—but no one here is judging her. It's just sex, for crying out loud. And here in Paris, where everyone's supposed to be sleeping with everyone else."

"And that might be her perspective in a few days," Hugo said. "Right now, she's had her privacy violated in the most extreme way possible. And then pasted all over the Internet for the world to see."

Pottgen sighed. "I know. And I don't mean to be insensitive, I really don't. I'd just like the chance to talk to her, figure out whether I should stay here in Paris or go home."

"Well, let's do this," Hugo said. "We're going to need to talk to her again, Lieutenant Lerens and I." He glanced at Maxick and gave her a little smile. "Whether the hotel staff like it or not. When we do that, I'll ask her to call you. In the meantime, as you pointed out, you're in Paris. That can't be so bad, can it?"

"If I had a lover of my own," she said, holding Hugo's eye for a few seconds.

"Mike Rice seems nice," Hugo said. "And you have the literary thing in common."

"Not my type." She glanced past Hugo. "Speak of the devil."

Rice had just stepped through the main doors, and when he spotted them he ambled over. "Is there a meeting I didn't know about?"

Hugo wasn't sure if he was joking. "Buzzy here was just looking for a lunch date."

She glared at him, but Rice didn't seem to notice. "I ate already." He turned to Maxick. "Can I call up to Helen Hancock's room, please? I need to talk to her."

"Good luck with that. I'm out of here," Pottgen said. She flashed them all a smile, but fixed her gaze on Hugo. "You know where to find me if you need me."

When she'd gone, Hugo turned to Rice. "Sorry, Helen's out of commission right now."

"What's that supposed to mean?" Rice looked back and forth between Hugo and Maxick. "She's sick?"

Hugo studied his face for a moment, then said, "No. More like an emotional time-out. You haven't seen the video, heard about it?"

"What video?"

"Someone posted one on the Internet," Hugo said. "Of Helen having sex with Ambrósio Silva."

"What?" The cool façade cracked for a moment. "You gotta be kidding me."

"I'm not."

"And she didn't know about it? In advance, I mean."

"No, of course not. She's pretty rattled."

"No fucking doubt," Rice said. He shook his head. "That son of a bitch."

"Who?" Hugo asked.

"Ambrósio Silva. Man, I thought when we first met we'd be good friends, but then I got the sense that there's something shifty about him."

"Shifty?" Lerens repeated.

"Like he was hiding something, or knew something you didn't."

Like his past in pornography? Hugo wondered. "So you're not friends?"

"We're not gonna be after this," Rice said emphatically.

"You think Silva posted that video himself?"

"Of course he fucking did!"

"Please keep your voice down," Hugo said firmly. "Why do you think that?"

Rice looked at Hugo and Lerens as if they were crazy. "Who the hell else would?"

"That's what we plan to find out," Hugo said. "But a lack of suspects isn't evidence that it was him."

"No—Ambrósio did it. Of course he did."

"So you keep saying. But why?"

"For his writing career, of course. I bet he's in the apartment right now, writing an article or essay, hell, maybe a book, about his secret love affair with the great Helen Hancock, about the humiliation of it being revealed to the whole world. Even if he's not, he'll forever be known as the guy having sex with her on YouTube."

"You think that'd help rather than hurt his writing career?" Lerens asked.

"Look, he's a nobody right now. Unpublished, unknown. But in a day or two *everyone* will know his name, and trust me when I say there's no such thing as bad publicity in the literary world. I mean, the guy can sell any romance book he wants now. He'll be publishing gold. Name recognition is everything in this business. Even bad reviews don't much matter because the reading public forget the substance of the review; they just remember the name of the writer—and when they're floating around a bookstore, looking for something to buy, and see that name, bingo."

"Except he doesn't have a book on the shelves yet," Hugo pointed out. "I think your theory would make more sense if he was promoting a new novel or something, but even if he got a publishing deal tomorrow because of this, he'd be a year or so away from hitting the bookstores, wouldn't he?"

"Well, that's true," Rice conceded. "But the hardest part is getting an agent and then a publisher, and this is bound to help him do that."

"Possibly," Hugo said. "But we talked to him, and he seemed pretty shocked by it."

Rice rolled his eyes. "Of course he did. Did you know he used to be a porn star?"

"We do know that," Hugo said.

"There you go, then. He's not going to mind performing for the camera, he's used to it. More to the point, he's got nothing to lose."

"We have no proof that he's the one responsible for the video and its distribution," Hugo said. "If he says anything to you, though, please let us know."

"I will," Rice said. "I guess Buzzy should be lucky he didn't do it to her. Although she's not famous, so why would he bother?"

"What do you mean?" Lerens asked.

Rice looked at them and smiled. "Oh, I guess he didn't tell you about that, either. He and Buzzy had a fling when they first met."

Hugo tried not to show his irritation. Not at the pleasure Rice took in breaking that news, but at Pottgen and Silva's deception. If nothing else, it meant they'd have to reinterview both of them to see if they'd left out any more pieces of the puzzle. Hugo was particularly annoyed because he saw no reason why they'd hide that information; he couldn't know if it'd be relevant to either Baxter's murder or the spy camera. But when people lied to law enforcement, or neglected to share key information, in Hugo's experience, it was usually for a good—or bad—reason.

"Well, thanks for the information," Hugo said. "We'll be talking to Helen soon and will let her know that you'd like a word."

"Thanks, I'd appreciate that," Rice said. "Well, I'll leave you guys to investigate. I guess I have a video to go watch."

CHAPTER FIFTEEN

Lionel Colbert lay on his bed, staring up at the ceiling, as Hugo and Camille Lerens found places to sit in his room, pulling up chairs as they had during Prehn's interview. As Lerens turned on her recorder, Colbert sighed deeply and rolled onto his side to face them.

Hugo judged him to be in his early thirties, a good-looking man, and Hugo guessed him to be around six feet tall, but slender. He wore his dark hair in a ponytail, and his eyes seemed to radiate both sadness and intelligence as he looked back and forth between his guests, quiet, waiting for them to break the ice.

Hugo did, remarking on the three pairs of shoes atop Colbert's locker. "Brand-new, or you polish them a lot?"

"Just spent a month's salary on them." He shrugged. "My weakness, shoes, and I'm in Paris so sometimes I can't resist."

"Paris will do that to you," Hugo said with a smile, one that Colbert didn't return.

Lerens spoke up. "*Monsieur, vous parlez français?*"

He nodded, and replied in French. "I'm fluent. In Spanish, too. My German's a little weak, as is my Arabic." He gave a small smile. "So you can ask me questions in French, no problem."

"*Merci,*" Lerens said. "First of all, as you can see, I'm recording this interview. You are Lionel Colbert, roommate of Andrew Baxter and Thomas Prehn, and you are speaking to myself and Hugo Marston from the US Embassy voluntarily. Is that all correct?"

Colbert nodded. "*Oui.*"

"*Bien, merci.*" Camille stated the date and time for the record. "*Alors*, how long did you know Andrew Baxter?"

"As long as I've been at the hotel, about a year and a half, I think. Andy was here longer."

"And you were roommates for that whole time?" she asked.

"Yes. It was just the two of us for a while, then Thomas got hired and moved in."

"I see. Monsieur Colbert, let me ask, do you have any idea who might have wanted to hurt your friend?"

Colbert's eyes started to slide away, but he caught himself, and his face remained impassive. "*Non.*"

Lerens continued. "Were there any problems between the two of you?"

"Not at all. We were good friends. I don't think we ever disagreed, about anything."

Again, Hugo noticed the slightest flicker in the young man's eyes, but he let it go, for now.

"What about Thomas Prehn?" Hugo asked.

"*Non.*" Colbert shook his head. "They weren't the best of friends, and Andy annoyed him pretty much every day, but I don't see Tom as the murdering type. And even if he was, it was just annoyance, nothing more. I've never even heard Tom raise his voice."

"Perhaps he was bottling it all up, then exploded," Hugo suggested.

"If that were the case, he'd have strangled him in here, not stabbed him in the stairwell." He shook his head again. "You're wasting your time if you think Tom had anything to do with it. Or me, for that matter."

"We have to look at everyone Baxter knew, or at least ask about them," Lerens said. "Do you know if Andrew had any dealings with, or was friends with, Wendy 'Buzzy' Pottgen, Ambrósio Silva, or Mike Rice?"

"None of them, that I know of. I've heard of Ambrósio Silva, but not the others. Don't think I've met any of them, and Andy never mentioned knowing them. Who are they?"

"How have you heard of Ambrósio Silva?"

"I don't know." He furrowed his forehead in thought. "I really can't tell you, but the name's familiar."

"Those three are friends of Helen Hancock," Hugo said, "if that helps jog your memory."

"What does . . . Oh. That whole camera business."

"You know about that?" Hugo asked.

"Of course, who doesn't? I mean in the hotel, that is. Word gets around real fast—this place can be like a high school sometimes."

"What are your thoughts?" Hugo asked.

Colbert smiled. "I think you're trying to connect Andy's death with what happened, and that's why you're asking about Ms. Hancock's friends."

"I meant, what do you make of Andy putting that camera in her room?"

"He didn't."

"Really?"

"No way."

"You seem sure about that."

"I am." Colbert pushed himself upright and sat on the bed, his legs dangling over the edge. "Andy's faults related to him being the stereo-typical loud American and blowing too much money on gambling. Definitely not that kind of failure of morality."

"You are a loyal friend," Lerens said. "But you may or may not know that we found recordings from her room on his computer."

"Then someone planted that computer in his stuff. Or planted that stuff on his computer."

"In *your* room?" Lerens asked pointedly.

"I wouldn't know. I guess it's possible."

"Apart from you, Tom, and Andy, did anyone have a keycard to get in here?"

"No. I mean, I guess the hotel management could get in if they needed to; they could make themselves a key. But room-service people don't clean in here, and we all signed a piece of paper promising not to share our keys with other people. Plus they only gave us one each."

"You ever lose yours and get a replacement?" Lerens asked.

"No."

"Did Andrew or Thomas, to your knowledge?"

"Not that I know about." Colbert thought for a moment. "In fact, if they had, I'm sure the hotel would have deactivated the lost card."

"Maybe," Hugo said. "Not suggesting either of them would do this, but is there anything to stop Andy or Tom from making their own duplicate key?"

"You didn't include me in that question."

"You already said you've only had one key." Hugo looked him in the eye. "And you wouldn't lie during a murder investigation, would you?"

Colbert ignored the question. "None of us can just make a duplicate key. Once a room is occupied, any keycard that's programmed automatically generates a message that goes to the managers. If they think it's suspicious, they can investigate. And they all know the policy that we're allowed just one key, so if someone did duplicate a key to this room, either it or the old one would be deactivated."

"So how would someone frame Andy by leaving a doctored computer in here?" Lerens pressed.

"Look," Colbert snapped, "this is a room in a hotel that three people share. It's not exactly Fort Knox, and just because I can't tell you how it happened, that doesn't mean it didn't."

"Except we have surveillance footage of him going into a store that sells spyware."

"You're making that up. Trying to trick me."

"Surveillance from inside and outside the store," Hugo added. "Not surprising that a place like that would use a lot of cameras, and very helpful for us. The footage is so good, we can see exactly what he bought, and it happens to be the precise make and model of camera found in Helen Hancock's room."

Colbert stared at him, then said, "That doesn't make any sense. For Andy to do that."

"Do you have a laptop?" Hugo asked.

Colbert nodded. "Sure. No room for a desktop in here."

"Would you let us look at it?"

"You mean the outside?"

"No," Hugo said. "I'd like to know what's on it, if you don't mind."

"I do mind, actually. What's on there is private and not anyone's business."

"I guess we could get a search warrant," Hugo said mildly to Lerens.

"Based on what?" Colbert asked. "I'm no lawyer, but in the States you'd have to have some reason to justify doing that."

Hugo kept his voice even. "How about you withholding information during this interview?"

"I haven't. What are you talking about?"

"When I asked you who might have wanted to hurt Andy, you thought of a name. Who was it?"

Hugo was fishing, but Colbert's involuntary responses to those questions suggested he was being dishonest. Colbert didn't bite. He stood up and walked to the door. "I haven't lied about or hidden anything, and I'm pretty sure a judge wouldn't sign a search warrant based on you saying that I did. And even if one does, I have nothing to hide. I just don't like the idea of you people fishing around on my computer for reasons I might have hurt my friend." He looked at Lieutenant Lerens, then at Hugo. "I have to get ready for work, so I don't think I have anything more to say right now."

Hugo and Lerens stopped outside Helen Hancock's room, but when she didn't answer her door they went downstairs and found Jill Maxick in her office. Hugo stuck his head in, as Lerens lingered behind him.

"Do you happen to know where Helen is?" he asked.

"Not in her room?"

"Nope."

"She didn't say anything to me." Maxick snapped her fingers. "I bet she's gone to see Ambrósio Silva. She was on the phone to some lawyers earlier when I went in to check on her. Before they decide what to do, they want to make sure he's on board with any plan."

"To make the websites take the video down?"

"Right. And make sure that in doing so they don't step on the toes of the police investigating Andy's death. You want me to call her?"

"No," Hugo said. "I'll take a walk over to Silva's place. Sometimes it's better to talk to people when they don't know you're coming. But thanks."

She gave him a tired smile. "Welcome. I'm clocking out for the day in about thirty minutes."

"This is pretty stressful for you, I bet," Hugo said.

"Helen is more than just a guest. She's become a friend, you know. I hate to see her go through all this humiliation; it's just so wrong."

"Do you read her books?"

"Oh, yes." Maxick blushed a little. "All of them. I feel silly liking romance novels at my age and stage in life, but I can't help it."

Camille tapped Hugo on the shoulder. "Hugo, we have to go."

He turned. "Something happen?"

"You could say that." Lerens held up the phone in her hand. "I just got a call about Wendy Pottgen. She's been attacked."

CHAPTER SIXTEEN

hree police cars sat outside the apartment building, lights flashing rhythmically but their sirens now quiet. A young police officer stood in the propped-open doorway, and he straightened up and dropped his cigarette when he saw Lieutenant Lerens emerge from the unmarked car.

"Third floor," the officer said. "No elevator in the building, but it's the first door you come to."

Lerens nodded and cast a disapproving, and obvious, look at the still-smoldering cigarette on the pavement. "Are you supposed to be smoking while on duty?"

"Technically, I'm off duty as of thirty minutes ago," he said. "I offered to stay late to help out."

"How diligent, I'm sure everyone appreciates that," Lerens said. She breezed past him and added in a mild tone: "No one appreciates a wise-ass, though, least of all your lieutenant."

Hugo gave the policemen a conspiratorial wink as he passed by. The *flic* may not know it, but the truth was that Lerens very much appreciated a cop who could think on his feet and speak up for himself. Rank meant something to her, of course, everyone respected the hierarchy, but that was less important to Lerens than staying late to help out, cigarette or not.

Hugo followed Lerens up the narrow staircase and at the third floor, the apartment door stood open. When they went in, Hugo saw two policemen standing over Buzzy Pottgen, who sat at a tiny, round table nursing a glass of water. She looked up but didn't say anything.

"What happened?" Hugo asked. The police officers moved aside, and he sat opposite Pottgen. She had a couple of scratches on her face and the beginnings of a fat lip. Her hair was mussed, too, and her eyes flicked around the room as if expecting another assault from someone hiding inside.

Pottgen shrugged. "I don't know. I was punching in the code to the main doors, and someone hit me from behind. Knocked me into the metal grill there. Like I told these guys, I didn't see whoever it was."

"They take anything?"

"No. I dropped my bag, but he just ran off, left it there."

"Do you need to go to the hospital? See a doctor at least?"

She smiled and nodded toward the two *flics*. "You're asking the exact same questions these guys did. And no, I'm fine, thanks, just a little rattled. And a headache."

"You have any painkillers?"

"I think so, in the bathroom cabinet. My legs are still wobbly, so if you'd grab a handful I'd appreciate it."

Hugo stepped into the tiny bathroom and opened the mirrored door of the cabinet over the sink. Out of politeness he tried to find only the pain medicine, but his eye fell on a prescription bottle, and he leaned in to read the label. He checked the date and rattled the bottle to confirm there was just one pill left, then replaced it and grabbed the painkillers.

He put the bottle in front of Pottgen, the lid off. "The label says to take two now, two more in four hours if that doesn't help." He gave her a serious look. "And I'd suggest a trip to the hospital; you may be concussed."

"I'm fine," she said.

"You really didn't get a look at who did this?" Hugo asked.

"No, I really didn't."

"Couldn't tell whether it was a man or a woman? Tall or short?"

"No." She looked down at the table. "I'm sorry. I'd like to be of more help but I really have no idea. I wasn't even going to call the police, but I ran into the apartment owner, Madame Petit, and she insisted on calling when I told her what happened."

Camille gestured to Hugo. "A quick word?"

"Sure. Excuse me, Buzzy, take those pills and I'll be right back." Hugo followed Lerens out of the apartment and onto the landing.

"Close the door, if you don't mind," she said.

Hugo pulled it shut behind him and gave her a quizzical look. "What's going on?"

"That smart-aleck *flic* downstairs decided to make amends, so he went across the street to the pharmacy and asked if they have surveillance cameras."

"And we're standing here talking about it, so clearly they do."

Lerens smiled. "Oh, yes. Inside and out. He downloaded the relevant moments on a thumb drive, put it on his phone somehow and texted it to me." She turned her phone toward Hugo, and he leaned in and oriented himself. The camera captured the sidewalk nearest it, the two-lane road, and the far sidewalk, with the doors to Pottgen's apartment off to the left side of the screen. People passed back and forth, their faces clear and visible on the near side, but a little harder to identify across the street.

Even so, Buzzy Pottgen was easy to spot. She came into the frame from the right, head down as if lost in her own world, her walk and figure recognizable despite her face being turned away from the camera.

Hugo watched the periphery of the screen on both sides, waiting for her attacker to show, holding his breath as if that'd help him not miss a frame.

Pottgen reached the double doors to the apartment building. She paused, as if trying to remember the code, her hand hovering over the key pad. Hugo noticed that Lerens was watching him, not the screen, as if she already knew who the attacker was.

Unless . . . she's watching me for my reaction because something's not right . . .

Pottgen's hand moved, entering the code, and the right-hand door clicked open. Hugo moved his attention to a man in a sports coat coming up behind her, his face impossible to make out, and his gait, his size, everything about him unfamiliar. In a second, he was past her, and Pottgen herself was disappearing through the doorway, the metal grill on the front of it slowly swinging closed behind her.

No one charged in behind her. Two men, one smoking a cigarette and the other waiving his newspaper as he made his point, passed by, but neither slowed or showed any interest in the closed door.

Hugo sighed. "She lied."

"Unless she was attacked inside the building, outside her apartment door," Lerens offered.

"That's not what she said. She was pretty clear about it being down there."

"Maybe she was confused."

"She lied," Hugo said again. "The question is, why?"

"Hugo." The policewoman's eyes narrowed. "You have that look on your face."

"Hang on . . ." Hugo looked at her, then at Pottgen's closed door. "If . . ."

"If what? Why don't we just go in and ask her?"

"No. Right now she thinks we buy her story. That means she won't . . . you know, interfere."

"With what, exactly?"

Hugo heard the exasperation in her voice and smiled. "With what we're doing next."

"Which is?"

"Well, what I'm doing next. You need to stay here and babysit."

"That's not how this works, and you know it," Lerens said firmly. "This is my investigation and you don't get to—"

But Hugo was halfway down the flight of stairs and didn't hear the rest, having no interest in finding out what it was he wasn't supposed to do.

Ambrósio Silva was home alone when Hugo rang the bell to his apartment. The main doors buzzed without Silva even asking who it was, and Hugo let himself into the small, marbled foyer. Silva's apartment, which he shared with Mike Rice, was on the *rez-de-chaussée*, or ground floor. He crossed the foyer and knocked, hearing the sound of steps before the door opened. Silva opened the door, filling the gap with his bulk.

"I was just going out," he said, pointing to his sneakers. "For a run."

"This won't take a moment," Hugo said.

"Another time," Silva moved toward Hugo, as if to shut the door behind him, but Hugo didn't budge.

"No, I think now would be best."

Silva turned and glared at him. "Unless you're here to arrest me, you don't get to decide that."

Hugo felt the big man's presence, his menace, just inches from him. "Why so hostile, Mr. Silva? This doesn't seem necessary in the least."

"Let's just say I've had a bad afternoon; I need to work off some stress."

"Yeah, I know."

Silva looked at Hugo for a second, then said, "What do you know?"

"Can we go inside and talk about it?"

"No. I've just finished stretching, and if I cool down I won't be able to run. I'll give you one minute."

"I want to know why you're hiding things from investigators conducting a murder inquiry. You hid that you were sleeping with Helen Hancock, *and* you didn't tell me about your fling with Wendy Pottgen."

"I've already explained to you why I kept my relationship with Helen secret; and, as for Buzzy, well, you didn't ask me about it."

"This isn't a game, Mr. Silva. One person is dead, and one other person has been publicly humiliated . . . maybe two people, though to be honest it's hard to tell."

"Don't judge me—you don't have that right." Silva had turned red and his eyes flashed. "I don't have to feel a certain way just because you think I ought to. You have no fucking idea what I'm going through, none whatsoever."

"Then explain it to me," Hugo said, his voice calm. "Explain to me why I just saw Wendy Pottgen with a fat lip."

Silva stared down at Hugo. "You think I did that?"

"Well, she has a fat lip right now," Hugo pressed. "She lied about how she got it; and she admitted that she didn't want to call the police to report it. Both of which suggest to me that it was a heat-of-the-moment thing and she's protecting someone."

"And that's me," Silva said.

"I'm asking."

They locked eyes for a second, then in one fluid move Silva pulled his front door shut behind him and took a large stride past Hugo, knocking him off balance as he sprinted for the main doors. Hugo recovered quickly, but his cowboy boots slipped on the marble floor as he took his first step, and by the time he hit the doors Silva was twenty yards ahead, his large body bounding down the sidewalk, the early-evening pedestrians ahead of him parting so they didn't get flattened.

Hugo had a split second to decide whether or not to chase him. Catching up was one thing, a likelihood, but then what? He'd never rugby-tackled anyone that big and strong, not without backup, and he didn't plan to start now.

"It's not like we won't find you," Hugo muttered. "You big idiot."

Hugo let the door swing closed behind him and called Lerens to update her.

"So chasing off like that worked well," she said, not hiding the sarcasm.

"Some you win, some you lose," Hugo replied, a little chastened. "And on that note I'm clocking out for the day, but call if something comes up."

Hugo tucked his phone away and started the walk back toward his apartment, prying his thoughts away from the murder of Andrew Baxter, away from spy cameras, and away from tight-lipped witnesses. He had a café in mind, one that sat on the corner of three streets, one that made very good Americano cocktails and served more than pass-able pizza. Maybe Claudia would join him; they could share a dozen snails and a bottle of wine.

And this was the difference for Hugo, in his new life as an RSO. At the end of the day, he could take off his gun, tuck away his badge, and switch off for the evening. Paris was a place to savor, its cafés and bistros spilling onto the sidewalks, giving those sipping wine and nibbling on olives the chance to critique or admire the style of those walking home, and giving those passing by a tempting suggestion for their own evening ahead. As an FBI agent he'd always been on call, always at the ready, especially as a behavioral analyst. Oh, sure, these days he might get a late call about a tourist in the slammer for being rowdy, but that was little more than a courtesy, not something he needed to deal with immediately. As he knew from his experiences with Tom, drunk guys can sleep it off behind bars as well as anywhere.

He decided he would call Claudia, and when she answered she sounded delighted.

"I thought you were stuck in a case, didn't want to bother you." Her voice turned coy. "Well, I did want to, but I knew I would've bugged you about the murder."

"Always the journalist," Hugo said with a smile. "You just can't help yourself, can you?"

"And what would you do, Mr. Lawman, if you saw an old woman getting mugged while you were out and about?"

"Good point—some things we just can't ignore. So, dinner?"

"Yes. Nowhere fancy, though."

"I was thinking about pizza and wine on our favorite corner," he said. "Not sure which café exactly, but we have several to choose from, so maybe I'll surprise you."

"Perfect! I will set a course for Rue Mazarine now."

Five minutes later, Hugo exchanged *bonjours* with a waiter and settled behind a small table. In front of him, the low evening sun cast long shadows on the street, and the not-unpleasant waft of someone's cigarette a few tables away reminded him that he was still in Europe, where one's pleasures may lean toward the wicked but are rarely indulged in guiltily.

He ordered a glass of red wine, choosing the slightly rough house Bordeaux over the downright raspy house Burgundy. He didn't mind suffering a little, at least until Claudia arrived to drop a pair of reading glasses on the end of her nose and choose something decent from the full wine list.

He sighed as his phone buzzed in his pocket, sighed again when he saw Tom's name on the screen. He hesitated, but Tom was a persistent one and, if Hugo didn't answer, his friend would either track him down in person or keep calling until he got some satisfaction.

"Yes, I'm enjoying a nice glass of wine," Hugo said, "and no, you may not join me."

"Yeah? Well, I'm gonna be drinking somewhere, so it may as well be with you."

"Try Camille, she's been working hard lately. I'm sure she could use the break." Hugo cleared his throat. "No pun intended."

"Oh, good one, real funny."

Hugo smiled. He remembered halfway through his suggestion that the last time Tom and Camille Lerens had met at a bar, Tom had been tanked. He'd picked a fight with some locals and, when she happened to show up and intervened, he clocked her in the eye, not even realizing who she was. For that he spent the night in a suburban Paris jail with a few bruises of his own, and neither Hugo nor the forgiving Camille Lerens gave up a chance to needle him about it.

"Thanks," Hugo said. "Something special you needed?"

"Yeah, I hate to ruin your lovey-dovey evening with Claudia—"

"Well, for one thing, I never said a word about seeing her tonight."

"Dude, just because you treat me like an idiot, doesn't make me one."

"Oh, Tom, I don't. I treat you like a child, because you are one of those."

"Fuck you. Anyway, be serious for a moment."

Something in his voice rang an alarm bell in Hugo's head. "OK, what's up?"

"Our old friend on the other side of the pond."

"Rick Cofer?"

"Yeah, that son of a bitch. You'll never guess what he's gone and done."

"Well, you're right about that, so just tell me."

"He's applied to the judge to let him leave the country. And he's coming here."

CHAPTER SEVENTEEN

Hugo straightened but was careful to keep his tone calm and measured as Claudia approached. "That's unusual."

"You think?"

"Tom, hang on a moment. Claudia just got here." He rose to greet her, and they exchanged kisses. "It's Tom, something of a crisis."

"For him or you?"

"To be determined. Tempest in a teapot most likely, but you know how he is."

"Oh, I know. He's adorable."

"Right, that's what he is. I forgot." Hugo rolled his eyes dramatically. "So then you take this call," he said, offering her the phone.

"No, thanks." She sniffed the carafe and wrinkled her nose. "You go sort him out; I'll order something drinkable. It's fine, Hugo, I'm in no hurry."

"Well, I am," Hugo muttered. He moved away so Claudia wouldn't be tempted to listen, moving past the café's tables and onto the sidewalk. "OK, Tom, I'm back. And let's not leap to any conclusions about this. How do you know he's coming to Paris?"

"Well, technically he's requested permission to go to Holland, if you want to be precise about it."

"Oh, so when you say he's coming here, what you mean is that he's not coming to Paris but in fact is going to a different country altogether."

"The one next fucking door."

"It's not next door; Belgium is between—"

"You know what I mean."

"I'm not sure I do." Hugo rubbed a hand over his forehead, trying to think. "Again, how do you know any of this anyway?"

"I made friends with his parole officer. Well, I had a colleague over there do that in person."

"In a nice way or in a Tom way?"

"It doesn't matter how, but it just needed to be done."

"A Tom way, then. What do you have on the poor guy? You know what," Hugo interrupted himself, "I don't even want to know. You're sure this news is straight from his PO, though."

"Basically, yes."

"Where in Holland is he going, and why?"

"Amsterdam."

"Why there?" Hugo asked.

"Because if he asked permission to come to Paris, it'd be too fucking obvious that he's coming after me."

"OK, take a breath here," Hugo said. "First of all, how would he know you're living here in France, let alone in Paris?"

"No idea. But you can bet he does."

"Second, if I'd been locked up in a Texas prison for more than a decade I'd be bursting to get away, too, and since millions of tourists go to Amsterdam every year, maybe it's just a coincidence."

"Oh, right, sure. I've just spent a dime plus a nickel bunking with some fat, farting sasquatch and as soon as I'm out I'm going to pack myself onto a plane like a sardine, probably next to another fat, farting sasquatch, and fly for ten hours to a place known for rain."

"And hookers. Legal ones."

"They have legal hookers in Nevada. And illegal ones everywhere. He's not making a transatlantic trip to get laid, Hugo."

"Maybe he built up a weed habit in the slammer; now he's coming to where it's easily available and very legal."

"Oh, you mean like in the much-closer Seattle or Portland, and the entire fucking state of Colorado?"

"Maybe it's the Dutch pancakes," Hugo said lightly. "I hear they're very good."

There was silence for a moment. "You're kidding me with this shit, right?"

"I grant you, it does seem unlikely, but unless you can convince me that he knows you're this side of the Atlantic, him coming after you is no more likely than him wanting to get out of America, the land that locked him up, that took away his freedom for so many years."

"It's a four-hour train ride from Amsterdam to Paris. And you don't have to show your passport or notify any authority you're leaving the country."

"I get it, Tom. Your theory is that he picks Amsterdam as a smoke screen."

"Right."

"Then he's the dumbest criminal I've ever heard of."

"Why?"

"Because here we are, discussing how easy it is to get there from here!" Hugo insisted. "Honestly, it's the worst smoke screen ever."

"Yeah, except you're not buying it, so you'll be looking the other way when he puts a gun to the back of my head."

"Well, that's another thing. Where's he going to get a gun, exactly?"

"Criminals find guns. Or maybe he'll hit me over the head."

"Or maybe you'll just die of paranoia."

"That's not a thing."

"So, what, you want to go to Amsterdam and confront him? Follow him?"

"Maybe I do. And maybe I want you to come with me."

"No chance. Not even close."

"Great friend you are."

"Agreed. I mean, here I am ignoring my beautiful, smart, journalist friend, Claudia, just to talk nonsense on the phone with you."

"Fine, hang up. Go choke on a fucking olive."

"No chance of that either."

"Yeah, what makes you so sure?"

"Simple," Hugo said. "I'm going straight for the escargot."

After dinner, they went back to Hugo's place, Hugo texting Tom on the way to make sure his friend was out of the apartment eating or, more likely, drinking somewhere. Hugo had a leftover slice of cheesecake that he suggested they share but, unsurprisingly, the giant mouse who lived in his spare room had found and devoured it despite the DON'T YOU DARE! note that Hugo had left on the lid.

Instead, he opened a bottle of Pichon Longueville, and they sat close to each other on the couch, resting their feet on the coffee table. Hugo frowned as his phone rang. He didn't recognize the number, so he waited for it to go to voicemail.

"Go ahead," Claudia said. "I know you; it's fine to listen to the message. It might be important."

He grinned sheepishly. "Thanks." He held the phone to his ear, his eyes longingly on Claudia, and it was Michelle Juneau's voice he heard: "Hugo, sorry to bother you, but I'm at the library and the police just left. We called them because there's been a theft. Burglary. Whatever. I thought I should call and let you know, though I feel a bit silly now. Call me back on this number when you get a chance. Thanks."

Hugo put the phone down. "Someone from the library. There's been a book theft."

Claudia's brow furrowed. "Why would you care about a book theft?"

"I wouldn't, especially right now." It was his turn to think. "Maybe she didn't mention a book. . . . But whatever it is, it can wait." He smiled. "I've had enough interruptions for one night."

"Very true," Claudia said. "So . . . what's going on with your case?"

"Let's not talk about that. Tell me about you, what stories you're working on."

"Let's both leave work at the office," she said. She leaned forward to pick up the wine bottle, inspecting the label. "Weren't we supposed to make plans to visit this place?"

"You were supposed to make plans and invite me along," Hugo reminded her.

"I think you're right, I *was*." She put the bottle down. "Naughty me, maybe I can make it up to you."

"Maybe." Hugo put down his glass and sat back on the couch. "I'm listening."

"It's got nothing to do with listening." Claudia leaned in and kissed his lips, gently to begin with, letting Hugo taste the sweetness of the wine and savor the soft aroma of her perfume. She pressed her body into his, and Hugo pulled her close, wanting to feel the weight of her on top of him, and a second later she was astride him.

"Oh, Hugo," she whispered. "We don't do this enough."

He didn't reply, just kissed her harder and let his hands drift down to the waist of her jeans. He flicked open the button and they separated for a moment, but their eyes locked as they undressed each other, hands careful but urgent, and when they were both naked she pushed him down onto the couch and stretched her naked body over him, covering him, kissing him again as his hands caressed the soft skin of her back and dipped lower to caress her bottom. She tried to pull away, but Hugo put a hand on the back of her neck and she moaned her pleasure at this small act of dominance, sinking back onto him, kissing him again and working her hands under him to pull him even closer.

He broke the kiss long enough to whisper in her ear, "You're making amends, my love, don't stop now."

Mischief flashed in her eyes as she reached down and picked up her blouse, then drew it slowly over his eyes as a makeshift blindfold. "I have no plans to stop," she assured him. "So you just lie there and accept my apology. It may take a while."

They dragged themselves to bed around midnight and were on the verge of sleep when the front door slammed.

"Tom's home," Hugo murmured, not bothering to open his eyes.

Claudia snuggled into him. "Hush, I'm asleep."

"Then pray he doesn't—" The bedroom door flew open and Tom staggered in. "So much for prayer," Hugo groaned.

"Yo, dude." Tom's silhouette swayed in the darkness, and he steadied himself by sitting heavily on the bed, just missing Claudia's feet. "Man, I been thinking about Cofer, what we need to do."

"We need to go to bed and talk in the morning," Hugo said.

"You're already in bed, stop complaining."

"Great, now you go and we'll be good."

"I said stop complaining," Tom slurred. "Seems to me, we need to be proactive, not give him any advantage."

"I'm not going to Amsterdam."

"Yeah, you are. We're sitting ducks here in Paris, and we need to finish what we started." Tom hiccupped. "Hey, that'd be funny as a spoonerism. We need to stinish what we farted."

"Tom. Sleep. I'll buy you breakfast tomorrow and we can talk about it."

"I shoulda taken care of that asshole when I had the chance." He slapped at the bed and hit Claudia, who squealed.

"Oh man, you have a girl here? Shit, dude. What if Claudia found out?"

"First of all, Claudia and I are not dating exclusively," Hugo said, then winced as he received an elbow in the ribs from under the covers. "And second of all, I'm pretty sure she'd approve of this . . . young lady."

Tom was silent for a moment. "It's not Camille is it? She likes her a lot, but even so . . . Camille, is that you?"

"It's not Camille, Tom, for crying out loud. It's Claudia." Hugo reached out and switched on his bedside light. "You happy now?"

"You naked under that sheet, girl?" Tom's eyes were red and he blinked in the light. "If so, I'd be a lot happier if I could—"

"Tom!" Hugo sat up. "If you pull this sheet away . . ."

Claudia propped herself up on an elbow and frowned at them both. "You two, you're like Neanderthals sometimes. If he pulls this sheet away, you'll do what, Hugo?"

"Wrap it around his neck," Hugo said.

"I'm not a delicate maiden, so I can do that myself—you don't need to protect me." She turned to Tom. "And, what, you want to see a naked woman? Like you've not seen a million before?"

Tom wore a look of confusion, like he knew he was being chastised but didn't really understand why. "Well, no, I mean yes," he stammered, "but not you, I mean, you're different, and I haven't . . ." His eyes dropped as his words tailed off.

"Yeah, I am different," Claudia said. "I'm your friend—not some piece of meat to ogle." She sat up and the sheet slid down, revealing her breasts, but Tom kept his gaze on the floor. "This guy next to me is the only one allowed to ogle me."

"Actually, I am—right now," Hugo said, his eyes glued on Claudia.

"Hush. The pair of you, really." In one fluid motion she swung her legs off the bed and stood. Tom's head twitched, but he stayed looking down, and Hugo saw Claudia fighting not to smile. She gave a dramatic sigh and strode in her perfect nakedness directly past Tom to the bathroom. "You sure as hell better sneak a peek, Tom Green, it's the only one you're ever going to get."

She brought Hugo coffee in bed the next morning, waking him up with a backrub but then resisting his clumsy efforts to increase the range of her motions.

"Not now," she chided him. "You have to go to work. And I wanted to ask you something."

"Keep massaging, and I'll answer anything you want to know. Very slowly."

"Last night, Tom said you and he were sitting ducks here in Paris. He said you needed to finish what you started."

"Oh, that was nothing. Drunk talk."

"I don't think so, Hugo. I didn't like his tone, he sounded truly concerned. For you and for himself." She stopped rubbing his back. "What was he talking about?"

"Something that happened a long time ago." Hugo rolled over and looked up at her. "He was referring to something that happened while we were in the FBI, but the copious amount of alcohol he no doubt consumed last night apparently distorted events in his mind, or outcomes. Or something. You can ask him yourself this morning; he'll tell you he was talking nonsense. If he even remembers."

"Yes, of course he'll say that, because he wouldn't have said anything at all if he'd known I was in here with you." She frowned. "If you guys have a secret, he's not going to suddenly admit it after a few loose words, is he?"

"Don't ask me to predict Tom's behavior, drunk or sober," Hugo said.

"It's OK for you to have a secret from me, Hugo. It really is. But if you're a 'sitting duck,' that doesn't sound good. It sounds dangerous, and now you're saying it has something to do with when you were in the FBI, which makes it sound more dangerous, not less. And if my boyfriend is in danger, I think I have some sort of right to know about that."

Hugo smiled. "'Boyfriend' now, is it?"

"You think I bring coffee in bed to every man I sleep with?"

"I have no idea. But to be my girlfriend, coffee needs to be accompanied by eggs Benedict."

Claudia snorted. "Good luck with that."

"Hey, I'm an optimist," he said.

"And I'm a realist, which means I know that you worked to catch dangerous people when you were in the FBI. I'm also a journalist, which means I know when someone changes the subject, is being evasive, and is hiding something from me."

That was one of the things he liked about Claudia. One of the many things. She was direct and honest about what she wanted, and what she wanted to know. He'd not told her much about leaving the bureau, had never felt the need, but she was right that he probably did owe her an explanation, especially if Tom was correct about Rick Cofer and his intentions. If nothing else, by putting himself close to Claudia,

Hugo was necessarily putting her at risk, so for that reason alone, he owed her at least part of the story.

Except she wasn't one to accept just part of a story and let the rest go. Not only was it her job to get a full accounting, it was her nature. And he wasn't ready to tell it all, not yet.

"I have to keep something to myself for a little longer," he said, and took her hand. "Not just for my sake, but for Tom's. I hope you know it has nothing to do with trusting you."

"No, I think you know you can trust me with anything." She wagged a finger. "So I will trust that you have good reasons and let you have your secret with Tom. But I will tell you one thing. If you're going to make me wait to hear it, this secret had better be a good one."

Hugo pulled her onto the bed next to him and kissed her forehead. "Oh, I think you'll find that as far they go, it's pretty decent."

CHAPTER EIGHTEEN

At ten that morning, Hugo and Camille spoke on the phone to discuss the next step toward solving Baxter's murder and the mystery of the spy camera.

"I wanted to check with you," Lerens began, "to see if you have your usual arrangement with Claudia."

"About press coverage?"

"Right. We're not getting any calls, not yet, and Claudia's not been bugging me for details so I assume if there's a story you'll give her the details once we figure out what's going on?"

"That's my plan. But if we take too long, or someone else finds out about the spy camera, she may not be able to wait. She knows she has an advantage when we're involved, and she doesn't abuse it, but she's still has a job to do. Which means printing something if another journalist is beating her to the story."

"I understand that," Lerens said. "I just hope Helen Hancock does."

"She won't like it, but she's been around long enough to know how the world works."

"That's true." Lerens nodded. "*Alors*, back to the case itself. We agree that the murder and the placement of the camera are almost certainly related?"

"Yes. We should keep an open mind, but . . . Well, let me tell you a story. Back in my bureau days, we were chasing this truck driver who'd killed at least three women that we knew of, but almost certainly more.

We'd managed to narrow the suspects down to two guys. Then one of them died in a traffic accident."

"Did the murders stop?"

"We waited two weeks, and a body turned up. Looked to be the exact MO—he'd cut some hair off her head, bound her with duct tape, and staged the body in the same way along the side of a major road. That left us with one suspect, Gary Lee Miller, thirty-six years old. Problem was, he stopped showing up for work, went off the grid entirely."

"Did he know you'd identified him?" Lerens asked.

"No idea. But he was gone. We put out a nationwide alert, of course, just in case, and then just had to wait. Two months later, Montana police pull over a car that has no license plates, and the driver gives his name as Lee Miller. No driver's license or other ID on him. The trooper ran his name and, of course, got the shock of his life when a picture popped up of a late-thirties white guy named Gary Lee Miller, wanted for serial murder." Hugo shook his head and smiled. "He had the driver out and on the ground in seconds, his gun in the guy's ear, screaming that if he moved he'd blow his brains out."

"Why would he give his real name?"

"Ah," said Hugo. "That's the point of this story. He didn't."

Lerens cocked her head. "What do you mean?"

"Turns out, the guy knew he had no license to drive and had several unpaid tickets, so he made up a name. Said the first name that popped into his head, which was Lee Miller. Just so happened that he looked a little like Gary Lee Miller."

"What happened to him?"

"They cleared it up pretty quickly, but not before the poor fellow had been told he was a wanted serial killer. Must have been quite a shock."

"No kidding," Lerens said. "Did you catch the real killer?"

Hugo shook his head. "Never did. We figured that he'd gotten the job with that trucking company under a fake name and Social Security number, even paid taxes under his fake name. I would guess that he got arrested for something else, was properly IDed through fingerprints, and went to prison under his real name. Or possibly his grave. But the murders stopped after that last one, so something happened to him."

"A sobering story, every which way."

"For sure. But I think most cops have something like that happen, a moment that makes them stop and think a little harder about what they're doing. Not you?"

"Yes, actually," she said. "Along those same lines, when I was a patrol officer in Bordeaux. I made a traffic stop. Totally routine, for speeding or something. I was backed up by a more senior officer who got to the scene a few minutes later, a man no one on the shift liked too much, kind of a loner who never really gelled with us. Oddly enough, now that I think about it, he was one of the least judgmental people when I was transitioning. Anyway, this businessman was waiting for me to write his ticket, he wasn't being difficult or anything. I was halfway through writing it when this officer came up to the window and saw me typing something on the computer. He asked if I'd finished the ticket and I said no, I was just replying to a colleague's e-mail about lunch plans."

"Important stuff," Hugo said.

"I thought so. I mean, we had to time our meals so they didn't overlap too much—to keep as many of us on the street as possible."

"Of course," Hugo said. "Makes perfect sense."

"Not to that other officer. He stuck his head right through that open window, put his face in mine, and said something I've never forgotten. He said, 'The most important right any human has is freedom. Freedom to come and go, to be with family and friends, or just go wherever we want.' Then he pointed to the guy I'd pulled over. 'This might just be a traffic stop to you, perfectly legitimate and routine, but right now you're depriving that man of his freedom. He is stuck where he is until you decide he can go. And you're depriving him of that freedom so you can discuss lunch plans.' Then he turned and walked back to his car and left me there."

"I think I like that *flic*," Hugo said.

"Yeah, I never forgot that lesson and definitely respected him a lot more after that."

"I trust you hurried up with that ticket."

"*Non.* Tore it up on the spot and went to apologize to the driver for taking more of his time than I needed to."

"Why am I not surprised?" Hugo said. "So let's you and I be careful about making assumptions, and curtailing other people's freedom. Good reminders."

"*Absolument.*"

"With that in mind, where do you want to go next in the case?"

"I am taking a few officers and interviewing everyone at the hotel. We started that Tuesday and did more interviews yesterday, but it's been hard catching everyone, with all those rotating schedules. I'm hoping we can finish today."

"Great. How can I help?"

"Can you go talk to Helen Hancock?" she asked. "She trusts you and we need to make sure she's told us everything she knows. Having lied about Silva, or at least hidden their little affair, I wouldn't be surprised if there's more to learn. Hopefully about any friendship or relationship with Baxter."

"You think she was having an affair with him, too?"

"It crossed my mind."

"It's certainly a possibility," Hugo said. "Baxter is sleeping with Hancock, finds out Silva is, too, and confronts her. She denies it but he's sure, so he puts a camera in her room to prove it. Silva finds out, they have a confrontation in the hotel . . ." Hugo stopped himself. "No. That would require Silva to be carrying a knife at the time of the confrontation, and a regular kitchen knife, not one for self-protection."

"True," Lerens agreed. "And those types of murders don't typically evolve that way, the escalating confrontation."

"I know, in a stairwell you'd expect a fistfight or something closer to that."

"Maybe Helen lured Baxter there and Silva killed him?"

"Maybe," Hugo said. "It's not like she stabbed him herself."

"Her alibi," Lerens said, frowning with thought. "Even if she didn't have one, we'd really be pushing the bounds of likelihood."

"Yeah, she doesn't strike me as a stabby woman," Hugo agreed. "But you're right; she could've lured Baxter without being there herself, for Silva to kill him. Sent him a message to be there."

"But why? What's her motive for having Baxter killed?"

"It's pretty far-fetched," Hugo conceded. "She could easily end the relationship with him if that's what she wanted, ended either relationship, no need for blood to be spilled."

"And that's assuming there *was* a relationship between them."

"Agreed," said Hugo. "And no one we've talked to has even hinted at one."

"That's true. Which means that as of now I see no motive for Helen at all, but, if you don't mind, talk to her and see if she can tell us anything new."

Hugo found Helen Hancock in the hotel's plush restaurant, in a corner booth with her back to the world. She had a cup of coffee in front of her and sat talking to Jill Maxick, who looked up as Hugo approached.

"Mr. Marston, you look so serious; do you have news?" Maxick asked.

"No, I just wanted another chat with Helen. Front desk said you guys were in here."

"They shouldn't be telling people where Helen is," she said. "I expressly forbade them."

"I think the guy recognized me," Hugo said, "so don't be too hard on him."

"Even so, they're all supposed to check in with me first."

Trying to make amends? Hugo wondered. He turned to Hancock. "Do you have a few minutes? Lieutenant Lerens asked me to come by and talk to you again."

Hancock sighed and wrapped her hands around her coffee cup, as if she were suddenly cold. "Yes, of course." She looked at Maxick, who slid out of the booth and gestured for Hugo to sit.

"Can I bring you some coffee?" Maxick asked him.

"No, thank you." *And no other interruptions*, he wanted to say, but didn't.

Maxick hovered for a moment, then left them alone without another word.

"I suppose you want to know why I didn't tell you about Ambrósio," Hancock began.

"Yes," Hugo said. "Investigators don't like surprises during murder inquiries, especially very public surprises."

Hancock look at him and snorted. "You think you were the one who was surprised? You think I liked that particular surprise myself?"

"I don't mean to sound harsh, Helen, but you knew someone had been recording you and you must have known there was a chance your encounters with Silva might have been filmed. That was a gross invasion of privacy, and no doubt very embarrassing to you, but I'm not sure you can label it as a *surprise* exactly. You should have said something to us."

"I had to make a choice, to try and protect my privacy. So here we are, and which do you suppose is worse, me hiding that or being splayed all over the Internet?"

"I think if we're making comparisons, then the worst thing to have happened is probably the stabbing death of Andrew Baxter, don't you?" Hugo softened his tone. "Look, I'm not here to argue with you, but Baxter is still dead and his killer is still out there. We know Baxter bought that spy camera, so it seems only logical that he was the one who installed it in your room. But he wasn't the one to put that footage online."

"I was thinking about that. Is it possible that he uploaded it and set it to be published a few days later?"

"No, I talked to Lieutenant Lerens this morning. They found the website it was first posted on, a pornography site, and it doesn't have a delayed publishing option. And if you think about it, why would he do that? Blackmail, maybe, but we've seen no evidence of any plan to do that. I can't think of any other reason."

"No, I guess not. I suppose I was just hoping..." She shook her head sadly. "I don't know. That there wasn't someone else out there looking to hurt me."

"Helen, there's a question I have to ask you. It's a personal question, but it's very important that you don't lie to me or withhold information. You may think it's irrelevant, or that we'll never find out, but if you hide something else important from the police, you're not only jeopardizing the investigation but you're putting yourself in a French jail cell for obstructing justice."

"But I was trying to protect my privacy. Don't I have a right to do that?"

"I'm afraid that in a murder investigation a great deal of very private information comes out. Mostly the police can contain it, though, and if you'd told them about you and Silva, maybe they could've done something to help."

"Like what?" she snapped.

"Helen, I came here because I don't want you running afoul of the police. It's my job to keep US citizens safe, and I want to do that for you. I also have to find out who killed Andrew Baxter; he deserves that. I promise you that I'll keep anything you tell me as confidential as possible, but you do have to be honest with me."

She sat back. "What do you want to know?"

Hugo leaned forward and kept his voice low. "I want to know the full extent of any relationship you had with Mr. Baxter. Friends, lovers, enemies, I just need to know."

"And of those, you suspect lover." A light seemed to come on in her eyes. "You think Ambrósio did it. You think I was having an affair with Mr. Baxter, then Ambrósio came along and replaced him and then, for some reason, killed him. Is that what you really believe?"

"You have quite an imagination," Hugo said with a smile. "That comes with being a writer, I suppose."

"But it's what you think." She wagged a finger. "If you expect me to be honest with you, then don't try and sell me a pile of horse manure in return."

"Fine. I can't tell you everything; but I won't lie to you, I can agree to that."

"Then admit that's what you think. That Ambrósio did it."

"Investigations don't work like that," Hugo said. "We don't come up with a single theory and go with it. We look at the evidence and consider as many options as fit that evidence." He held up a hand to silence her. "And, yes, that possibility did cross my mind. Of course it did; I'd be a pretty poor investigator if I didn't consider that as a possibility."

"Do you consider me as a possibility?"

"You have an alibi, and, even if you didn't, I can't think of any reason why you'd want to hurt Mr. Baxter, so no. Maybe that'll change as we investigate more, but as of right now, you're in the clear as far as I'm concerned."

"Even though I misled you about Ambrósio?"

Hugo smiled. "Let's call that an evasion rather than an outright lie, shall we?"

"Thank you, I do like the sound of that better."

"Good. Now, how about my original question?"

"I've forgotten what . . . Oh, right, the extent of my relationship with poor Mr. Baxter."

"Right."

"I do know him by sight, of course." She frowned in thought. "And I'm sure I've spoken to him, chatted with him here at the hotel. But I don't think I even knew his name until this happened. I absolutely wasn't having an affair with him, nor did I have any kind of problem with him. The thing about me is, I kind of latch on to people whom I get on with. By that I mean, I prefer a small circle of people. I'm terrible with names, so it's much easier that way." She nudged him and smiled indulgently. "Plus, I have my favorites, and I've never been good at sharing. But poor Mr. Baxter, I wish I had known him, because I'm sorry that I can't help more."

"OK, thanks. Is there anything else from our previous conversations that you need to correct or add to?"

"I don't think so, no."

"Good." Hugo looked around the room, but the few people in the restaurant seemed to be ignoring them. "How are things going?"

"You mean since the video was published?"

"Yes," said Hugo.

"Not well." She shook her head. "You have no idea how many ugly e-mails I've received. Some from people who are shocked I'd actually have sex with a man, which is pretty ironic if you think about the books I write. And that those same people read."

"Very ironic," Hugo agreed.

"And far too many e-mails from people wanting to . . ." she grimaced at the thought. "Well, wanting me to re-create what was on that video with them. Complete strangers."

"How delightful. Can you have your publisher intercept them?"

"I'm doing exactly that right now, yes. Although they're not very happy with me."

"They don't blame you for this, surely?" Hugo asked.

"Yes and no. They can't say so, of course, because I didn't do anything wrong, but me naked on the Internet isn't exactly the image they've spent years cultivating. It's one thing to be sexy and to have your characters make love behind a veil of euphemisms, but apparently the person who creates it all has to stay pure as the driven snow. All demure lipstick and floral dresses."

"That's silly."

"Maybe, but for the people who put out my books, it's business."

"Have your sales been impacted?"

"Far too soon to know," she said. "But my editor seems to think they will be, at least judging from the way she's acting about all of this. I'm sure they'll let me know if there is a negative impact, no question." She slurred the last word just a little, and Hugo wondered whether there was something other than just coffee in her cup. Not that he would blame her, necessarily. After everything she'd been though, a little noontime lubrication didn't seem unreasonable.

"Are they finding you a new hotel?" he asked.

"A new hotel?"

"Yes. I mean, someone was murdered here and your room was rigged with a spy camera."

"That's the last thing I need, to move all my stuff to somewhere unfamiliar." She shook her head. "No, I've been coming here for years. I know the place, the staff, the chef even."

"And Jill Maxick, of course."

"All of the managers, but yes, of course her. She's been wonderful, and I think she feels a great responsibility for all this."

"Well, she's not just the hotel manager," Hugo said. "She's also a Helen Hancock fan."

"I know, she's been an absolute dear; I always sign a ton of books for her and people she's bought them for."

"That's nice."

"And since the incident with the camera, she's stopped charging me for that room, said I can stay as long as I want to on the hotel's dime." She smiled. "I haven't paid for a single drink at the bar since then."

"That's kind of her," Hugo said.

"It's good business sense, too. I mean, every business wants to keep their regulars happy, don't they?"

"And you feel safe and secure here?"

"I do. The hotel is sweeping my room every single day, now, and with everyone on guard, it's hardly likely to happen again." She shrugged. "And if it can happen here where people know me and where I have such a long-standing relationship, it could happen anywhere."

"One would hope not, but I get your point," Hugo said. He reached into his pocket as his phone buzzed. "Excuse me, it's Lieutenant Lerens. I should probably take this if you don't mind."

"Not at all."

Hugo stood and walked to an empty part of the restaurant. "Camille, what's up?"

"*Salut*, Hugo. It's Ambrósio Silva, and it's bad news, I'm afraid."

"What's he done now?"

"That's to be determined, whether he did it to himself or someone else did," Lerens said. "Either way, he's dead."

CHAPTER NINETEEN

At any crime scene, Hugo liked to get a wide-angled look first, if at all possible. In houses that wasn't always an option, but outside, like at this crime scene, it was easier and gave him a broad picture of what the killer saw, and where he might have gone to. For that reason, Hugo walked down from the busy road beside the Seine to the wide walkway that carried foot and bicycle traffic. He stopped short of the three policemen blocking access to the crime scene and spent a minute looking at it from afar, gazing around him.

Silva's body sat in the shade of Pont de Sully, on the walkway but tucked underneath the cast-iron arch that stretched directly ahead of him, out across the River Seine. The bridge connected the Left Bank with the Right, running across the southeastern tip of Île Saint-Louis, offering tourists a view of Notre Dame and giving Silva a canopy from the elements. His back was to the stone wall, his head slumped forward and his legs stretching toward the river twenty feet away. Up above him, orange nets sprang out sideways from the side of the bridge, on top of which workers had temporarily halted renovations, their curious faces peering down at the collection of police below.

Hugo looked up at the bridge and made his way back up the stairs toward it. He stood with the workers and gave himself another wide-angled look, a different perspective of the same scene. After a minute he saw the medical examiner, Doctor David Sprengelmeyer, trot down from the street to the walkway beside the river, and then head toward the crime scene that lay beneath them, out of view. Hugo took one more look from above and then made his way back down to the walkway himself, waiting with the policemen until Lerens waved him through.

"This area was cordoned off to pedestrians," she said, pointing to the "DO NOT CROSS" construction tape stretching across the sidewalk under the bridge.

"So no tourists coming and going, like they usually are."

"*Exactement.*"

"Who found him?"

"One of the workers. They're not supposed to smoke on the job, so he came down here to be out of sight."

"Needed a cigarette after seeing that, I'd bet," Hugo said. "How did the poor guy die?"

"Shot. Once in the chest."

"While he was sitting there, or did he fall into that position?"

"Not sure yet, I'm hoping Sprengelmeyer can enlighten us."

"How about the gun?"

"No sign of it, so definitely not suicide."

The setting of the bridge, the river, the missing gun, and even the aspiring writer himself . . . it all called to mind a story crafted by Sir Arthur Conan Doyle. Hugo smiled grimly. "Remember our conversation earlier, about jumping to conclusions?"

"I think it was about making assumptions, but perhaps it's the same thing. What are you thinking?"

Hugo remembered the conversation he had with Silva the first time they met, remembered, too, the death of Claudia's father and the way he'd emulated a trick pulled by a character in a Sherlock Holmes story. Something felt off, somehow, and Hugo's instincts were telling him to look closer. He eyed the distance from the body to the riverbank, then walked to the water's edge. Lerens followed him.

"It's unlikely that he killed himself," Hugo said. "But there are no impediments between him and the drop into the water."

"Impediments?"

"Silva was a Sherlock Holmes fan. Have you read any?"

"When I was younger, I'm sure."

"I'm thinking about 'The Problem of Thor Bridge.' In that story, a woman shoots herself on a bridge after tying a rock to the gun, which dragged it over a bridge balustrade and into the river."

"Why would she do that?"

"To make her suicide look like murder and frame someone else."

"You're not suggesting that Silva was suicidal and trying to frame someone, are you?"

"No idea," Hugo said. "But, as I said, he was a big Holmes fan, and it's the kind of emulation a writer might try."

Lerens looked at him skeptically.

Hugo raised his hands in mock surrender. "OK, maybe being around all of these romance writers is finally getting to me, kicking my imagination into high gear. It could be that someone shot him and ran off with the weapon, of course. That seems reasonable. Or maybe the killer tossed the gun into the river as a countermeasure. Either way, I'm just saying that it's worth dragging the riverbed."

"Not if you're the one who has to do it," Lerens said. "Or put in a request for it to be done."

"Red tape?"

She nodded. "Yes, but not just that. Putting divers in attracts attention to the crime, which isn't ideal for tourism. Something I'm not concerned with, but my bosses are."

"That so?" Hugo smirked. "Glad I'm not the one putting in the request, then."

She threw him a dirty look and took out her phone. As she made her call, Hugo edged closer to the crime scene. Dr. Sprengelmeyer was finishing his work, and when he zipped his bag closed, he looked up and saw Hugo waiting. He walked over to him.

"Monsieur Marston." He held out a hand. "Don't worry, I was wearing gloves."

"Doc." Hugo shook his hand. "Sorry we have to keep meeting like this."

Sprengelmeyer jerked his thumb at Silva's body. "Not as sorry as he is."

"True enough. Learn anything we can use?"

"Maybe, maybe not. He was shot once in the chest, straight into the heart, so he died pretty much immediately. You want to know when and who, am I right?"

"Of course." Hugo had never met a medical examiner who'd give a straight answer, especially at a crime scene, so he was patient, let the doctor do it his own way.

"I can't tell you if it's suicide or murder. I know the crime-scene techs swabbed his hands for gunshot residue, but that's hardly a definitive test, as you know. I'm guessing they'll have those results by tomorrow morning."

"Can you tell what caliber was used?"

"Not right now. Large, I'd guess. It plowed right through him and took some chips out of the wall. Crime-scene people will have that at the ballistics lab by now, so another answer you'll have to get tomorrow."

"Any sign of a struggle?"

"No. The only wound I see on him is the gunshot, no other bumps, bruises, or scrapes at all."

"And time of death?"

"No more than a couple of hours would be my estimate."

"Can you tell if he was standing or sitting?"

"Sitting, it looks like."

Hugo looked over the doctor's shoulder at Silva, still propped against the stone wall as if he was taking a nap. "You ever see someone shoot themselves in the heart like that?"

"Heart, head, mouth. Stomach even."

"Why would someone do that, the stomach?"

"No clue. Painful as hell." Sprengelmeyer shrugged his shoulders. "That's the thing about my job; I never get to ask my patients any questions."

The medical examiner turned and walked away, so Hugo moved in front of Silva and knelt down. He took a moment, as he always did, out of respect for a dead man and to let the discomfort of seeing a dead body shift into a more dispassionate professionalism. Hugo tried, in every case, not to treat a corpse as merely a blob of evidence to be inspected, poked, and prodded. Somewhere, people would mourn this man; and, despite the hundreds of dead people Hugo had seen, he always made himself remember that each had been a living, breathing individual who deserved respect. Even, or perhaps especially, in death.

There was very little blood on his blue shirt, and the entry wound was clean and round. Hugo tried to see the exit wound, wanting to gauge for himself the size of the weapon used, but he couldn't see it without moving the body, and he didn't have permission for that yet.

"Well, Mr. Silva," Hugo said quietly. "I don't know whether you did this to yourself, or whether someone else did. But either way, I promise I'll do my best to find out. And I'm sorry we didn't figure out what was going on before this had to happen."

He stood and turned to see Camille Lerens walking toward him. "The divers will be here within the hour."

"How deep is the water here?"

"No idea. The river averages about thirty-five feet, and I'm sure there's a nice layer of sludge at the bottom they'll have to deal with."

"I bet that's fun."

"Hey, they get well paid for it, so as long as they do a thorough job, I'm not worried."

"I've generally found the Paris police to be pretty good," Hugo said with a smile.

"Thanks." Lerens looked left and right, then said, "So there's something I wanted to mention."

"Sounds serious."

"I've been offered a job. Back in Bordeaux."

"That is serious."

"*Oui.* I haven't responded, but it'd be a pay increase, more responsibility, and close to my parents."

"A promotion?"

"Assistant chief."

"Fancy," Hugo said. "And even though I'd be very upset at you breaking up this crime-solving thing we have going, you know I'd support you."

She put a hand on Hugo's arm. "I do know that, thank you."

"Tom, on the other hand, I can't promise anything."

"He'll have to find another policewoman to punch."

"Oh, that won't be a problem for him, I'm sure. But I'm guessing whoever it is won't be as cool as you."

"You mean forgiving," she laughed. "I should have let him stay in jail a few more days."

"Probably. When do you have to decide on the job?"

"They want an answer by the end of the week."

"Just curious, did they seek you out or the other way around?"

She laughed gently. "The former. I'm very happy here, you know that. But I'd be a fool not to consider it. Although . . ."

"Although what?"

"Part of me wonders how much of the offer is for PR purposes."

"In what way?" Hugo asked.

"Come on, Hugo, don't play dumb with me. In the modern world, demographic statistics mean something. To some people, anyway."

"Ah, I see. And having a transgender police lieutenant, and one of color, in a high position looks good."

"And a lesbian one, at that."

"Is that what you . . . I mean, you're a . . ."

"Labels are tricky, I know," Lerens said kindly. "Especially for dinosaurs like you."

"A good reason to do away with them, if you ask me."

"*Certainement*," Lerens agreed. "We should do away with any and all modernities that make cis-gendered, arrow-straight, white males like Hugo Marston uncomfortable."

"Glad we're on the same page, Camille. Warms my heart to know that."

She threw him another dirty look, then cracked a smile. "Funny man."

"Not often, but thanks." Hugo straightened, as if remembering why they were there. "Well, you know I'll support whatever decision you make. In the meantime, what do you want me to do to help here?"

"I have to wait for the divers and for Sprengelmeyer's people to take the body. We'll have autopsy, ballistics, and gun-shot residue test results back sometime tomorrow morning, so I'm not sure there's anything else to be done today."

Ballistics, Hugo thought, Michelle Juneau's voice surfacing in his mind. *Surely not.*

"Excuse me a moment," he said, "I need to check on something." Camille Lerens nodded and drifted back toward the crime scene to give him privacy. Hugo pressed the Call Back feature on his phone and waited.

"This is Michelle Juneau."

"Hi, Michelle, how're you?"

"Oh, Hugo, hi. I'm fine, but something's happened at the library, and I thought you'd want to know."

"You mentioned a theft."

"Yes. After you were here talking to those people, Helen Hancock's students, it seems like it might be related. Or it might not be, I really don't know." She was talking quickly, her voice high and excited. "I didn't think of a connection until after the police left, sorry."

"Calm down, Michelle, and tell me what's happened."

"You know that glass cabinet in the conference room?"

"Of course, yes."

"Well, someone broke into it."

CHAPTER TWENTY

Hugo's heart sank. "What was stolen?"

"A gun. Hunter S. Thompson's gun."

"What else?"

"Nothing. Oh, except the bullets that go with it."

"All of the bullets?"

"No," Juneau said. "Just two or three of them. I think so, anyway."

"When did this happen?"

"That's the thing, we're not sure." She sighed. "Sometime in the last few days, we think."

"You think? Explain that to me, Michelle, because the timing of this, it's potentially a huge deal."

"I know, I know. And I'm sorry."

"Just tell me when you think it happened." Hugo caught Lerens's eye, his tone of voice had evidently alerted her that something was wrong.

"We don't really use that room a lot. It's not covered by any of the security cameras, obviously, because people have important meetings in there and wouldn't want to be recorded."

"But no one noticed a smashed cabinet?"

"It wasn't smashed, sorry, I didn't explain that bit. We reported it to the police yesterday, and when they came they said it looked like someone had used a glass cutter to do a controlled break. Like, a circle they could put their hand through."

"OK, but no one noticed the gun was missing?"

"That's the crazy part," Juneau said. "Whoever took it left most of the bullets behind and put a replica in its place. I guess it's a toy or something, but it looked real, or real enough that no one looked very closely. And the hole in the glass was at the far end of the cabinet, not really visible from the front."

"Who noticed it was the wrong gun?"

"A library patron. He wasn't even sure at first, asked if we'd substituted one Hunter Thompson gun for another one, so we took a look and discovered the fake."

"And called the police."

"Yes, of course, since it was a gun. Well, we would have anyway, and I think the gun was disabled, inoperable."

"What makes you say that?"

"I don't know, just some thought I had, a memory from when we acquired it. I can't think we'd have displayed a fully functioning gun like that. I guess it was technically locked up, but . . ." Her voice tailed off. "I can't be entirely sure it was disabled, to be honest."

"When did you report it?"

"Yesterday evening, right after we found out. I was talking to some people here about it and realized that you'd want to know, so I left you a message after we talked to the police. I wasn't sure if there was any connection with what you're doing, so I didn't know if they'd tell you right away."

"I appreciate that, Michelle, and you're right—I definitely want to know, because the police haven't passed that on yet. I guess there's no reason they'd make the connection, though. And I'm sorry I didn't call you back right away. Do you have any idea at all who might have taken it?"

"The police asked the same question. No, I really don't, none of us do. We all made a list of people we know who've had access or definitely have been in the room this past week, and we gave it to the police. I can e-mail it to you, if you want, but it's long and everyone working here is on it."

As are all the people associated with Helen Hancock, Hugo thought. "No, that's OK, I can get it from the police. But thanks again for the call; I'll be in touch if any other questions come to mind, if that's alright."

"Anything, Hugo, call anytime."

They disconnected and Hugo explained the new development to Lieutenant Lerens as two men placed Silva into a body bag and zipped it closed, then lifted it onto a gurney. They moved out of the way as the medical techs wheeled it to their van, and Hugo could hear the whir of cameras from the bridge, the press and public alike fascinated by the anonymous but familiar sight of a dead body sealed in a black bag, the gruesome details hidden but the end result clear.

Hugo and Lerens moved into the lee of the bridge, away from prying eyes and cameras as they continued their conversation about the gun theft.

"You think it might be the gun that killed Silva?" she asked.

"One hell of a coincidence if not."

"Agreed. Whoever they reported it to will have asked this, probably, but if not we'll need the library people to check to see whether the purchase records, or donation records I guess, say anything about it being usable or not."

"Good idea. I'll ask them to look if they haven't already." They turned as the sound of engines rolled in from the river behind them. "Your divers?" Hugo asked.

"I'd say so; it's a police launch."

"I'll leave you to it, then," Hugo said. "My boss called me earlier; he wants to get together so I can brief him on the investigation. Maybe we can do it over wine and pizza."

"Sounds delightful," Lerens said, checking her watch. "Looks like I'll be here for the next few hours, so enjoy it for me."

"I'll do my best." He gestured toward the river. "But if you find anything interesting in there, please let me know."

At six that evening, Hugo met Ambassador Taylor at Chez Maman, the last place anyone would expect a senior representative of the United States government to go for drinks. Despite its location near the river, no tourists ever troubled its orange-haired bartender-owner, known to everyone as just "Maman." The place had been functioning as a bar for a hundred years or more, and its floor and walls were coated with the smoke from the million-plus cigarettes, pipes, and cigars that had been lit within its walls. That history and a lack of windows meant that even now, when smoking inside a bar like this was banned, every time he stepped outside, Hugo's clothes and skin smelled like he'd been firing up strong Cuban cigars for hours.

The floor was uneven, the chairs and tables sturdy and worn, but it was a safe place. Safe from tourists, yes, but also from prying eyes and ears—really from any kind of interference. You could sit alone and nurse a drink for two hours and not be bothered by anyone. Or you could drink yourself into oblivion, and someone would heft you into a cab and send you home without emptying your wallet. Hugo knew this place through Tom, of course, and after thirty or forty visits had finally been welcomed as a semiregular.

Welcomed was a strong word, perhaps. It just meant Maman didn't shoot dirty looks his way anymore, although she looked a little disappointed Tom wasn't there to flirt with.

Hugo and Ambassador Taylor sat against the back wall and nursed glasses of the house scotch. In truth, it might also have been Irish whisky, or possibly even some form of cheap, small-label bourbon; one didn't go to Chez Maman for top-shelf liquor, vintage wine, or craft beer. You got what you asked for more or less, and it cost half what you'd pay in any other drinking establishment in Paris.

"Not been here in a while," Taylor said. "Last time was with Tom, I think."

"Same here," Hugo said. "I'm half expecting him to burst through the door and yell at us for not inviting him."

Taylor smiled at the thought. "How's he doing these days?"

"Same old Tom. A little lighter on the booze than he used to be, I think; he's getting older after all."

"Aren't we all?" Taylor said. "What's going on with the Helen Hancock case? Any updates?"

"Yes. One of the players was found shot to death under the Pont de Sully."

Taylor sat up straight. "Murdered?"

"Could be."

"That is news. Who was it?"

"Ambrósio Silva. You may have seen his recent online shenanigans with Helen Hancock."

"Ah, yes, I did see something about that." As a former CIA operative himself, J. Bradford Taylor had seen a whole lot worse than two consenting adults having sex, but even so he sighed deeply and shook his head. Hugo wondered if perhaps his boss was disappointed in Hancock, reinforcing what she'd said about the destruction of her clean image that her publisher had worked to create. Hugo couldn't help but smile at the idea of an ambassador and former spook being affected by the downfall of his favorite romance writer, but Taylor seemed to shake himself out of the doldrums. "So, a fresh mystery for an already-strange investigation."

"Right. A new twist every day, it seems," Hugo said. "And of course Silva's death ups the ante considerably."

"He have any connection to Andrew Baxter?"

"Passing acquaintance at most, best we can tell. In my opinion," Hugo went on, "the central mystery is the spy camera in Helen's room. We figure out what that was about, and everything else will fit into place, I think."

"Any more footage come to light?" Taylor asked.

"No, not that we know about anyway. I know Lieutenant Lerens has people monitoring the Internet in case something new pops up, but nothing as of yet."

"That's good."

Hugo took a sip and sat back. "You OK, boss? You're looking a little pale."

"I'm fine, thanks. This job, it gets to you sometimes." He looked around the dingy little pub. "That's why I wanted to come here. Zero chance of having to glad-hand someone, play the charming ambassador, listen to someone's problems or complaints."

"Nice to cut loose a little," Hugo agreed. "We need to get you a false mustache and send you out drinking with Tom."

Taylor snorted. "I can see the headline now. *US Ambassador Arrested after Drunken Brawl with Pack of Nuns.*"

"Nuns come in packs?"

"Don't they? No idea. Anyway, I'll have a few here, and that'll be a nice-enough change." He gave a small smile. "Drinks, that is, not nuns."

"Can't imagine too many of the latter have set foot in here in the past century." Hugo raised his glass. "So here's to unwinding just a little bit."

Taylor chinked glasses with Hugo but didn't look him in the eye, so Hugo set his scotch down gently and said: "Boss, I know something's bothering you. And I'm guessing we're here because you want to tell me, so why not spit it out?"

Taylor looked around the room, but the half dozen customers paid them no mind, and Maman herself was nowhere to be seen. *Probably dragged her oxygen tank out back where she can smoke in peace*, Hugo thought.

Taylor ran a hand over his bald head and down across his face, sighing deeply. "Helen Hancock found you at Isabelle Severin's funeral," he said. "She knew you were there because I told her."

"OK," said Hugo. "I already knew that, so no big deal. Go on."

"The thing is, I'm a little more than just one of her million or so readers."

"I didn't know that," Hugo said. "But I think I'm beginning to see."

"Do you? I've not said anything yet."

"We wouldn't be having this conversation if you and Helen were just coffee-drinking buddies."

"I guess." Taylor looked around the room again. "It's not what you're thinking, though."

"So tell me what it is."

"She did a signing here a number of years ago, and I went. It was just after a terrorist threat; nothing came of it, but I had a couple of your guys with me, suits and earpieces, you know the look. Anyway, it got her attention, and we ended up chatting, then going to dinner. A case of a couple of slightly lonely people who like books having a good meal."

"Nothing wrong with that at all."

"Right. So the next couple of times she came to Paris, for research or whatever, we got together for dinner. One night we both had a little too much, let our guard down and then . . . well, pick your cliché."

Hugo smiled. "One thing led to another? Biggest mistake of your life? Or hers, more likely."

Taylor flashed a smile. "Funny. But that's the thing, it was . . . good fun, and neither of us felt remotely bad about it afterward. So on her next visit, we did the same again."

"How very French of you both."

"Trouble is, Hugo, that next time was this past week."

A silence opened up between them as Hugo realized what Ambassador Taylor was saying. *You think you might be on candid camera, too,* he thought. "When *exactly* did this encounter happen?"

"A few days before she discovered the camera."

Hugo pursed his lips in thought. "I don't mean to get personal, boss, and I surely don't mean to judge, but was she sleeping with you and Silva at the same time?"

"I don't know if it was the same time exactly, and it's not that I really mind her sleeping with someone else." He shrugged. "I just didn't think it appropriate for her to sleep with one of her students."

"He's a grown man."

"Sure, one who looks up to her and places a degree of professional trust in her. It just," Taylor struggled for the right words. "I don't know, it just didn't seem like something she'd do. Not without telling me, anyway."

"I hear that," Hugo said. "But if your thing was no-strings-attached, why would she have to tell you about it? Maybe Silva asked her not to, and she was honoring his request."

"Like I said, I don't know, it just didn't sit right with me."

"Ambassadors aren't immune to jealousy, you know."

"But it wasn't like that," Taylor insisted. "Really, I mean it." He slumped back in his chair. "I'm doing a shitty job of explaining it."

"Thing is, you don't need to. What's important is whether or not that camera was in place and recording while you two were together."

Taylor leaned forward, his head in his hands. "Can you imagine?"

"Yeah, that one's hitting the headlines," Hugo said. "Ambassador's big white ass all over the screen, making love to his hero, a romance writer."

Taylor looked up, surprise on his face. "You're not taking this seriously. Jesus, Hugo, this could end my career."

"I am, and it could. Look, if that film is out there, then there's nothing you can do about it. I mean, maybe we'll come across whoever put up the Silva footage and snag it before anything happens, but it's not looking promising. So, if it does happen, the best thing you can do is hold your head up and say, 'Yes, I was having a relationship with a beautiful woman, in the city of love. So damned what?'"

Taylor thought for a moment. "Easy for you to say."

"And easier for you, I would suggest, than making excuses or being defensive about something you did that wasn't wrong."

Taylor took a slug of his scotch. "Damn, Hugo. You're a good man and you give good advice. I think."

"Have you spoken to Helen about this?"

"We haven't talked in a few days. Ever since I found out about Silva."

"OK, do me a favor and don't speak to her yet. Definitely don't tell her that you've told me about your relationship."

"Sure, that's fine, I won't."

"This does add one more technical complication," Hugo said.

Taylor looked at him, confused for a second, and then his eyes widened with worry. "Shit, if Silva was murdered, this makes me a suspect."

"Can you establish your whereabouts for the whole of today?"

Taylor's shoulders relaxed. "You know I can. Hardly ever get a moment to myself in this damn job."

"Well," said Hugo. "In that case, on this occasion you should be grateful to your entourage."

"You'll need to tell your lieutenant friend."

"I will, but I imagine she'll want to interview you herself." Hugo saw the worry on his face. "Please don't worry; she'll be discreet."

"You think so?"

"I know so." Hugo gave him a reassuring smile. "If there's anyone on this planet experienced with, and sympathetic to, public judgment, it's Camille. Trust me on that."

"I'll drink to that." Taylor straightened his back and raised his glass. "After all, I don't have much choice at this point, do I?"

"Not really." Hugo started to raise his own glass, but his phone buzzed into life on the table in front of him. *Camille Lerens*, the display said. "Mind if I get this?"

Taylor shook his head. "Not at all. I'll get us another round."

Hugo answered. "Camille, what is it?"

"Divers found a gun. We recovered the bullet, so ballistics will run some tests to confirm, but it's got to be the murder weapon."

"It's the gun from the library?"

"It is, yes."

"Do you have any good suspects in that theft?"

"*Non*," she said. "We have a lot of them but not many good ones."

"What do you mean by 'a lot'?"

"Well, everyone who used that conference room between the last time the real gun was seen in the cabinet and when it was discovered missing."

"How much time is that?"

"Several days, we're not even sure about that."

"How many people?"

"All the people in the writing group, including Helen Hancock herself, all ten of the library's staff, plus four volunteers, and twenty-three library patrons. And you."

Hugo smiled. "True. That *is* a lot of people. Including Silva himself."

"Oh, yes," Lerens said. "So, like Juneau told you before, there's no camera inside the room, but we did find that one outside of the room does catch the door, so we may be able to figure out who was in there alone during our flexible time frame. I have officers looking at the tape and doing interviews, but it's going to be hard to prove who took that gun unless someone saw it happen."

"Which no one did, or else they would have come forward already."

"*Exactement.* And just so you know, Hugo, you and your boss are both on the list of people who've used the conference room this past week."

Hugo looked at Taylor, who was leaning on the bar and telling Maman a story with a drink in each hand. "Is that right?"

"It is. And one more thing. The gun was tied to a rock with a long piece of string."

"Well, well," Hugo said. His thoughts immediately went back to Claudia's father and his untimely demise. "Then we have either a suicide or a killer with literary tastes."

"Right," Lerens said. "Which might normally be good information to have, but not when we have a library full of suspects. Literally."

"Very true."

Lerens sighed. "Well, I'm tired and going home. Coffee in the morning?"

"Yes. I'll text you first thing." Hugo disconnected as Taylor returned to the table, a little unsteady on his feet.

"News?" the ambassador asked.

"You could say that."

"Can you share?"

"I'd like to." Hugo gave him a wry smile. "But I probably shouldn't, what with you being our newest suspect."

CHAPTER TWENTY-ONE

On Friday morning, Hugo met with Camille Lerens in a quiet café off Rue Jacob. They sat at the back of the small space and talked as the breakfast crowd ebbed and flowed around them. Hugo gave in and ordered two croissants with his coffee, remembering Oscar Wilde's comment about being able to resist everything except temptation.

Sitting across from him, pastry-free and her hands throttling a tiny coffee cup, Lieutenant Lerens was less than happy.

"He should have told me," she said. "He should have told me the moment that camera was found, and if not then at the very least the moment a murder victim was identified as the person who was monitoring Helen's room."

"He should, you're right. But I hope you can see why he didn't."

"Yes, I do, but one day you Americans will realize that having sex is quite normal and not something to be ashamed of." She shook her head. "*Merde*, this complicates things a little."

"A lot, and he's sorry about that. He'll be in his office all day today. I told him you'd take his statement yourself, and I assured him how discreet you are."

"*Bien sûr*," she said. "And as long as his alibis check out, this will be the end of it. Unless a new tape surfaces."

"Wait, alibis—with an 's'?"

"*Oui.* For the Baxter murder and Silva's." She held his eye for a second. "We agree that they are connected, don't we?"

"Yes, of course. Somehow an ambassador being questioned about two murders seems worse than just one, but I get your point." Hugo changed tack. "What news on the gun?"

"Ah, yes. Our ballistics people confirmed it was the weapon that killed Silva. Other than that, nothing useful. The water and mud took care of any fingerprints or DNA, and the string is the kind you can buy at any *tabac* in the city."

"*Tabacs* sell string?"

"Don't they? Anyway, you know what I mean—easily available and untraceable."

"And the rock?" he asked with a smile.

She threw him a dirty look and sipped her coffee. "You're in a hilarious mood this morning. Claudia spend the night or something?"

"Nope. Just slept like a baby and had a nice walk here. Why're you so grumpy?"

"Hormones. One of the joys of being me, they fluctuate without warning me first."

Hugo said nothing, painfully aware of the superficiality of his knowledge when it came to Camille and transgender issues in general. He felt her watching him but still couldn't find anything to say. Finally she spoke.

"I'm sorry, Hugo, I didn't mean to make you uncomfortable." She gave him a reassuring pat on the hand. "But I'm curious why you never ask me about my transition. About any of it."

"Well," Hugo said. "The truth is, I feel like I don't know as much about this stuff as I should, and I sure as hell don't want to say something dumb and offend you."

"That'd be Tom's job," she said with a smile.

"Precisely."

"Then let's do this," she said. "If you have a question, or want to know something, you have *carte blanche* to ask. If it's a stupid question, I might let you know, but I'll never be offended."

"You're sure about that? I can be pretty oblivious."

"Yes, I'm sure. Look, I know how different my path has been, especially compared with that of someone like you. Think about it this way, I'm fairly certain that in your shoes I'd be curious and end up asking dumb, and possibly offensive, questions."

"OK. And you can ask me about being a Texan any time you like."

"Deal." She looked at her watch. "Well, I better pay your ambassador a visit."

"Got your tape recorder?"

"Always. What are you going to do?"

"Well, with Silva's death our suspect list got shorter by one, so I thought maybe I'd go and chat with each of the others. Starting with Andrew Baxter's roommates."

"Good plan," Lerens said. "You have appointments with them?"

Hugo grinned and shook his head. "You know me better than that. I prefer the element of surprise." He pictured Lionel Colbert's pinched, angry face. "Especially when it comes to people who don't like authority."

"Yes, you do, don't you?" She stood. "Just be careful with that. One of these days you're going to pop up in front of someone who doesn't like surprises."

"It's happened," Hugo said. "And trust me, I'm careful. Back home there was always a chance that unhappy person carried a gun, so you better believe I'm in the habit of not taking stupid chances."

He walked to the hotel, in no hurry and so drifting along in the wash of people on Rue de Seine. In front of him, an old couple clung to each other, the man in a blue blazer and the woman in a loose white dress, going at their own pace, creating their own little wake for Hugo to drift in.

Hugo meandered behind them and wondered about how to get more from Colbert and Prehn. One step they'd not taken was a thorough search of the room they'd shared with Baxter. Searching shared spaces always posed a problem for law enforcement, given the varying expectations of privacy that were protected by law—going through Baxter's stuff was one thing, but with no good reason to search his roommates' space, they'd not sought a warrant.

An image of his friend Tom flashed into Hugo's mind. How many times had Hugo suggested ideas to Tom of actions he himself couldn't or wouldn't take, and let Tom do his dirty work? Most of the time it was to avoid red tape and procedure, not to skirt the law; but, even so, Hugo always hesitated before calling on his friend like that. And on the occasions he hadn't hesitated, he made sure to ask himself later why not.

As he headed toward the hotel, Hugo felt the hair on the back of his neck stand up. He slowed and pretended to be interested in the modern art in the next store's window, but he focused his eyes on the reflection in the glass, not what was behind it. He didn't see anyone he recognized but was dimly aware of someone to his right moving into the shoe store he'd just passed. Hugo pulled out his phone and opened the camera app, reversing the image and holding up the phone so he could look behind him while walking. He acted like he was studying the phone, maybe about to talk on it, and kept going.

Ten steps farther on, a familiar figure slipped out of the shoe store, his head down and his hands deep in his pockets and—like any amateur trying to tail someone—making himself stand out like a sore thumb.

Hugo quickened his pace and turned the corner onto Rue de Buci, stepping off the sidewalk behind a white van. He stationed himself on the road, able to look through the side and front windows of the vehicle as the man following him came closer and closer. The person tailing him had hurried, too, and as he turned into Rue de Buci Hugo saw the worry on his face. *Worried you've lost me?* Hugo wondered. *Or is something else bothering you?*

He decided to find out.

As his follower passed on the other side of the van, Hugo stepped out, right in front of him. Lionel Colbert sprang back and held up both hands to ward Hugo off, as if he were a mugger.

Hugo moved closer. "Lionel, right?"

"Right. Lionel. Or Leo."

Hugo could see the man almost literally pulling himself together after the surprise and decided not to let him get too comfortable. "Why are you following me?"

Colbert stared at Hugo for a second, long enough to muster some of that disdain from their previous encounter. "I'm not."

"You spent last month's salary on shoes. Doing the same this month?"

"You have a good memory."

"A requirement of my job."

"And what is that, exactly?" Colbert asked.

"At the moment, it's to find out who killed an American citizen." Hugo took a step closer. "And, right this second, it's to find out exactly why the dead man's roommate is following me."

"I told you, I wasn't."

Hugo relaxed his body and smiled. "You know, I used to be in the FBI. I got real good at telling when people were lying to me or hiding something. I'm getting that feeling right now."

Colbert looked at him with deep, dark eyes, as if trying to study Hugo's mind, his soul even. But Lionel just shook his head.

"Let me guess," Hugo said. "You know something about this, something you wish you didn't. And you're worried that if you tell me this information, I'll think you're more involved than you are, than I already think you are." When Colbert said nothing, Hugo continued. "Thing is, when people hide stuff from me, that's when I tend to think they're involved. When they tell me things, even bad things, I'm far more inclined to give them the benefit of the doubt. When we first met, my alarm bells were set to ringing pretty quickly, because you were so hostile and, as far as I could tell, you had no reason to be."

"Maybe I don't like cops."

"Yeah, maybe. But even people who don't like cops like them involved when their friend is murdered. I mean, it's a joke in law enforcement that everyone hates cops until they need one. Kind of like lawyers."

"Wow, you cops are hilarious."

Hugo shrugged. "Our humor is a little darker than most people's, but otherwise not much different. Point is, you have no reason to distrust me or to be hostile. Not that I know of, anyway. But you may have a reason to lie or to withhold information. People do that all the time, and usually it's because they think that what they know or what they've done is irrelevant to the investigation. . . . Maybe something embarrassing that they did, and they're sure it has no bearing on anything. Am I close?"

Colbert took a slow, deep breath, but his eyes never left Hugo's. "I'm sorry you thought I was following you. Have a nice day."

Hugo nodded. "OK then. You have a nice day, too." He brushed past Colbert, heading back toward Rue de Seine, toward the hotel. He barely made it around the corner when he heard footsteps rushing up behind him. He turned.

"Wait." Colbert swung around in front of him, breathing hard. He looked up after a moment, and his shoulders slumped as his eyes slid away from meeting Hugo's. "You were close. Very," he said. "But it's not information I have. It's something a little more tangible."

"And what's that?"

"I want you to know that I *found* it; I didn't take it. Not before and not recently; I just found it."

"Found what?"

"Andy's computer. I'm moving into another room at the hotel, and I was clearing out some boxes. It was in one of them. At first I didn't recognize it. Or realize whose it was. I didn't know what it was doing in my stuff—so I fired it up to see." He shook his head. "I ended up looking at everything on it."

"You 'just found it'?" Hugo pressed.

"Yes. And I should've turned it in straightaway but, man, I'm not wild about being sucked into any of this crazy shit."

"How does that suck you in, exactly?"

"It was in *my* stuff, how do you think? Look, Jill Maxick was with me when I found it—she'll tell you what happened. And some of the crap on there . . . I can't believe he'd record that. I can't believe he did."

CHAPTER TWENTY-TWO

Fifteen years previously.

1530 hours, Houston, Texas.

Hugo adjusted the car's visor and tried to get a better view of the bank's entrance, maybe see through one of the windows. He and Tom both stiffened as a sound echoed across the shopping-center parking lot, muffled but unmistakable. Hugo reacted first and opened the car door with his left hand as his right grabbed the handset of his radio and held down the call button. "Shots fired, we're going in."

Tom was already out of the black SUV, moving in a low crouch between the rows of parked cars, his gun drawn. Hugo swung the door closed as he got out, not caring about making a noise, worried only about his friend heading into the bank alone. He hurried to catch up with him, and did so at the last row of cars. He pulled Tom down into a full crouch, and they watched the bank for a moment.

"We need a plan," Hugo said. "Any ideas?"

"I got a plan for you—"

"No, a real one. We can't sit tight for backup, but let's not get shot before we get through the door."

"I'm OK with that, but we ain't waiting around." Tom pointed at the front of the bank, which had large glass windows on either side of double glass doors.

"Let's just play it cool," Hugo said. "I'll walk in like a customer, and you come in behind me, gun drawn."

"Works for me."

They straightened and started across the lot to the bank. Hugo wiped his palms on his pants and made sure his jacket covered any view of his gun. At the twin doors, he took a deep breath and breezed into the main lobby, adrenaline surging through his body and only dimly aware of Tom coming in behind him. Hugo knew he didn't look casual, like any old customer wandering in, but he couldn't help it and, when he saw three bodies on the floor, he no longer cared.

Hugo couldn't see either of the gunmen, but he drew his weapon anyway. The lobby was an open square with windows opposite where Hugo and Tom had just come in and with closed office doors to their left. Against those doors, half a dozen customers cowered, several of them crying. He looked to his right, where the tellers were stationed, but they were either hiding or had fled.

To his left, Tom moved past in a blur, heading for one of the people who'd been shot, a woman wearing a yellow sundress and cowboy boots. He knelt beside her, muttering and cursing, and when he looked back at Hugo there was rage and horror on his face.

Ahead of Hugo, in the middle of the open area, a security guard lay face up, unmoving. Hugo strode over to him and went down on one knee to feel for a pulse, and saw a pool of blood spreading out beneath his head. When he got nothing, he rolled the man over and saw why. One of the robbers had put a gun in the man's mouth and blown most of the back of his head off.

Hugo left him and went to the third prone person, a middle-aged man in shorts and a T-shirt that had once been white but was now mostly red from the two bullet wounds in his stomach and chest. *Also dead*, Hugo thought, and silently cursed himself for not listening to Tom, for not following the men into the bank immediately.

"Tom, how is she?"

Tom was still down on both knees, unable to answer. He shook his head, which told Hugo all he needed to know. He turned to the huddled customers.

"We're FBI—police are on their way. Where did those men go?"

An older white-haired man pointed to his left, to the double doors leading out to the smaller parking lot behind the bank. "They just left, that way."

Hugo nodded and went to Tom, resting a hand on his shoulder. "Hey. We have to go. There's nothing we can do here."

Tom stayed still for a second, then nodded. "Yes. Yes, I know."

"Come on, let's get those bastards."

"Too fucking right." He looked up at Hugo, his eyes blazing. "Too fucking right we're getting those bastards."

"See if you can spot them." Hugo pointed the way the robbers had gone. "I'll get the car, come get you."

Hugo heard Tom clatter into the back door as he himself hit the front one, sprinting to the SUV, his gun still in his hand. As soon as he reached the SUV, a black Chevy Impala squealed around the corner of the bank, heading right at him.

Where did they . . . ? Did they just carjack someone? But Hugo had no time to ponder. He stepped away from his vehicle and raised his gun, but the sun glinted off the windshield, and Hugo couldn't be sure whether an innocent was in the car, his trigger finger stilled by the inclination *not* to shoot, *not* to kill. In seconds, the car was just feet away, almost on top of him, and instinctively he threw himself sideways, wincing as his left arm slammed into the grill of his vehicle and the Impala sped by, missing him by inches.

Forty yards away, Tom was sprinting toward him, face red and arms pumping. Hugo ran to the driver's side, ignoring the pain in his arm. He started the engine and pulled out of the parking spot, leaning over to open the door so Tom could dive in. Before the passenger door was even shut, Hugo flipped on the lights and sirens and gunned it. The SUV leapt forward, tires squealing, and both Hugo and Tom held on for dear life as the back end slid wide before gripping the pavement and shooting them toward the exit of the parking lot a hundred feet away. Hugo fixed his eyes on the back of the Impala as it swung onto the main road, and pressed his foot all the way down.

"Those motherfuckers," Tom said. "You better not let them get away."

"Working on it," said Hugo. He slammed on the brakes to avoid rear-ending the Prius in front of him, then bumped the SUV up on the curb and accelerated through the red light. "But when we get them, we do this the right way."

"We do this however we have to," Tom growled.

Hugo glanced over and saw anger burning in his friend's eyes, and for the first time he didn't want to be Tom's leash—because he felt it too, a sudden burn of rage deep in his gut. "Yeah. Maybe this time you're right."

CHAPTER TWENTY-THREE

Inside the lobby at the hotel, Hugo pulled out his phone and activated the recording app.

"Tell me again I have permission," he said calmly.

Leo Colbert leaned toward the device. "You have permission to look around my new room."

"And you give that permission freely and voluntarily," Hugo said. In the old days when he was with the bureau, a judge would have taken his word that Colbert had given consent to search his things, but these weren't the old days. And he wasn't an FBI agent anymore. Camille Lerens had told him numerous times how she liked the officers working for her to record every conversation, every request for and grant (or denial) of consent.

"Yes, you can search my shit," Colbert said testily. "I told you like four times."

Good enough, Hugo thought, turning off the recording. "Your room key?"

Colbert dug it out of a back pocket; as Hugo took it, he said, "Wait here, please, I won't be long."

"Whatever. You believe me that I just found it, don't you?"

"Right now I do, yes. But if you're not right here when I get back, I may change my mind."

Hugo left Colbert mumbling to himself and went to the concierge table. The man behind it looked up and smiled. "Can I help you, *monsieur*?"

"*Bonjour*. Do you have one of those plastic bags for wet umbrellas?"

The man's brow creased and he looked from Hugo's empty hands to the front door. "But it's not raining, *monsieur*."

"I know." Hugo tried not to sigh heavily. "I need it for something else."

"*D'accord.*" The man shrugged and reached into a drawer, pulling out a roll of bags. "Just one?"

"*Oui, seulement un.*" He took the bag with a *merci* and headed for the elevator bank. In two minutes, he was letting himself into room 424. He could see why Maxick would chose this one for an employee. It was smaller than the other rooms he'd seen, with no kind of view. And it was situated between the elevator shaft and the room with the ice and snack machines. The kind of room in which your average guest, paying upward of 600 euros a night, would be less than happy to rest his head for the night.

Colbert hadn't unpacked, probably because there wasn't much space to put everything. Three cardboard boxes sat on the queen-size bed and two laptops sat on the built-in desk, between piles of papers. According to Colbert, the small Dell on the left belonged to Baxter. Hugo left it where it was and instead looked through the stacks of papers. Nothing of any interest, so he moved to the boxes. One was full of books, and he started there, flipping the pages of each one, not sure what he was looking for, and stacking them on the bed as he finished.

Decent taste, he thought, noticing the titles—two nonfiction works by Erik Larson, three heavy biographies by David McCullough, and some self-help books. Hugo paused at the one he might find on his own shelves, *The Ultimate Sherlock Holmes Collection*. He flipped through the book, as he had with the others, but also made a mental note of the stories contained within its pages.

When he was done, he put the volume down and finished going through Colbert's other belongings. He found nothing else of interest, so he used a clean pillowcase to pick up the laptop and put it in the umbrella bag, relieved that it fit, if only just.

He made his way down to the main reception area, where a police officer put there for Hancock's peace of mind lounged against a back wall. Hugo handed him the computer in its bag and said, "Hop on your radio and have Paul Jameson come get this, please. Don't touch the computer inside and tell him not to, either. He'll understand."

The *flic* straightened, seemingly glad to have something to do. "*Oui, monsieur, immédiatement.*"

Hugo turned and saw that Colbert was making a beeline for a pretty receptionist.

"Leo," Hugo said, stopping the young man in his tracks. "Here's your key, thank you."

"Find anything?" Colbert watched Hugo intently.

"You have good taste in reading material."

"That surprise you?"

"Nope. You seen your boss?"

"Jill? I can have her paged; she's working today."

"Thanks, I'd appreciate that."

Colbert continued his journey to the reception desk and was greeted with a big smile from the young lady behind it. He talked for a moment, then she picked up the phone and punched some numbers into it, presumably paging Maxick.

Maxick appeared after five minutes, flustered.

"What's going on?" she asked. "I was in the middle of helping Helen switch rooms."

"Why is she moving now?" Hugo asked.

"Because one of the larger suites just become available, and I thought it was the right thing to do, letting her have it. After all that's happened, all she's been through . . ."

"Quite right," Hugo said. "Nice of you."

"So what's the emergency down here?"

"You were helping Mr. Colbert here move, too, this morning?"

"That's right."

"Why?"

Maxick glanced over at Colbert, who was slouching over the front desk as he spoke to the receptionist. "Did you ask him?"

"I was interested in your perspective."

"Right now, my priority is saving the reputation of this hotel," she said.

"Meaning?"

She didn't answer but gestured for Hugo to follow her into her office. She shut the door behind them, perched on the edge of the desk, and shook her head slowly. "I feel like I'm losing it. The murder, the spy camera . . . everything's going wrong, and it's like it's all my fault. At least, my fellow managers are acting that way."

"They're blaming you?"

"Yes. Helen's become my friend, so I should be making sure her stay is perfect. I'm American and so was Andy, so somehow that's my fault, too. And now Leo and Thomas have gone from roommates to murder suspects and don't trust each other; they're at each other's throats, and both threatening to quit. If I oversee an exodus of employees on top of everything else, I'm done for here."

"And you like your job."

"I really do, yes."

"Well, I'm sorry this is all rolling downhill to you; that's not right." In the face of Jill's distress, Hugo changed tack, asked about the real reason he was here. "Tell me what happened with finding the computer. I need to know exactly how it went down."

"I don't understand."

"I'll explain after. Best you just tell me without knowing why, if you don't mind."

"OK." She shrugged. "Like I said, Leo and Tom were about to assault each other, so I agreed to split them up. We have a couple of smaller rooms I'd prefer to keep for paying guests, but we're headed toward a slow period and I'm really focused on keeping people happy right now."

Hugo gave her a reassuring smile. "Nothing wrong with that."

"I'm sure someone will find fault with it. . . . Anyway, I went up there to make sure the switch went smoothly; I could just picture them getting into blows over the toaster or something stupid. But Tom wasn't there, so I grabbed a couple of boxes of Leo's stuff to put them onto the luggage cart we were using. One of the boxes split open and spilled everywhere."

"One of the things in it was a computer?"

"Yes, that's right. I guess an old one, because Leo acted surprised, like he didn't know it was there."

"Did that seem odd?"

"Not really. I mean, I only use laptops and never throw them away. I probably have three or four lying around my apartment."

"OK, so what happened then?"

"Nothing. We cleaned up and moved his stuff to the new room." She cocked her head. "What's this all about?"

Hugo was deciding whether to answer or stall when the door flung open, narrowly missing him. Tom stood there, his face dark as thunderclouds.

"You and me. Outside, now."

"Excuse me," Hugo said to Maxick.

"Wait, you were going to explain what—"

"Whatever it is can wait," Tom snapped. He turned on his heel and marched into the reception area, heading for the exit.

"Is everything OK?" Maxick asked. "If it's something to do with the hotel . . ."

"It's not. My friend has it in his head that some bad guy from our past is coming to Paris to . . . do something or other—maybe start trouble. I'd better go." Hugo gave her an apologetic smile and then hurried after Tom, catching up with him outside, at the top step.

"Tom, what the hell's going on?"

"He's here. I saw him."

"Rick Cofer?"

"You don't believe me." He set off, with Hugo in tow. "We're in a hurry, because he's at a café half a mile from here."

"And we're headed there to do what?"

"Let him know we know he's here. Find something he's done, and get him pulled back to the States."

Hugo put a hand on Tom's shoulder and planted himself in his friend's path. Over Tom's shoulder he saw Jill Maxick standing outside the hotel, just a few feet away, with a worried look on her face. "Wait, stop. There's no way Cofer got here already. No possible way."

"What the fuck are you talking about? I saw him, with my own two fucking eyes! Face it, Hugo, he's gunning for us!"

"Calm down," Hugo growled. "Even if you did see him, if it is him, we're not going off half-cocked here. If he's here, it may be legally."

"Which is bullshit."

"Yeah, it is. But I hate to tell you, what that means is this situation requires us to think about what we do, not go in guns blazing."

"Leave it up to you, in other words."

"Yeah, well," Hugo said with a wry smile. "I know that's not going to happen. But this isn't Texas, and we're not cops here. We have to be smart about this."

Tom shrugged off Hugo's hand. "We're putting eyes on him right now, though. I want you to see him."

"Fine." Hugo gestured ahead. "Lead the way."

Tom set off again, and Hugo trailed slightly behind, hoping his friend would lose some of that built-up steam before they got there. He turned to check on Jill Maxick, who raised a tentative hand and waved before turning back into the hotel. As they walked, Hugo watched the people around him, the row of mopeds parked alongside Rue des Écoles, a man and a teenage boy perching sidesaddle on one of them, sharing a baguette sandwich as a trio of hopeful pigeons loitered nearby.

They walked for ten minutes, the tension growing as they got closer, the sights and sounds of Paris blurring to Hugo as he focused on what he might see in a nearby café. *Could Rick Cofer really have made it here?* He tried to think of alternative explanations, but the only possibilities seemed to be that Tom was mistaken, or delusional.

That, or Cofer was indeed in their city, and there could only be one reason for that. For the first time in many years, Hugo felt a twinge of resentment toward his best friend, one that Tom apparently sensed.

"I told you once before I'm sorry, right?" he said, breaking his silence.

"We both made choices, Tom."

"I made mine first, didn't give you too many options."

"Maybe that's true. But I still could have done things differently."

"Let me dangle in the wind?" Tom gave a rueful smile. "That's not you."

"Hey, it's not too late, so let's just worry about whoever you think you saw."

Tom shot him a dirty look for the use of the word *think*. But Hugo knew he was right, that Tom had put him into a box that day, made him choose between two very rocky paths. As long as Cofer had been in prison, and they'd continued with their own successful careers, Hugo had been able to put any feelings of resentment into their own compartment and hide them away. But if that sonofabitch was making another appearance in their lives, then at some point he and Tom would have to talk a little more.

They continued on in silence for a while, but at the beginning of Rue Thouin, Tom stopped. "The place next to the Indian restaurant—it's called Café Ursula."

"Wait, how in a city of more than two million people did you happen to spot one guy in a café down some little side street?"

"I didn't. I spotted him from a distance in the Luxembourg Garden and followed him here."

"Why didn't you just call me?"

"Because." Tom chewed his lip for a second before speaking. "I went out last night. Someone stole my phone."

"You mean you lost it."

"For fuck's sake, Dad, does it make a difference at this point?"

"It might if you took LSD while you were out drinking."

Tom, apparently, had also lost his sense of humor. "I'm not fucking imagining this. Let's go."

Hugo didn't move. "So what's your plan, exactly?"

"Simple. We go in there, provoke him into making a scene, record the whole thing, and get him yanked back to Texas. And hopefully a tiny prison cell."

"Provoke him how?"

"Good grief, man, do you need a script for this?"

"It might help. Or just, you know, a vague outline of how this goes down."

"Hugo, I swear to God," Tom fumed. "For once in your life, do something a little rash. Let go of the reins and fucking gallop while shooting from the hip. You don't have to map out every little frigging step you take—sometimes you can just wing it and everything turns out the way it should."

A moment of silence opened up between them, and Hugo knew that those words had triggered in Tom the same images they raised for him, images of a blistering day in Houston, gunfire and emotions running hot, and Tom leading them away from the rule book, insisting that to make things right they should, together, *just wing it*.

"You might be right," Hugo said quietly. "And you know that I'm thinking about the one time I did fly a little high with you. Didn't work out so well, did it?"

"Maybe not." Tom nodded slowly, but his eyes glittered with anger, and when he spoke his voice was firm. "But that just means it's time to put things right." Without another word, he turned and started down the narrow street toward Café Ursula.

CHAPTER TWENTY-FOUR

The café was small, a narrow strip of a building wedged in between an Indian restaurant and what looked like a lawyer's office. Hugo brushed past the empty outside tables and entered the café two steps behind Tom, who'd obviously opted for the aggressive approach. The go-to mode when it came to Cofer.

The bar was at the back of the room, a dozen square tables and their chairs taking up the rest of the space directly in front of them. The café had been updated recently, which surprised Hugo for no particular reason he could identify, and the place was full. Hugo moved to Tom's right side, indicating that he'd scan that side of the café for Rick Cofer, but it was quickly obvious that unless Cofer had changed his appearance drastically and picked up a companion, he wasn't on that side. Tom finished his search just as quickly, and he threw Hugo a dark look that said, *He was here, I saw him.*

"Maybe the restroom?" Hugo said, ignoring a diminutive waiter who waived an impatient arm at them and then toward the one empty table.

"Maybe." Tom started forward and Hugo followed, the reassuring weight of his gun holster shifting as he moved. They paused outside the door marked *Hommes*, just long enough for Tom to take a deep breath.

"Wait," Hugo whispered. "Are you carrying?"

Tom shook his head.

"I'll go first, then."

Tom hesitated and then gave a small smile. "Probably look better for you to shoot this one anyway; I've reached my quota."

"Nice," Hugo said. "But just so you know, I'm gonna try very hard not to shoot anyone. They're not used to it over here."

Tom moved aside. Hugo stepped forward, gave him a nod, and shouldered the door open, sending it crashing into the wall. Hugo stepped into the small white-tiled room and saw a man staring at him, eyes wide over a white drooping mustache, his ancient hands frozen around a paper towel he'd been using to dry them. Behind him was the closed door of a toilet stall.

"*Excusez-moi,*" Hugo said, then nodded to the stall. "*Il y a quelqu'un?*"

"*Non.*"

Hugo nodded and moved out of the way, the old man in a sudden hurry to finish up and leave. Hugo looked back at the closed door of the stall, which reached the floor and ceiling. No way to know if the old fellow was right. Hugo stepped forward and tried the handle. Locked.

He and Tom turned as a figure appeared behind them. He wore the white shirt and black pants of an employee, and his face was creased with annoyance.

"What's going on here?" He demanded, hands now on hips. "You scared poor Monsieur De Kruyff. And you better not have damaged my door."

"We're waiting," Tom said, indicating the stall.

"It's locked," the man said. "It's not working. You have to use the women's, but wait until the two in there leave."

Tom hesitated, but Hugo put a hand on his arm. "He's not here, Tom. Let's look around, see if he's in the neighborhood."

The waiter switched to English. "Who's not here? Who are you looking for?"

Tom reached into a pocket and pulled out a crumpled piece of paper. Hugo raised an eyebrow. "You carry his photo now?"

"It's from his prison file, latest picture."

"So that's a yes, then."

"Fucking right," Tom growled. "I wanted to know what the bastard looked like after a decade or more in prison. You know, so I recognize him when he comes for me."

Hugo turned his attention to the increasingly agitated waiter. "Have you seen this man recently?"

The waiter studied the picture after taking it from Tom. "I don't know. Maybe. Maybe not. I'm not good with faces."

"Very helpful," Tom said, snatching the paper from the man's hands. "Let's get out of here."

"I don't know," Hugo said lightly, "since we're here, I could sure use a coffee. Maybe a pastry?"

"Shut up, Hugo," Tom said on his way to the door.

Out in the street, Hugo stopped him. "Tom, what's your plan now?"

"Run around like a chicken with its head cut off until I find him. Then beat him to death."

"Yeah, that might work. But I have a better idea."

"Oh, let me guess," Tom said testily. "It involves talking or phoning someone or looking something up on a computer."

"It does. If that's too inactive for you, then go do your chicken run and I'll do my talking thing and we'll see who comes up with a result first."

"Yeah, we will." Tom turned and started to walk away. "I may have to stop for a drink first, though."

Hugo shook his head and took out his phone. He scrolled through his list of contacts and found the name he was looking for. After half a dozen rings, a familiar voice came on the line.

"Is this really Hugo Marston calling me?"

"It is. Andy Whitener, how are you?"

"Surprised, to put it mildly." Whitener was a former police officer for the city of Austin, Texas, quitting after fifteen years to become a federal probation officer. He and Hugo had met when Whitener was assigned to the joint FBI–Austin PD robbery task force. They'd worked several cases together and become friends, drifting out of contact when their job paths diverged. "I heard you were with the State Department."

"Best job in the world," Hugo said. "And I get to live in Paris."

"Nice." There was a brief pause. "So, I heard about your little issue, or should I say Tom Green's issue. Sounded to me like the bad guy got a hug and a kiss rather than the sentence he deserved."

"Yeah, that was kind of a mess."

"Well, I'm sorry it went down that way. I didn't know Tom, met him a couple of times, but you were the best agent I ever worked with. Best cop, period."

"Thanks, Andy, I appreciate that. How's the probation business?"

"Getting old, like me." Whitener chuckled. "I'm retiring in three years, go live on a beach somewhere."

"Sounds heavenly. Come see me in Paris, though, if you can."

"I'd like that, very much. Now then, tell me what I can do for you; I presume this wasn't just a social call."

"You're right. It has to do with that little issue, as a matter of fact. The guy got released from prison."

"Jesus, already?"

"I'm afraid so. Tom Green is over here with me. He thinks he saw the dude."

"In Paris?"

"Right," Hugo said.

"Coming for revenge, eh?"

"That's what Tom believes. It seems a little far-fetched to me."

"You said he saw him? What was the guy's name again?"

"Rick Cofer. And what I said was, Tom *thinks* he saw him."

"You don't think he did?"

"I have no idea," Hugo said. "That's why I'm calling. I want to know if we can find out whether he's being tracked, whether he asked for and was issued a passport. I had my people at the embassy check, but our system will only tell us when and where it was last used, not if someone has possession of one."

"Well, that's not so useful."

"Exactly. Think you can help?"

"I don't know." Whitener chuckled. "But I can surely try. I'll call you back later today."

Hugo spent the next thirty minutes walking in circles, one eye out for Tom and the other for Rick Cofer, or anyone who might look like him. He took a moment to call his second-in-command, Ryan Pierce, and confirm that Cofer hadn't used a passport in his own name in the past few days.

"I told you, boss, I'll stay on it and let you know if that changes." Pierce didn't like his competence or diligence being questioned, and Hugo knew he shouldn't be doing so. "We have this great alert system, you know, been in place a couple of decades now."

"I know, I'm sorry, Ryan. Thanks for putting up with me."

"For now, boss, for now." There was humor in his voice, which Hugo was grateful for.

Hugo took a shortcut down a narrow side street, keeping his eye on a couple of homeless people who looked desperate enough to take his wallet, but other than stare, they left him alone. Hugo half expected to see Tom at a jog, crisscrossing the streets and alleys around him, increasingly desperate to find his nemesis, who may or may not even be on the same continent. Hugo soon gave up, assuming Tom had meant what he said about that drink.

He checked the time, pondering his next move. He needed to check in with Camille about the second laptop, and to get back to the hotel to finish up with Colbert's interview. But his mind was foggy, distracted by Tom's distress and the possible presence of Rick Cofer. He pulled out his phone and called Camille. He briefed her on the developments at the hotel.

"You're going back?" she asked.

"I was going to ask you to. I'm a little distracted right now."

"Pretty lady?" Her voice was coy.

"No, an ugly man. Named Tom."

"Understood," Lerens said. "Paul just brought in the computer you bagged at the hotel. Our techs will get to work on it soon. In the meantime, I'll head over to the hotel and talk to Lionel Colbert."

"Thanks."

Hugo wanted to clear his head, and he considered calling Claudia for a bite to eat but had a sudden urge to sit quietly in his apartment and read a book. After his recent book discussion, he'd bought a new release, *A Thousand Falling Crows* by Larry Sweazy, immediately loving the protagonist, a one-armed Texas Ranger forced into retirement after taking a bullet from Bonnie Parker. The book brimmed with atmosphere, bleak, desolate, and threatening, yet somehow a delightful escape from his own recent swirl of murder and intrigue.

Ten minutes later, he turned onto Rue Jacob, his thoughts on the comfy chair and book he was about to sink into. Twenty feet from his building, he heard footsteps behind him, closer than they should have been, and he started to turn around, his mind snapping back into the real world around him. Too late. He felt a searing pain above his right ear, and then a warmth overwhelmed him. He dropped to his knees, and his last view was the sidewalk speeding toward him, then nothing more than a deep, enveloping blackness.

CHAPTER TWENTY-FIVE

Hugo lay motionless, his mind grappling with his whereabouts, with what had happened. He knew *something* had happened, but his mind was a fog and the memories drifted through it like ghosts, faceless and unrecognizable. He tried to open his eyes, but the light was too bright and he squeezed them shut, wincing as the streak of yellow stabbed through the back of his eyes and into his brain. He took a slow, easy breath and was relieved that his torso seemed intact. He moved his arms and felt someone hold them down.

"Stay still, *monsieur*, you might make it worse." A woman's voice.

He tried to speak, but it came out as a mumble, unintelligible even to him.

The same female voice. "You're in an ambulance. You had an accident, looks like you fell and hit your head."

This time his voice was a slur. "*Non*, someone hit me." He wanted to add, *I fell after, after someone hit me*, but it seemed like too much.

Other voices floated over him. *How long was I unconscious?* he wondered. He could tell that the ambulance wasn't moving. The engine was idling, the sirens quiet.

"*Alors*, Monsieur Marston, the police are here," the woman said. "They're saying someone hit you. Can you speak to them?"

"I don't remember anything." His voice was stronger, and he fluttered his eyes to let a little light in, not too much. "But I can talk to them. Quietly."

191

Hugo heard the paramedic relay the message and then add, "He has a sense of humor, so I'm guessing he'll live."

Live. Die. Someone hit me.

Shit.

He reached a hand into his jacket.

"Shit," he said aloud. His gun was gone. He struggled, tried to sit up, but a firm hand on his shoulder held him down.

"Relax, *monsieur*, your head is bleeding and you likely have a concussion." Hugo opened his eyes further. A burly paramedic in a blue uniform was looking down at him, her hands on each of his shoulders. "You'll stay still if I let go?" He caught a glimpse of Rue Jacob behind her.

"*Oui*," Hugo confirmed, starting to get his bearings. Even that slight attempt to sit had sent jagged streaks of pain through his skull. "I'll stay still."

"*Alors*," she said. "I'll have the *flic* come in and talk to you." She smiled, and added, "Quietly."

"Wait, I need you to call someone for me, it's important. Her name is Camille Lerens; she's a lieutenant with the Brigade Criminelle." A thought struck him. "My phone. Did they take that too?"

"*Non, monsieur*, we took it out of your pocket before lifting you up. So that it wouldn't fall out and break. That's how I know your name. I also found your wallet. You are an American policeman?"

"Something like that. How bad is the damage?"

"Like I said, bleeding and concussion. You should go to the hospital for a scan, at least have a doctor look at you."

"I feel OK," Hugo lied. "I don't need any of that."

"Your choice, *monsieur*. Here," she said, offering him his phone. "You want me to make that call?"

"No, thank you," Hugo said, wanting to show her that he was fine. "I'll do it. If you could just tell the *flics* I'll be right with them."

He swiped at the touch screen and started to look for Lerens's number, but he paused when he heard raised voices outside.

"What the fuck is going on here?" said a familiar one. A moment later, Tom stepped into the ambulance.

"*Monsieur, s'il vous plaît*, you cannot just—"

"The hell I can't; this idiot is my landlord."

Hugo couldn't help but smile. He turned to the paramedic and two flustered police officers who were just outside the ambulance and said, "It's OK, you can let him through. Just make sure he keeps his voice down."

"What happened, dude?" Tom asked, squeezing himself in beside the gurney.

"I think someone took a whack at me." Hugo went for some humor, to show he was all right. "If it was with a bottle, you'll be the prime suspect."

Tom snorted. "I'd have finished the job."

"Can you call Camille and let her know? I'm assuming it's related to the case. Cases. Maybe one of the stores has surveillance cameras." Hugo's heart sank. "And, Tom, call the ambassador. The bastard took my gun."

Tom shook his head slowly. "That's gonna be a mess of paperwork, you dumb shit."

"Yeah, I know." He groaned at the thought of it. "Just what I need."

"Any witnesses?" Tom asked.

"I think so. No idea who, though."

"You see anyone?"

"Tom, I just woke up. He hit me from behind. Stop asking me questions."

"Now, now, don't get feisty with me. I'll let the uniforms quiz you; they're also short-tempered for some reason." He patted Hugo's arm. "I'll call Camille and Ambassador Taylor, let them know. You going to the hospital?"

"Yes," said the paramedic, at the same time as Hugo said, "No."

"Well, you two sort that out. I'll make some phone calls and poke around a little." Tom hopped out of the ambulance, his phone already in his hand.

"Just bandage me up; I'll be fine," Hugo said, hearing the desperation in his own voice.

"I strongly recommend that you let a doctor check you out," responded the paramedic as she hopped back into the bus.

"Of course you do; that's your job. But I have one to do as well, and I can't do it from a hospital bed."

The paramedic shrugged. "As you like, it's your head. But please have someone look at you later today, or first thing tomorrow."

"I will." Hugo sat still as she finished winding a bandage around his head.

"There. I put some butterfly stitches in, and the bleeding's stopped, so if you take it easy for the rest of the day, you might be OK."

"*Merci*," Hugo said.

"You understand what I mean by *taking it easy*, right?" she said sternly. "And like I said—"

"I know, see a doctor sooner rather than later."

"And have your tenant keep an eye on you, if he can," she added.

"My tenan . . . Oh, right. I will." Hugo closed his eyes and took a moment to collect himself as a uniformed *flic* replaced the paramedic in the back of the ambulance. He introduced himself as he flipped open a notebook.

"*Je suis Julien Steinberg, monsieur.* First of all, I have some good news. We found your gun in the gutter. Can you tell me the make and model?"

"*Bien sûr.*" Hugo gave him that information, also rattling off the serial number.

"*Merci.*" Steinberg slid the gun gently into Hugo's holster beneath his jacket. "Are you able to answer a few more questions?"

"*Oui.*" Hugo closed his eyes for a moment, suddenly tired, then opened them again. "I can try, anyway."

"Do you remember what happened?" The officer's tone was calm, his voice low, as if he was aware of Hugo's throbbing head.

"I was walking home, heard some footsteps behind me, and then . . . woke up here. How long was I out?"

"I'm not sure, *monsieur*, but I can ask when we're done, if you like."

Hugo forced himself onto one elbow, fighting the wave of nausea that swept over him. "The paramedic said there were witnesses. What did they tell you?"

"Let me get your statement first, if you don't mind."

Smart cop, Hugo thought. *He doesn't want my memories tainted with someone else's.* "I really don't remember anything else," he said. "I didn't see anyone, hear anyone's voice. I know someone crept up behind me and then . . . nothing."

"*D'accord, merci. Un moment, s'il vous plaît.*" The officer hopped out of the back of the ambulance and spoke to his colleague. Hugo sank back on the gurney, his head nestling into the pillow, and he fought the urge to close his eyes. A minute later, the officer returned. "Two witnesses. Neither one saw you get hit, they just saw the person running away."

"You have a description?"

"Not one we can use to identify anyone. Both witnesses say he was short, but one says stocky and the other skinny. They agree on the hoodie, either red or orange."

"Did you find what they hit me with?"

"Yes, most likely. There was a heavy stick in the gutter; we think that was the weapon, but we'll test it for his prints and DNA. Yours to make sure it was used, and his to find the bastard."

"Assuming it was a man," Hugo prompted.

"Right, with that description, it might not be."

"How long will the DNA testing take?"

The officer grimaced. "Probably a while. Weeks would be my guess. Months, maybe, since they didn't manage to kill you."

"I thought so." With some effort, Hugo reached over to his phone again. He typed out a text message and hit send. *They think the stick is the weapon. Cops to send it for DNA testing . . .* "By the way, the other officer here, I think I met him once." He propped himself up again, trying to see out of the back.

Steinberg yelled at his colleague. "*Jean, viens ici!*" and gestured for him to come over.

The second *flic* appeared at the end of Hugo's gurney. "Have we met before?" Hugo asked.

"*Non, monsieur*, I don't think so."

"You look very familiar . . . maybe you have a relative in the force?"

"My father, but he retired years ago."

"Well, I'm sorry to have wasted your time; I must be mistaken."

"Not a problem," the cop said. "How are you feeling?"

"A sore head, a little dizzy, but I'll live."

"You'll go to the hospital?"

"At some point, yes. Thanks for all your help today. I appreciate what you do."

"You're very welcome." The officer turned as Tom's face peered into the ambulance. "Can I help you, *monsieur*?"

"He's with me," Hugo said. "You guys mind helping me up? I have a couch waiting for me."

"Is it far?" Steinburg asked. "Be happy to give a colleague a ride home."

"It's about twenty feet away," Tom said. "Idiot got mugged on his own doorstep."

"Technically I wasn't mugged," Hugo said. "They didn't take my gun, phone, or wallet—just hit me and ran."

Tom grinned. "Well, we've all had that urge."

With a few grunts and groans, the officers helped Hugo off the gurney and out of the ambulance. He felt a little light-headed, and his skull throbbed like someone was still drumming on it, but he was glad to be upright.

He shook hands with the *flics* and paramedics, thanking them, then started toward his apartment building, Tom falling into step close beside him.

"You get it?" Hugo asked.

"Won't Camille be pissed?"

"I bet she would've authorized it if we'd asked."

"But we didn't. And so she didn't."

"We've used your lab before, and we don't have weeks or months to wait," Hugo said.

Tom glanced over his shoulder as they reached the steps of the building. "OK, just make sure she knows it was your idea." He put a hand on Hugo's arm to help him up the stone steps.

"I will," Hugo said.

Inside the foyer, Tom unzipped his jacket and pulled out a plastic evidence bag. The weapon was about two feet long, and they both studied it for a few seconds.

"Thanks. I don't need a tampering-with-evidence charge on my record."

Hugo looked up at him. "Totally unrelated question, but did you have any joy with your earlier escapade?"

"Fuck no. But if he's here, I'll find him—and for your sake, if not for mine." Tom held up the bag. "Apparently you've become a very soft target."

CHAPTER TWENTY-SIX

Camille Lerens showed up with half a dozen red roses and a smile on her face.

"I just saw Tom on the way out," she said.

Hugo was lying on the couch, his bandaged head on two pillows. "Let me guess, something about me being old and incapable of looking after myself."

"Exactly." She walked to the open kitchen and lay the flowers down on the counter. "Got a vase here somewhere?"

"You recall who lives here, right?"

"Oh, good point." She pulled a water jug from a cupboard. "This'll do."

"You're very sweet, Camille, but it was just a bang on the head."

"Whatever you say." She finished arranging the flowers, then leaned down to sniff them. "There. Lovely." She turned back to Hugo. "This have anything to do with the conversation we had before, about you leaving Houston?"

"No, I don't think so. But maybe."

"Then I think I deserve an explanation," she said.

Hugo rubbed his head gingerly and grimaced. "Yeah, probably."

He told her the basics, about the robbery, the men they were chasing, the abandoned house in Houston where the Cofers holed up. He left out some of the details and was careful not to apportion blame; but what he said, and his tone, gave her the gist of it.

"And now this Cofer is after some revenge?" she asked, when he'd finished.

"Again, maybe. I guess we'll know more after that club is tested."

Lerens turned, hands on her hips, her face serious. "About that."

"Right," Hugo said, forcing himself to sit upright. "You see, Tom tried calling you but had to leave a message. Purloining the weapon was my idea, not his."

"That so?"

"Really, it was. We can't wait that long, and he'll have us a result by tomorrow."

"Fingerprints *and* DNA?"

"Yes, both. And whether it's related to the hotel case or . . . the other thing, we need to know who wielded it as soon as possible."

"It was definitely the weapon?"

"I . . . I don't know, to be honest," Hugo said. "I wasn't in any shape to look around for something else, and the two *flics* there seemed to think so."

"Did the witnesses say what was used?"

"I really don't know."

Lerens looked at him for a moment. "Happened about an hour ago?"

"Yes, roughly."

"Then I'll be right back."

"Take a grocery bag in case you find something," he said. "You know where to look?"

She picked up a bag from the counter and looked over her shoulder, a smile on her lips. "I'm guessing near the blood smear just outside your front door."

When she'd left, Hugo picked up his phone and checked his voicemail. He'd heard it ring earlier but had been half asleep and not inclined to reverse the direction he was headed. The message was from Andy Whitener.

"Hey, it's me, Andy. Put down the baguette and call me."

Hugo did, straightaway. "It was a beautiful French model, not a baguette," he joked.

"Well, shoot, I'd never ask you to put down one of those." Whitener chuckled. "Anyway, I've got some info for you. First of all, your man Cofer *did* make a request to be allowed to travel abroad. That request was denied. He has a passport, though. I guess he went through the application process with the hope he'd get permission to travel. Like I said, he didn't, but I don't have a way to see if the passport's been used."

I do, and it hasn't, Hugo thought.

"But here's the thing. He's also AWOL."

Hugo perked up. "Meaning?"

"He has certain reporting conditions, by phone and in person."

"He's not been doing that?"

"He's been making his phone calls," Whitener said. "But not the in-person meetings. Three times he's phoned in and made excuses; he leaves a message each time about why he can't be there."

"Do you have those dates?"

Whitener hesitated. "I do, but I can't give those out—you know that."

"Andy, look. You know the situation, what happened and who he is. If he's not making those meetings but is calling in, it could be because he's no longer there. It could mean that Tom's right about where he really is, and that puts me in a very dangerous position."

"Hugo—"

"Tell you what. I just need to know if he's been missing in action this past week, that's all I care about. That he's not resurfaced there."

"That's what I'm trying to tell you. Right now, we're not able to put eyes on him."

"OK. Last question: Is it possible to see where he's been calling from?"

"Not that I know of," Whitener said. "At least, there's nothing in his file that his PO noted."

Hugo thanked him and hung up. He lay back on the couch and let his mind wander over the possibilities. The truth was, he had no idea whether Rick Cofer had revenge in his heart, but he certainly wouldn't put it past the guy. He'd profiled him while studying the bank robberies, looked at his movements and his methods, the care with which he and his brother had planned and carried out the raids. But that was different; it was more like a job to them, the robbing and getting away with it both essential elements to ensure a successful venture. This, if it was happening, was more personal. That suggested to Hugo that Cofer might take more risks, be more unpredictable the closer he got to his targets. But it made him much more dangerous, too, which meant it was best to assume the worst.

One possibility, a reach but hovering in his mind, was that Cofer had clocked him, knowing it'd bring Tom close, put them together. But if so, why hadn't he done something right away? Maybe he didn't realize how close they were to Hugo's apartment, to safety? But if Cofer had traveled that far to search them out, he would have known where he and Tom both lived. Tom was right about how inattentive he'd been—a soft target indeed. He had no doubt Cofer could have followed him to the building on a previous occasion without Hugo noticing.

Maybe he was planning to do something at whatever hospital they wanted to take me to? Hugo wondered. But Cofer didn't fit the description—his attacker had been called short and stocky. Cofer was taller than most people, which an eyewitness should have spotted. Then again, he knew how unreliable eyewitnesses were, had seen horribly wrong descriptions more times than he could count. Even so, Hugo reasoned that most hit men struck in isolated places with as few people around as possible, which hardly described a Paris hospital. He returned to the bait idea, because if Cofer had been the assailant, he could have killed Hugo there and then. If not with the club, then with his own gun. But he didn't.

Why not? Because it wasn't Cofer at all? . . . But why would Andrew Baxter's or Ambrósio Silva's killer attack me? And, again, not finish the job?

Hugo reached over and took a sip of water. The only thing that made sense to him was that this was a warning. But from whom, and about what, he had no earthly idea. He put his glass down as Camille Lerens knocked softly and let herself back into his apartment.

"Find anything?" Hugo asked.

"Honestly, I'm not sure." She held up the grocery bag. "You should take a look. And we should get Tom back in here to check this out."

CHAPTER TWENTY-SEVEN

The next morning, Hugo downed two aspirin and three glasses of water to try to relieve the throbbing of his head. Tom was nowhere to be seen, and he didn't feel like sitting around his apartment and feeling sorry for himself, so he decided to follow up on a few loose ends, starting with Buzzy Pottgen and Helen Hancock.

Feeling a little bit steadier after a full night's rest, Hugo took off his bandage and set off for a slow walk to the Sorbonne Hotel, dialing Helen Hancock's number as his boots hit the sidewalk. He wanted to check in with her, press her on a few of her misdirections, and explain that even if they seemed irrelevant to her, he and the police ended up wasting time when they didn't know the whole truth.

"Yes, I'm still here," she said. "I'm about to work with Buzzy and Mike; they're on their way. Trying to get some sense of normalcy around here." She lowered her voice. "And hopefully not get sued for taking these people's money and giving them nothing in return."

"They wouldn't do that, would they?" Hugo asked.

Hancock sighed. "Who knows, these days. Good way to an easy buck, especially if someone famous is on the other end. Anyway, we'll be in the conservatory. Go through the main lobby, past the restaurant, and it's at the end of the hallway."

Outside the hotel, Hugo saw Buzzy Pottgen and got her attention with a wave as she was about to jog up the steps to the main doors. She paused, uncertainty in her eyes.

"Oh, hey," she said.

"Got a moment?" He gestured for her to move to the side so they could talk without blocking the entrance. She went with him.

"Look, I've talked to that lieutenant," she began. "And I'm sorry I lied about the assault."

"Camille Lerens interviewed you?"

"Yeah, at my apartment, yesterday. Recorded it and everything."

"And you told her the truth?"

"I did." She gave a small smile. "I like it when you're stern."

"Buzzy, come on. This is incredibly serious."

Her shoulders slumped. "I know. I think I'm in denial, mostly. It's all so bizarre."

"So what did you tell Lieutenant Lerens?"

"That I went to Ambrósio's apartment to talk to him after I found out about him and Helen. That we argued. That I slapped him a couple of times and he stopped me by hitting me back."

"You argued about his affair with Helen?"

"Yes."

"You were jealous."

"I was a little, but I was more angry that he'd not told me. I wanted to know if I'd put my health at risk, if he'd been sleeping with us at the same time."

"And?"

"Yes, there was overlap, but he said he'd used condoms."

"Well, that's good," Hugo said. "But I don't get something. Why were you were so angry with him? You two had only been here a short while, no?"

"Here, yes. But we'd chatted a lot online back in the States. One of the reasons I came here was to be with him, and he knew it. I spent every last penny to be here; I'm eating bread and water." She looked away. "How did this all happen? None of it seems real." She looked back at Hugo. "Why would someone kill him?"

"I don't know. Did you talk to Lerens about that?"

"Yes, and she said it's possible he killed himself, but no way." She shook her head emphatically. "No way in the world."

"What makes you so sure?"

"You met him; you saw how he was. Have you ever known anyone so full of life? Sure, he was a selfish jerk, but most guys are, in my experience. And what reason would he have for killing himself?"

"I was going to ask if you knew of anything like that."

"No," she said. "Like, he didn't have depression or anything, either."

"Let me ask you this, and I'm sorry if it seems insensitive. Do you think his attraction to Helen was real or something a little more . . . career oriented?"

That small smile again. "I accused him of that. I mean, seems pretty obvious, doesn't it? All that time courting me, then suddenly he's madly in love with Helen?"

"Did he say he was in love?"

"No, I guess not. In lust, or whatever it was."

"Had he ever hit you before?"

"No. I wouldn't have anything to do with someone who hit me. Once and you're done," Pottgen said. "And I meant it when I said he hit me to stop me from hitting him for real. I have quite the temper when the right buttons are pushed, and I guess he pushed them."

"Are you doing OK? With his death, I mean."

Pottgen hesitated. "Yes and no. I mean, we had an intense thing going for a short time, but after learning about his affair with Helen, I'm starting to feel like maybe I never really *knew* him, you know?"

"I do."

"And it all seems so unreal, unbelievable that this could be happening. I mean, just being here in Paris with Helen is unreal enough, but adding all this to it . . . I think I haven't really processed it yet; I'm just carrying on as if nothing is happening. Is that weird?"

"People process death and tragedy differently. In my experience, there's no right or wrong way." He gestured to the door. "We should go in; I think Helen's waiting for you." He followed her into the hotel. "Go ahead, I need to talk to someone first."

He crossed the lobby and stuck his head into Jill Maxick's office, wanting to be courteous and let her know he was there. He was surprised to see Lionel Colbert sitting behind her desk.

"Promotion or stealing stuff?" Hugo said lightly. From Colbert's reaction, he didn't like the joke.

"Because everyone's a criminal in your world, I get it," Colbert said sourly.

"Or they get promotions," Hugo said, resisting the urge to sigh. "Jill around?"

"Running late. Cut her hand in the kitchen yesterday, so she asked me to fill in this morning while she gets a tetanus shot." He kept a straight face. "So call this a promotion, I guess."

"She's not badly hurt, I hope?"

"She'll be in later. Typing with one hand, probably, but other than that she's OK."

"I just wanted to let her know I'm here."

"Poking around again," Colbert added. He was back to being surly, Hugo noted.

"Yeah, we do that when someone gets knifed in a stairwell." Hugo's patience was beginning to run out with this kid, and his head was still throbbing. "So what's your problem with authority?"

Colbert shrugged. "Not really your business, is it?"

"Maybe not. But on the other hand, if you're being uncooperative in a murder investigation, then maybe it *is* my business. And that of the police."

"Look, I've answered your questions, haven't I? And I gave you that computer, too." Colbert glared. "Look, I may not have the protection of the US Constitution here, but I'm pretty sure even in France I'm not obliged to have a good attitude while I'm cooperating."

"First time I met you, you stormed out of the room."

"That's putting it a little dramatically, don't you think?"

"Murder brings out the dramatic in me." Hugo leaned against the door jamb and studied Colbert. "Seems like, as Andy's roommate and friend, you might be a little more affected yourself."

"People react to tragedy in different ways," Colbert said. "You should know that, in your line of work. I don't tend toward the melodramatic."

"Fair enough. But mind if I ask a few questions? Seeing as we're here and you're cooperating, and all."

Colbert sat back and spread his hands. "Captive audience."

"Did you know about Helen Hancock and Ambrósio Silva?"

"Nope."

"And, as far as you know, there was nothing between her and Andy?"

"Not as far as I know."

"What about Helen and anyone else?" Hugo asked.

"Like who?"

"That's what I'm asking you. Anyone."

"Besmirching her reputation, are you?" Colbert's eyes narrowed, and he leaned forward a little. "Or did you have someone specific in mind?" Hugo said nothing, not about to mention his boss's name, and eventually Colbert sat back again. "I don't know a damn thing about her love life," he said. "But this is Paris, and if she was banging every guest and employee in the hotel, I'd be all for it."

Hugo wondered if that apparent lack of interest masked something else. *What if Colbert was one of her lovers?* Before all of this, Hugo would've doubted it, but Helen Hancock was proving to be more romantically active than he imagined. *Why not Colbert, too?* Hugo decided not to press the issue, instead letting it sit in the back of his mind in case a synapse or two might later connect the possibilities and come up with an answer.

"When did you last see her?" Hugo asked.

"Yesterday. I was here covering for Jill after her accident, and she stuck her head in just like you did."

Hugo smiled, unable to help himself. "I trust you were friendlier with her than you were with me."

"Of course," Colbert said, returning the smile. "But then she wasn't peppering me with questions."

"She's nice like that. Well, thanks for your time, I'll go find her."

The hotel's conservatory was a picture of relaxation. The large space was a little warmer than the hallway leading to it, instantly making it feel cozy. Lazy fans kept the air moving, though, flapping slowly above plush wicker chairs and tables, and a couple of floral sofas. *The perfect place to take tea*, Hugo thought, *or come up with romantic story lines.*

Helen Hancock saw him as he walked through the door, and waved him over. She sat with her charges at a low round table, and each had a computer and a few papers in front of them. Hugo took the one spare chair.

"I hate to interrupt; looks like you're all hard at work."

"We're discussing the merits of plotting versus pantsing," Hancock said with a smile. "Any opinion on that?"

"Well, I don't write, I just read," Hugo said. "And, to me, pantsing is what you do to your annoying little brother to embarrass him in front of other people. But something tells me you don't mean that."

Buzzy flashed those white teeth at him. "Silly. 'Pantsing' means writing by the seat of your pants. Making it up as you go along, as opposed to carefully plotting everything out."

"Ah, that makes more sense in this context," Hugo said. "What do you all do?"

"I like to pants," Buzzy said, large eyes pouring over Hugo.

"I'm a careful plotter," Hancock said. "Things don't always go as I plan in my books. Or in life, I guess." She sighed and seemed to bring herself back to the moment, smiling at them. "Anyway, my being a plotter is a professional secret, so don't tell anyone."

"How about you, Mike?" Hugo looked at Rice.

"I plot the hell out of things," he said. "That's part of the fun for me. I enjoy mapping it all out—plus it takes the stress out of the actual writing."

"And the point I was just making," Hancock interjected, "is that a lot of new writers come into this with a couple of misconceptions. First, that one is the 'right' way and the other wrong. It's whatever works best for you. The other misconception is thinking that you have to do one or the other. You have to do what works for you, and even though I use notes and diagrams and charts, someone else may not be able to function that way."

"Makes sense," Hugo said.

Hancock took a breath and said, "Anyway, I could talk about this forever." She rose to her feet. "Why don't you guys look over my critiques of your first chapters? I need to talk to Hugo for a moment."

"Sure," Rice said. He picked up a sheaf of papers. "Take your time; I see a lot of red ink on mine. Although I'm going for a run at four, so I'm hoping we'll be done by then."

"Where do you run?" Hugo asked.

"Around and through the Luxembourg Garden. I love that place."

"That's where I run, too," Hugo said. He patted his stomach. "Although not as often as I should. As for all the red ink, I'm sure it's all complimentary, right, Ms. Hancock?"

"Of course, as always," Hancock said with a smile. "Now then, you all let me know if you have any questions; then I want to talk about research before exercise hour." She picked up a folder that was stuffed with papers and tapped the top of it. "This is for my work in progress. I want you guys to understand the importance of getting certain things right."

She turned, and Hugo followed her to the far side of the conservatory, where two comfortable chairs sat facing each other, separated by another small round table. She put the folder on it and sat back.

"Any news?" the writer asked once they were seated.

"Not a lot," Hugo said. "How about you? How are you doing?"

"People keep telling me I need to turn this into a story, all this weirdness. But it's just so personal. . . . I don't want to plunder my emotional distress for a mere book."

"Books are supposed to capture and retell powerful events in people's lives, no?"

"I write fiction," she said. "That would be way too close to nonfiction."

"Sometimes it's hard to tell with you," Hugo said.

Hancock eyed him for a moment. "And what's that supposed to mean?"

"You've not been forthcoming." He held up a hand to silence her. "Now, I get why, I really do, but I'm worried you don't understand how serious this is. Andrew Baxter is dead. Murdered. So is Ambrósio Silva. We need to find out who did this and why, because right now there's someone out there who has two deaths to his name, and we have no idea if more are on the way."

"You know that Ambrósio's death was murder?"

"Yes. Gunshot-residue tests were pretty conclusive. His hands were clean of it, which tells us that he didn't handle the gun."

Hancock was quiet for a moment, then she looked up. "Do you really think there might be more deaths?"

"I don't know, Helen, I really don't. I hope like hell the answer is no, but if the major players in this investigation are hiding information from me and the French police, then how can I be sure of everything?"

"Look, I know I—"

"I'm not finished," Hugo interrupted. "You're about to tell me that your private relationships have nothing to do with these murders. My response to that is twofold. First, how can you possibly know that? When we don't know who's doing this or why, that's not a statement you're in a position to make. Second, I don't care who you're having sex with, and neither does Lieutenant Lerens. But we do care about your relationships. All of them. Friends, acquaintances, lovers, whatever. Most murders are about relationships, and if people are hiding theirs from us, we'll be flapping about in the dark—and I don't like that."

"OK, I get it," Hancock said.

"Do you?" Hugo countered. He maintained firm eye contact with Helen but rubbed his right temple to still the returned throbbing in his skull.

"Yes, I do. And I'm sorry. I should have told you about Ambrósio, I know that." She sighed. "How's your head?"

"I'm OK, thanks," Hugo responded, distracted by the pounding. "But about Ambrósio . . . how are you coping? With his death, I mean."

"I think, like everyone else, I'm having a hard time accepting it, believing it. When you spend so much time in a fictional world, where all of that serious drama like breakups and death are all pretend, it's somehow harder to really face what's going on." She smiled sadly. "If that makes any sense."

"It does. I can connect you with a counselor, if you think it'd help, someone confidential to talk to Paris, in English."

"Oh, no, thank you. I have a therapist back home. I've talked to her a couple of times. The miracles of modern technology."

"Well, that's good. I'm always available to listen, too, if you think I can help."

"Thank you, that's kind of you. Jill is a good listener, too, although she's so busy all the time."

"Have you spoken to her today?" Hugo asked. "I wanted to ask her a couple of things and she's not answering, and not calling me back."

"Oh, how odd. She and I spoke on the phone last night. I tried calling her once this morning, too, and she's not responded to my message yet."

"Well," Hugo said, "like you said, she's a busy woman. But I'm glad she's your friend and a good listener."

"She is." Hancock hesitated. "On that note, and as a gesture of good faith, there's another relationship I have to tell you about, though I am absolutely positive it has no bearing on what's been happening. I also want you to promise me that you will be as discreet as humanly possible, because I don't want to cause problems for him."

Hugo was tempted to preempt her confession about his boss, but he wanted to make sure that was who she meant. His head was spinning with all of these secret liaisons cropping up throughout the investigation.

"You have my word that I will be as discreet as a murder investigation will allow me."

"I suppose that will have to do." She took a deep breath. "I have become close friends with the ambassador. If you know what I mean."

"Thank you," Hugo said, giving her a reassuring smile. "I needed to hear you say it, but he already told me."

"Oh, he did?"

"Yes. You should talk to him."

"I think he's upset with me."

"Nothing you can't get past," Hugo said. "And if he is upset, it's only because he has feelings for you, which isn't necessarily a bad thing. Listen to me, talking like I'm your shrink."

"You'd make a good one, I'm sure."

"I doubt it. I'm better at catching bad guys. To that end, I want to make sure we're on the same page, that there are no more surprises."

"None, I promise," Hancock said. "Not from me, anyway."

"Good." A thought struck Hugo. "On that note, did you tell Ambrósio to stop seeing Buzzy Pottgen?"

"You won't tell her, will you?"

"No," Hugo said with a smile. "But did you?"

"I told you once before," she said in a quiet voice. "When I want something . . . or someone . . . I'm not very good at sharing. At all."

"You wouldn't be the only one," Hugo said kindly. He nodded to the folder between them. "Research, eh? I thought you made everything up."

"Oh, goodness, no. I mean, the main story line, the characters, all that I make up. But let me tell you, as an author, if you get certain things wrong, you'll hear about it from readers."

"Like what?"

"Well, the big one is weapons. If you put a silencer on a revolver, or misname a gun . . . major no-nos." She picked up the folder and handed it to Hugo. "Have a look, you'll see the kinds of things I'm talking about."

Hugo flipped open the folder. Sure enough, the first four pages were printouts of various handguns. He felt like he was being nosy, looking at someone's diary, but Hancock gave him a reassuring nod. The next few pages were street maps of Paris, printed from her computer, and behind them some correspondence with a lawyer in Dallas dated the previous year, apparently answering some questions about French civil law. Hugo saw the words *libel . . . Article 9 . . . damages*, before he moved on to the next sheaf of papers, all relating to Marie Antoinette's life and death.

"She's featured in the book you're working on?"

"Obliquely. My heroine is going to be obsessed with her, so I need to make sure I get my facts right. If I don't, I'll hear about it. History and guns, I'd say those are people's sensitive areas, where they like their authors to get things right."

"So how does it work—does your publisher approve a story line in advance?" Hugo grinned. "I'm such a big reader and I've been to book launches before, but I know next to nothing about your end of the business."

"In my case, they just let me get on with it. After so many books, I guess they trust I'll come up with a good story." She grimaced. "Or they used to."

"Things still rocky with your editor?"

"Yes, that's one way to put it. I guess their marketing department is working overtime to make up for the damage of that tape."

"I'm sorry to hear that." Hugo handed the folder back. "Well, I should let you get back to educating your people."

CHAPTER TWENTY-EIGHT

By two o'clock, Hugo was hungry, but even more than that, he was worried. Camille had sent Paul Jameson to Jill Maxick's apartment, but after ten minutes of knocking no one had answered the door. Lionel Colbert had mentioned that Jill needed to get a tetanus shot—something about cutting herself with a kitchen knife—but that was hours ago. She should have been either at home or at work by now. After getting no response at her apartment, Jameson called Hugo and explained that Camille Lerens's phone was busy, and he wasn't sure what to do next.

"You think I should kick the door in?" the Scot asked, half joking.

"Better not," Hugo said. "We don't have any evidence that she's hurt or in danger, or that she has done anything wrong."

"Aye," Jameson said. "Wouldn't look good, if that's the case. And she might not appreciate it, either, if she's just out at the movies or something."

"Right. Did you talk to any neighbors?"

Jameson chuckled. "Several came out when I knocked on her door for the fifth time. No one's seen her this morning, but that's not unusual, according to them. One of those places where people have different schedules and don't really know each other. Keep to themselves, and all that."

"Of course," Hugo said.

"She's not answering when you call?" Jameson asked.

"No. I tried calling earlier; so has Helen Hancock. And I texted her, too, but . . . nothing."

"And no one at the hotel has seen or heard from her?"

"Nope. Not since early this morning, when she had asked Colbert to cover for her while she got a tetanus booster. Which is unusual. She's normally very diligent—checks in at the hotel regularly, even if she's not on duty. I was going to ask Camille if we could ping her phone."

"Good idea. Want me to take point on that?"

"Let me talk to her first, if that's OK. I'm worried that we don't have a good-enough reason. I mean, back home, we make sure to have probable cause and then get a warrant. I assume it's the same here, or close to it."

"And since all she's done is not answer her door or the phone . . ."

"Exactly," Hugo said. "She's not a victim, not a suspect, none of that."

"Aye, you're right. You can call Camille, but I'm betting we're out of luck. Next course of action?"

Lunch, Hugo thought, but he said, "Not sure. I'll call you when I figure it out. Let me get a hold of your lieutenant, and then one of us will get back to you." He disconnected and decided to find himself a comfortable seat, a few more aspirin, a sandwich, and maybe a coffee while he worked. It didn't take long for him to settle into a small chair under an awning on Rue de Condé. He ordered an espresso and a salmon-and-caper sandwich, then he dialed Camille Lerens.

"Thought we should talk about where we are," Hugo said. "Because I'm at something of a loss."

"My main concern right now is finding Maxick," she said. "I don't have enough to get a warrant to go into her apartment, or to ping her phone."

"That's what I told Jameson. Are you really worried for her safety?"

"I don't know, to be honest. The way things have been developing, anything could happen at any minute. I feel like we're behind in this investigation and not catching up."

"OK." Hugo flipped open his notebook and readied his pen.

"Then let's forget about Maxick for a minute and talk about some of the others," Hugo said. "I mean, we do have a limited pool of suspects."

"And it's getting smaller," Lerens said. "Buzzy Pottgen, Mike Rice, Thomas Prehn, and Lionel Colbert. Maybe even Helen Hancock herself, despite that alibi and just because she's in the middle of all this. Who else?"

"I hate to mention it, but did you talk to my boss?"

"Yes, and he has an alibi for both murders."

"Good, so we can cross him off."

"And we're assuming our killer is working alone," Lerens said.

Hugo paused and sat back in his chair. "That's true. If only we could figure out a motive, some reason for both Baxter and Silva to have been killed."

"The sole connection is Helen Hancock," Lerens said. "Baxter was spying on her, and Silva was sleeping with her. I don't know why or how, but I get the sense that somehow she's the key to this."

"Which makes me wonder if she's in danger."

"You want her in protective custody?"

"She wouldn't do it," Hugo said. "She won't even leave the damn hotel, get a room somewhere else."

"Stubborn lady, I can admire that."

"Not if she gets herself killed." Hugo signaled for another coffee. "OK, so it looks like the ambassador is in the clear. What about our other folks? Let's start with Buzzy Pottgen."

"She had a motive to do in Silva. Two of them, in fact. First, he cheated on her, and later he hit her."

"She admits to having a temper."

"More than that," Hugo said. "At her apartment, I looked in her bathroom cabinet. She's taking Prozac. It's an antidepressant, but it's also prescribed for people with anger-management problems."

"Oh, really?" Lerens said. "And yet Silva's murder doesn't seem like a spur-of-the-moment killing, does it? At least given the Sherlock Holmes aspect."

"We're agreed on that, I think. Silva's murder seems premeditated. But what reason would Pottgen have for killing Baxter?"

"That one's harder to explain," Lerens admitted. "Maybe he made some unwanted advances in the stairwell, she overreacted and stabbed him. Or maybe they were more than advances; maybe he tried to force himself on her and she was genuinely defending herself."

"And she just happened to have a kitchen knife on her, stabbed him to death, and decided she'd be better off not reporting it?"

"People make rash decisions, bad decisions, in the heat of the moment. And we know she has already lied to the police."

"Maybe, but Baxter's murderer seems more . . . cold-blooded than she is. And it still doesn't explain why she would have a kitchen knife on hand." Hugo nodded his thanks to the waiter who dropped off his coffee. "Let's keep her as a maybe in the Baxter murder. Who else?"

"Michael Rice. You told me he has a cold-blooded approach to this writing business, to making money."

"A lot of people do. Doesn't make them remotely capable of killing."

"We're all capable of killing, Hugo. You know that as well as anyone."

"Fine, but you know what I mean. What specific reason does Rice have to murder Baxter or Silva?"

"Well, remember how he reacted to the video going online? He was very angry at Silva, blamed him."

"True, he thought it was a callous act of self-promotion."

"And it may have been." Hugo heard Lerens sigh; then she said, "But enough to kill him?"

"Doesn't seem likely, I agree. And that still leaves us with our friend Andrew Baxter."

"Whom no one seems to have a reason to kill. Or even dislike, that we know of."

"Nothing fruitful on the gambling angle?"

"Yes and no," Lerens said.

Hugo sat up in his chair. "Camille, have you been holding out on me?"

"I'm not sure. But we've been going through his bank records, and the history on that computer found in Colbert's belongings. We've also got some of the records from the online sites where he was spending his hard-earned money. And yet we've found no credit cards, and he seems to have been spending more than he was making."

"How is that possible?" Hugo asked. He watched as a grubby teen in a red cap paused at the row of tables fronting the café. He was eighteen years old, *maybe*, and all but genuflected as he asked café patrons for a spare cigarette, a broad smile never leaving his face. A woman in her fifties handed him a half-empty packet and shooed him away, glancing around as if worried people might judge her.

"Maybe he had a third job, cash only. But then how does he convert that to money to spend online without it going through his bank account?"

"You think someone was lending him money?"

"The only way I can think of is if someone gave him prepaid credit cards to use. Which amounts to lending him money, yes."

"You can't tell by looking at the website records?"

"We're going through it now; I have a forensic accountant doing it."

"So the question is," Hugo began, "who would be lending him money, and why?"

"It has to be one of his roommates. Or possibly Maxick?"

"I think we can rule out Thomas Prehn; he wouldn't give Baxter the time of day, let alone money to gamble with."

"Unless he disliked Baxter so much that he wanted to put him in a financial hole so deep he couldn't climb out," Lerens suggested. "I mean, if you were Baxter and you owed a bunch of money and couldn't pay it back, what would you do?"

Hugo thought for a moment. "I'd up sticks and move. Just disappear."

"Prehn might have been shooting for that."

"Seems like a convoluted way to get rid of someone."

"Easier than murder, though," Lerens said. "Unless it turned into that in the stairwell."

"And Silva?" Hugo asked. "Why kill him?"

"I'm starting to wonder if Silva witnessed Baxter's murder. Or knew something about it. Maybe he was blackmailing the killer and got himself murdered for it."

Hugo ran a hand over his face, frustrated at the amount of speculation they were making. "Thing is, Camille, all these scenarios are possible, but they seem like too much of a stretch. It's like we can explain one murder, maybe, but the second one we're shoehorning into place."

Lerens laughed. "What is it you tell me, from Sherlock Holmes?"

"Ah, yes. 'When you have eliminated the impossible, whatever remains, however improbable, must be the truth.'"

"*Précisément!*"

"But what have we eliminated?" Hugo said, hearing the exasperation in his own voice. "Basically nothing. We've created a whole bunch of scenarios, all of which are improbable but not impossible. We're doing the exact opposite of what Sherlock suggested."

"If it's any help, we have solid alibis for Lionel Colbert, for both murders."

"Tell me."

"Starting with Silva's death, he was working. Several people vouched for him, said there's no way he was gone long enough to get to the bridge and back without being missed."

"And Baxter's murder?"

"Same thing. He was working in the lobby at the time Baxter was killed. He took one bathroom break and one cigarette break, and while no one had eyes on him those times, of course, he came back inside after the latter smelling of cigarettes; and with all that blood. . . . Several people assured Jameson they would have known."

"I'm glad, and not surprised," Hugo said. "The kid doesn't like authority, but Baxter was his friend and I see no reason he'd kill him. Or Silva. And Silva didn't kill himself, the GSR tells us that."

"The GSR indicates that very strongly," she corrected. "Although I'm inclined to agree with you. But what makes you so certain?"

"I just know." Hugo realized how that sounded. "Look, I've been dealing with people close to the abyss a long time."

"What does that mean?"

"It means he wasn't one of them. He was mentally and emotionally stable, and other than being exposed on that tape, he had no reason to harm himself."

"Public humiliation isn't enough of a reason?"

"Not when you've already got pornography out there, no, I don't think so." Hugo frowned into the phone. "I just know he didn't kill himself."

"Oh, well then," Lerens said, with humor in her voice. "I'll be sure to put that in the report for the investigating magistrate."

"Are you really thinking it might have been suicide?" Hugo asked, disbelieving.

"No. I'm messing with you; I agree with your assessment, and the gunshot-residue test."

"What about Michael Rice?"

"We have a statement from him but haven't had a chance to double-check his alibis. I think Jameson is having someone do that right now." Hugo heard a beep, then Lerens said, "I have a call coming in from the hotel; can you hold a moment?"

"Sure." Hugo waited patiently, setting his pen down and turning his attention back to a half-empty cup of mostly cold coffee, slugging it back and imagining the shot zipping caffeinated energy, and maybe inspiration, into his veins—not to mention his still-pounding head. Lerens was back in less than a minute.

"Interesting turn of events," she said. "I need to go. Call you later?"

"What happened?"

"It's Thomas Prehn. Looks like he's taken off."

"Does that mean what I think it means?"

"Yes. Or as Paul Jameson might say, he's 'done a runner.'"

CHAPTER TWENTY-NINE

Hugo signaled to the waiter for his check. "Tell me how I can help, Camille."

"If I figure that out, I will."

"How do you know he's gone?"

"Earlier today I went to talk to him and Lionel Colbert, at the hotel. Their room was cleaned out."

"Oh, no, wait. That doesn't mean he's left," Hugo said. "Jill just moved them to their own rooms."

"That's what Colbert told me, but it was the manager there today who just called me. He said Prehn sent him an e-mail saying he was quitting and going back to Germany."

"Dammit. Did he say why?"

"Yes. He didn't feel safe in Paris anymore."

"I guess that's possible," Hugo said. "It's certainly not impossible."

"Except I expressly told him, told all of them, not to leave the city without my permission, without telling me even."

"You think this is suspicious?"

"Of course it's suspicious," Lerens said. "How could it not be?"

"I guess he wasn't on my radar as a likely candidate," Hugo said. "And he told us once before that he was worried for his safety, so it's consistent at least."

"*Peut-être.*" Perhaps. "But I don't like it. I'm going to see how far he's made it, bring him back if I can."

"OK, Camille, but remember what I just told you—he may be genuinely afraid."

"I now have him and Jill Maxick out of my sight, Hugo, and I'm not looking to baby a grown man because he's scared." Her tone was sharp. "I'll talk to you later." She hung up without saying good-bye.

Hugo thanked the waiter on the way out of the café, his thoughts drifting away from the case and to Tom Green. He called his friend and left a message. "Tom, it's Hugo. Checking in, seeing if you have any info. And to make sure you're OK, not on the way to Amsterdam or anything silly. Call me."

Hugo checked his watch. The timing was perfect, but he'd need to pick up the pace just a little bit.

At a newsstand on Rue de Vaugirard he dodged a Lycra-clad woman charging down the sidewalk with a stroller in front of her, oblivious to those around her and, Hugo thought, the safety of the child inside the arrow-shaped device. Since he was there, and a couple of minutes early, he bought a newspaper before crossing the street into the Luxembourg Garden. He could have read the news on his phone, and in English, but he hadn't become fluent in French by taking the easy route. And he hated seeing people staring at their phones, no matter how valid the reason.

He wandered around for a few minutes, and at five to four he found a park bench that maximized his view of the park, and sat down to wait.

Michael Rice was, if anything, a prompt man. At one minute after four o'clock, he jogged into the park, his jaw set and eyes straight ahead, a determined runner if Hugo had ever seen one. He felt bad about waving to get the man's attention, but Rice didn't seem to mind. He pulled the ear buds out of his ears and plopped down next to Hugo, panting softly.

"Sorry to knock you out of your stride," Hugo said.

"Oh, no problem. I detest running, to be honest. Back home I'm a member of a gym and do my workouts there. Swim, bike, anything but run. Here I can't afford it, so I have to run or get fat, because I do like to eat."

"You and me both," Hugo said. "I just haven't had a chance to talk to you lately, one-on-one."

"I gave a statement to the police; you need something more from me?"

"Not so much more, just different."

Rice cocked an eyebrow. "What does that mean?"

"It means I want to know how you feel about all of this. Particularly Silva's death."

"Oh, boy." Rice sat forward, his hands clasped and his elbows on his knees. "The police said I was a suspect in his murder." He glanced at Hugo. "Which is fucking ridiculous."

"Tell me why."

"Because I was mad at him for posting that video online, for humiliating Helen. And if I'm honest with myself, for him sleeping with her, trying to get that edge." He shook his head. "*I'm* supposed to be the crass, commercially oriented one."

"You haven't slept with her, too, then?"

"Are you serious?"

Hugo smiled. "I've had more surprises this week than I've had all year, so I guess I am."

"It never even crossed my mind. I'm all for exploiting her knowledge, if you want to put it that way."

"You're paying for it, though."

"Right. I guess that's what I mean. I'm taking advantage of her, but not unfairly. Don't get me wrong, she can sleep with whomever she wants. I just didn't get the sense that he was doing anything but looking out for himself. It wasn't like he *liked* her that way, as far as I knew. He certainly never said anything to me."

"Did he like Buzzy that way?"

"Seemed to. I actually thought they knew each other already, the way they were thick as thieves. I was surprised they didn't get a place together."

"They'd only met and chatted online, I think," Hugo said. "How do you feel about his death?"

"Honestly, I can't fucking believe it. Even if he was a manipulative jerk, jeez . . . I mean, maybe a punch in the gut or something. But who shoots someone? In Paris? It's all beyond me."

"Do you have anyone in mind?"

"No. I don't know many people here, of course, but neither of those. Buzzy or Helen. No way."

"Buzzy has a temper though, right?" Hugo prodded.

"Yeah, sure. A door slammer and, maybe, a face slapper. But a woman with a temper in a city where she barely speaks the language would have to also be pretty ice-cold to get mad, then go find a gun, lure Silva to that bridge, and murder him."

And maybe try to make it look like suicide, Hugo thought.

"Also," Rice was saying, "where the hell do you get a gun in Paris? I suppose she could manage in the States, but Paris?" He shook his head again. "No, you want my opinion, whoever shot him, it was either a robbery or . . . someone cold and calculated."

"I tend to agree, but it wasn't robbery; we know that much."

"So you don't think Buzzy did it?"

"Do you know Lionel Colbert or Thomas Prehn?"

"They work at the hotel, right?"

"Correct," Hugo said. "Andrew Baxter's roommates."

"I know Leo, didn't know his last name, though. Nice guy the couple of times I talked to him."

"About what?"

"Just chitchat while I waited for Helen. We've lived in some of the same places; he's an interesting guy."

Hugo gave a wry smile. "Not one for authority, was my impression."

"That's not so unusual."

"What about Prehn?"

"The German guy, right? Efficient, polite, not overly friendly." Rice frowned. "Seems like he doesn't like Americans, but I'm not sure if that was my impression or if someone told me that. I know a few days ago, shoot, maybe a week, Buzzy was being loud in the main lobby, just herself, nothing obnoxious, but he got all huffy."

"Ever see Silva interact with either of them?"

"Nope, can't say I did."

Hugo scuffed the gravel with his heel, frustrated. "OK, thanks."

"Trying to find a connection between all these people?"

"Right," Hugo said. "And not succeeding yet, which is getting a little frustrating."

"Maybe there isn't one." Rice suggested.

"There is. With these particular deaths and such a closed circle, the connection is there; I just have to find it. Anyway, not your problem." Hugo felt like he was giving too much away, so he changed the subject. "How was the writing session, productive?"

Mike sighed. "You were wrong, you know."

"About what?"

"All that red ink. Most of it wasn't very complimentary."

"Sorry to hear that," Hugo said.

"No, it's fine. I like her honesty. Anything else would be much less useful."

"So she's been helpful overall?"

"Oh, for sure. I'm actually starting to appreciate the writing itself more, the creating and telling of the story. Imagine that—there's more to writing books than making money."

"I've heard that," Hugo said with a smile.

"That said, we met with her French editor yesterday, one-on-one, which was cool. Good to know how the process works once a writer turns a book in."

"I'm surprised her editor took time to do that."

"Oh really? She seemed happy to do it, had nothing but praise for Helen. Talked about the new book, when that's coming out over here, the process. Bestselling author and all that, I'm sure she'd bend over backward to help her."

"True enough," Hugo said. "Well, I won't hold you up any longer, thanks for the time. And you have my card, so if anything comes to mind, call me."

"Will do." Rice shook his hand and then stood, stretching his back.

"I'd prefer you delay me another hour or two so I can avoid torturing myself. But I'll just think about the pastries this'll let me eat."

Hugo watched him jog off into the park, slow but steady progress through the trees and out of sight. Hugo sat back and closed his eyes for a moment, letting the breeze wash over his face as something Rice had said percolated in his mind. *Interesting*, he thought. *Very interesting indeed.*

He opened his eyes when his phone rang, and sat up when he saw Tom Green's name on the screen. "Hey, where are you?"

"Have a guess."

"Are you right behind me?" Hugo asked. "Maybe in that trash can beside the homeless guy. Is he poking you right now?"

"Shut up, Hugo. You guessed it, I'm in Amsterdam."

Hugo slowly sat back into the bench and closed his eyes again.

Just sometimes, he thought to himself, *I really do hate being right.*

CHAPTER THIRTY

Fifteen years previously.

1500 hours, Houston, Texas.

Hugo Marston turned the black FBI vehicle into the parking lot and looked for a spot in the shade, one with a good view of the bank's entrance.

Beside him, Tom fidgeted. "This is so stupid," he said.

"Maybe. Maybe not," Hugo said. In front of them, the parking lot baked in the Houston sun, not a tree or other shade in sight. Which meant he'd have to leave the engine running for the air-conditioning, not ideal when they were trying to be surreptitious. "They've got to hit one of those banks."

"So *you* say."

"So the profile says."

"*Your* profile, Hugo, unless I'm much mistaken."

"Well, makes sense that it would be; I've been tracking these guys since last December."

"Tell me again why they're wasting a profiler on a couple of bank robbers," Tom said. "You guys have your specialty, and it's killers not thieves."

"No clue," Hugo said. "Although I suspect someone down here pulled a string in Washington. Or it could be that eight similar bank robberies going unsolved makes the local cops and FBI look bad. I just do as I'm told, go where they want me, and the sooner we can snag these guys the sooner I can get back to DC."

Hugo had been with the Behavioral Analysis Unit for eight years, rising quickly in the estimation of his superiors. He'd actually wondered why they chose him for this assignment. Usually a more junior agent would be sent off to help with something like this, something that didn't involve murder. Maybe that was why. They certainly wanted to catch these two before someone did get killed, which was inevitable given how aggressive they'd been.

The MO was the same each time: Two white men, possibly brothers because they looked so alike, saunter into a bank and once inside they pull out two handguns apiece, one covering the lobby and the other demanding cash. Any customers inside are made to lie facedown on the floor and get a hard kick in the ribs if they move or even look up. In and out in three minutes or less, quick enough that the eyewitness descriptions had mentioned the similarities but otherwise been vague on other details. No one knew what the getaway car looked like, or even if a third person was driving it.

With so little to go on, someone in the bureau had obviously decided that an agent from the BAU would be able to help. Hugo hadn't minded; it meant he got to see his best friend, Tom Green, catch up on old times, and maybe needle him a little. Tom lived with his sister, Christen, in her house about three miles from the bank they were surveilling, and she was everything Tom wasn't. Beautiful, refined, kind, and responsible. She was five feet five inches, with pretty blue eyes and naturally dark hair that she'd dyed red since middle school.

She'd lived alone in Houston until Tom had come to the house, her security taking the form of a German shepherd named Maddie, who took great delight in chewing up the newcomer's shoes whenever she could, just to show who was boss. Christen and Hugo had come close to dating a few years back but, after one awkward kiss, had decided to stay close as friends, for their sakes as well as for her brother's. That one kiss was perhaps the only secret Hugo had ever kept from Tom.

Before he'd even arrived at the Houston field office for this trip, Hugo requested the two men be able to work together on the case, and he'd swung by Christen's house to pick up his friend twenty minutes ago. She'd not been there, had left for work hours before, and Hugo was disappointed not to see her. But he quickly focused on the job at hand. On the way to the bank they'd gone over some of the plan but chatted about other things, too, like how after this case Hugo was looking forward to being in DC again.

"The Texan wanting out of Texas so soon?" Tom unbuckled his seatbelt, settling in. "For shame."

"I'm from Austin, which isn't quite the same," Hugo reminded him.

"There's an understatement." He nodded to the bank. "So why this one in particular?"

"Because it's the closest one to my hotel."

"Seriously, you were going to tell me," Tom insisted.

"They never hit the same part of town twice in a row. I mapped each bank they robbed, and they bounce around, in a pattern. I wouldn't be surprised if the ringleader has some sort of compulsive disorder."

"How come?"

"They hit north, then south, then east, then west. Then they started filling in the gaps, but always opposite the last one. It's like they're trying to be random but can't quite manage it."

"How many banks are there in this part of town, though?" Tom asked.

"A lot. There are more than a thousand in the city, so, depending on where you start drawing lines, a lot." Hugo adjusted his visor to keep the sun out of his eyes. Even with the air-conditioning on, the bright sun burned its way into the car. "But they choose smaller banks with no cameras, though I fail to understand why there's any bank in the country that doesn't have a camera in this day and age."

"No shit," Tom said.

"They also hit banks that have open teller counters, which is most of them."

"Also not smart."

"From a security perspective, sure," Hugo agreed. "I can see why they don't, though. Customer service is important, that face-to-face transaction. And most banks have a policy that even if you have protective glass, if someone points a gun at a teller, they're supposed to hand over the cash."

"And God knows if those things are as bulletproof as they claim."

"Exactly," Hugo said.

"So what else?"

"Well, they hit mid- to late-afternoon, when a lot of cash deposits are in. Between three and closing time. Also, each bank hit so far has been within half a mile of a major road, with easy access to it," Hugo said. "In other words, they're not making themselves turn left across traffic to get to the freeway."

"Smart, I guess."

"We'll see. I came up with four banks in this general area that fit the description. Wilson and Rodriguez are watching one, city police the other two."

"Great, one in four chance," Tom said grumpily. "More to the point, three in four that we sit here like chumps for two hours."

"Three hours," Hugo said lightly. "They close at six."

"Do I have time for a nap?"

"Feel free, as long as you don't mind me putting it in the report."

"And as long as you write the report," Tom said, "you can put whatever the hell you like in there, I don't care."

Hugo ignored that. "I don't like that we have to keep the engine running. I have no idea whether they case the place beforehand or not."

"You could've picked a more subtle car. I mean, a black SUV, really?"

"I didn't choose; I was given," Hugo said.

They settled down to wait, and Hugo glanced over at his friend every few minutes to make sure he wasn't taking that nap. Every time, Tom's eyes were open and fixed on the doors of the bank, or scanning the parking lot.

"You can stop checking on me," Tom said eventually.

"Sorry, all that talk of naps . . ."

But Tom was peering through the windshield, seeing the same thing Hugo was: two men in jeans and T-shirts who'd pulled into a parking space way to the agents' left, giving the men access to the front and back doors of the bank. They were standing by their car, watching the building, occasionally looking around as if for cops.

"You see any guns?" Hugo asked.

"Nope. Baggy T-shirts though."

The man by the passenger's side of the car reached into the open window and pulled out what looked to be an empty duffel bag. Adrenaline shot through Hugo's body as the two men moved forward in unison, their body language purposeful, determined.

"That's gotta be them," Hugo said.

"You wanna call it in?"

Hugo hesitated. "I'll have Houston PD stand by, but we don't want the cavalry here yet. Let's get close, make sure. But if it is them, we won't have much time." He flipped open the computer that sat between them and was about to type a quick message to the coordinating agent back in the office when Tom grabbed his arm.

"Oh, my God, Hugo. Look who's going in right behind them."

Hugo looked up and saw the woman walking slowly to the bank on what must have been her lunch hour.

"Oh, shit," Hugo said. "That's not good."

Tom jerked forward, his nose to the windshield. "Shit, Hugo, we have to stop her from going in."

Hugo gripped the steering wheel and watched the woman push her way into the bank. "Too late for that. She'll be fine, Tom, they haven't hurt anyone yet." *Not seriously, anyway*, Hugo thought. "She doesn't carry a gun, does she?"

"No, she hates them." Tom's voice was a whisper. "Thank God."

Hugo nodded. "That's good. She'll do what they say, like the others will."

"And we just sit here? Fuck that."

"No, we're going to get closer, try to get eyes on them and be there to catch them," Hugo said as he readjusted the visor to get a better view of the bank entrance.

They both stiffened as a sound reached them across the parking lot, the muffled but unmistakable *Crack!* of a gunshot. Hugo reacted first and opened the car door with his left hand, as his right grabbed the handset of his radio and held down the call button. "Shots fired, we're going in."

His feet hit the pavement, and a blast of hot air scorched his face, but all Hugo could think about was Tom's sister. Sweet, funny Christen, who looked as happy and relaxed as Hugo had ever seen her, headed into the bank, wearing a pretty yellow sundress and cowboy boots, with her confident walk and not a care in the world.

CHAPTER THIRTY-ONE

Of course, that day, and every one since, Tom had blamed himself.

He was too slow to stop her from going in, too dumb to figure out that she used that particular bank, too uncaring to warn her not to use *any* bank until the robbers were caught.

Tom and Hugo both knew who was really to blame, who's always to blame, but Tom's already-volatile personality was given a nudge by whatever forces had steered his beloved sister into the path of the Cofer brothers; and despite their culpability, Tom punished himself. Then and every day after.

Sitting on that park bench, Hugo listened to his friend rattle on about how and why he went to Amsterdam, how he planned to get to Rick Cofer before Cofer got to him. But running through Hugo's mind were the times he'd pulled Tom from a bar, from a fight, from the gutter. And, not too long ago, from a French jail cell. Good metaphors for his friend's state of mind, because for a long time now Tom had fueled his anger and self-loathing with booze, which usually landed him in a worse place than he started, literally.

He'd reached an equilibrium, Hugo thought, just in the last year or so. The occasional drunken bender would be followed by a patch of relative sobriety, even teetotalling it a few times. But his sister was still dead, and one of the men who'd killed her was now breathing clean, fresh air again.

"Just one chance," Tom was saying. "You know I'm good, and you know I'll do it."

"Yes, I do know, Tom," Hugo said. Listening to the cold anger in his friend's voice. Hugo realized that if Cofer *had* come to Europe seeking revenge, the man had made a serious mistake. He was on Tom's home turf, without a lick of training, and probably with very few friends or contacts. And, sure, revenge is a powerful motivator, but Cofer was absolutely mistaken if he thought he was the only one looking for it. For closure, maybe, if such a thing even existed.

Cofer might be smart and could have been planning this for years, but he'd done so from a prison cell with few resources and a vivid imagination.

No, Hugo thought. *If you're here, Rick Cofer, I've been wrong. Tom's not the one who needs protecting from a vengeful killer. It's you who should be afraid, not Tom.* Hugo smiled to himself. *Good luck with all that, Mr. Cofer.*

The next morning, Hugo woke early and began the long walk to the embassy. He didn't mind working, even though it was Sunday, and he particularly enjoyed the relative emptiness and quiet of the city at this time. But he walked a little faster than he normally would on a weekend morning, wanting to check something on his computer at his office, a set of files Camille Lerens's expert had couriered to him on a thumb drive. They were from Helen Hancock's computer, turned over willingly by the author to the police so they could check whether someone had been plagiarizing her work.

As he stepped into his offices, he heard a noise; and when he poked his head around the door, he saw his secretary, Emma, peering at her computer screen.

She looked up and asked, "What are you doing here? And how's your head?"

"Much better, thanks. Almost free of that headache," Hugo said. "Also, I think the real question is, what are *you* doing here?"

"It's my secret to being organized," she said. "An hour or two on the weekend and Monday sails by without a hitch."

"Really? But I've worked many weekends and have never seen you here, not once." Hugo narrowed his eyes. "Wait a minute. Aren't your brother and his wife staying with you this weekend?"

She gave him her most angelic smile. "Files. They don't organize themselves, you know. If we're going to be here a while, should I make coffee?"

"That would be fantastic." He decided to let the other thing slide without further comment, because her family was her business, and if there was one person in the office who'd cover for him, it was Emma. And if she was making coffee . . .

Hugo slipped behind his desk and into his chair, going through the comfortable routine of firing up his computer. His e-mail inbox held half a dozen messages that could wait, so he opened a web browser and searched online until he'd found several provisions of French civil law. His eyes glazed over with boredom as he finished reading Article 9, so he switched gears to what he had initially come in for and took out the thumb drive Lieutenant Lerens's expert had sent over. He plugged it into his computer, clicked on its icon, and ran his eye over the options.

He double-clicked on the document that was her manuscript in progress, then sat back to think. The smell of coffee wafted in from Emma's office, along with the sounds of her bustling about and clinking cups. Truth was, his office was as much home to him as his apartment. He loved the people he worked with—Emma; his second in command, Ryan Pierce; and even his boss, Taylor, was more his friend than his superior. And that was good, because he did his best thinking when he was comfortable and free of distractions.

Emma walked in, two coffee mugs in her hands, and put Hugo's in front of him.

"Anything I can help with?"

"Sure," Hugo said. "Have a seat. You said before that you have contacts in the publishing business?"

"Over here, yes, not back home. You planning to write a book, or is this Helen Hancock–related?"

"The latter."

"Well, unless it has something to do with her books over here, you're out of luck."

"Actually, it is. If I send you a list of questions, do you think you can get answers?"

"I know I can try," Emma said. "No promises, but I'll do my best."

"The sooner the better, if you don't mind."

Emma cocked her head. "I know that tone, and that look. You have an idea."

"I have the inkling of an idea. A seedling, perhaps."

"And of course you won't deign to share it until you're sure," Emma said.

"Correct."

"Not even a hint?"

Hugo thought for a second. "Two hints. One from Sherlock Holmes, one of my favorite sayings of his, and the other from Michael Rice."

"Ah, then let me try. Something like, 'if you've examined all the possibilities, then it must be one of the impossibilities.'"

Hugo smiled. "Something like that. And clue number two?"

"I don't even know who Michael Rice is. Another author?"

"Working to be one. He's a student of Helen Hancock's. He told me that if you look for connections and can't figure out what they are, maybe they don't exist."

Emma frowned, obviously unimpressed. "Sounds like one of those wise but rather obvious statements, if you ask me."

"Sometimes those are the best ones." Hugo opened up a new e-mail and filled in Emma's address. "If you find out what I think you're gonna find out, I'll try to come up with something more profound."

"Deal." Emma rose and on her way out of the door said, "Now I can tell my visitors I have important investigative work to do. Thanks, Hugo."

He typed up a list of questions and sent them to Emma, then spent the next thirty minutes scrolling through Helen Hancock's newest manuscript. He didn't read for the story but for the elements, a way to assess both the subjects Hancock included, factual stuff like locations, points of law, even historical events. He wasn't sure why, necessarily—if she'd made a mistake, so what?

One thing he didn't want to do, though, was read the book with an eye to inputting the traits of her characters onto Helen Hancock herself. He'd talked to enough writers to know that one question they get a lot, and don't particularly care for, is whether a character's trait is their own. At one book launch Hugo had attended, someone in the audience had asked whether an author's cutthroat businessman character reflected the his own approach to getting ahead. Everyone there had thought it a rude question, given the reaction of people around him, but the author had smiled and said, "We get those questions, sometimes. But let me turn it around and ask you something. Hundreds of authors are out there writing murder mysteries. Are they all killers? And if I wrote a transgender character, would you assume I was myself going through that process? No, I didn't think so. It's the same with the smaller things, too, so please never assume that just because you see something in a novel, it reflects the author's own personality or interests."

The manuscript file Hugo had access to was 62,017 words long, a few chapters from completion. But there was something missing from the story, something he'd expected to see in there. He scrolled back through the manuscript, and then he spent ten minutes crafting word searches to make sure he was right.

He e-mailed Emma one more question to ask her publishing contact, then drained his coffee cup. Beside him, on the desk, his phone buzzed to life.

"Hugo, it's Camille."

"I know," he said. "Your name pops up."

She laughed. "Technology, a wonderful thing."

"Unless you're trying to surprise someone."

"True enough. Are you busy?"

"At the office doing a few things. What's up?"

"I want to send a car and Paul Jameson to you. Assuming you have time for me," she added hurriedly. "I know it's the weekend, so if you have plans, let me know. I just thought you'd want in."

"Stop being coy, Camille. In on what?"

"Jill Maxick missed her shift at the hotel. Didn't show up. First time she's done that. Ever."

"You have a search warrant for her apartment?"

"I do."

"Based on missing one shift at work?"

Lerens chuckled. "Well, that's part of it. The other part was based on the fact that the piece of wood found nearby wasn't what was used to knock you out. At least, that's my theory since Tom's people found no DNA on it, but did identify yours and someone else's on a piece of the broken glass I found at the scene."

Hugo nodded. "OK, well, that's good. So we know for sure now that I was hit with a bottle. But what does this have to do with Jill and the warrant?"

"Since we have voluntary samples of DNA from the relevant people at the hotel, as well as Helen Hancock and her merry group of writers, we now know who was wielding it. I'll give you one guess who it was."

CHAPTER THIRTY-TWO

They didn't talk much on the way over, what with Paul Jameson focusing on the traffic and getting Hugo to Maxick's apartment in the Thirteenth Arrondissement as quickly as possible.

"You got any theories on why she attacked you?" Jameson asked as they got close.

"Working on it," Hugo said, and sank back into silence. The few ideas he had were like tendrils of mist, without real form or definition, and constantly shifting.

The address was Rue du Moulinet, and when they got close Jameson swore under his breath at the construction that spilled onto the narrow roadways and slowed traffic. A large woman in a colorful print dress and headscarf stepped out in front of them, staring at her phone and oblivious to the proximity of the police car's bumper to her knees. They eventually passed Square de la Montgolfière and made it onto Rue du Moulinet, where the construction had reduced the street to one very thin lane. Several police cars sat on the sidewalk up ahead, and Jameson bumped their car up behind one of them. Lerens was perched on the hood of one car, and Hugo got out and walked over to her.

"Thanks for waiting," he said.

"*Pas de problème.* Wouldn't want you missing the show, assuming there will be one."

Hugo looked up at the apartment building in front of them. It was modern, all straight lines and white and off-white colors, with none of the ornate stonework or ironwork of the older buildings. Function over form, the emphasis on cost not appearance. A shame, from Hugo's perspective, but then he didn't have to pay the rent.

"How do we do this?" he asked.

"Knock on the door first, and if there's no answer I have a large gentleman who's very good with a battering ram. Ready?"

"I am," Hugo said.

Lerens already had the code to the building, and she led the way up the stairs to the third floor. A central corridor ran down the middle, leading to four apartments on each side. Lerens seemed to read his mind.

"Ugly building and small apartments," she said. "Doesn't seem like a fair trade-off."

"Close to work, though, and the center of the city."

She nodded to the first doorway. "They're all one-bedroom units. Small hallway with a kitchen on the right, then a living room with a bedroom off to the left. Bathroom is next to the bedroom, accessible from the living room too. Want to see a floor plan?"

"Not unless you're sending me in first," Hugo said.

Lerens smiled. "Not a chance. You'd pull a muscle or get shot or something, and I'd have a lot of explaining to do to my superiors."

"And mine."

"Aye, we're the expendable ones," Jameson said from right behind Hugo. "Foot soldiers."

"Very true," Lerens said. "Although I prefer to think of you in particular as cannon fodder. Anyway. It's the farthest door on the left, so let's see if she's home." Lerens looked around at the six men behind her, four dressed in tactical gear in case of forced entry, and, satisfied everyone was ready, she started down the hallway.

They were marching as one unit when a door opened up on their right. A young man with floppy blond hair and wearing a red backpack stood in his doorway, his mouth falling open at the sight of the entry team closing in on him. Lerens waved him back into his apartment and, Hugo thought, he looked only too happy to comply.

At Maxick's apartment the team separated, lining up on either side of the door. Once they were in place, the tactical officers switched on their helmet cameras and nodded to their leader, Lerens, who stood to one side of the door, reached out, and rapped loudly.

No response, so after thirty seconds she tried again. "Police, open the door!"

Still silence.

A third knock, and this time several of the team shifted as if they'd heard something from inside. Hugo strained to listen but heard only distant voices, from other apartments or maybe the street outside.

"Policy requires three, so I give it four," Lerens said to Hugo, and she knocked one last time, loud and hard.

"Police! Jill Maxick, open the door; we have a search warrant."

Ten seconds later, Lerens checked her watch and stood back, gesturing for the burly officer with the battering ram to step forward.

"You couldn't get a key from her landlord?"

"We tried, briefly. We got the DNA back from Tom about two hours ago, so I focused on getting the warrant. Jameson identified her landlord but couldn't get hold of him, and I'm not inclined to wait."

"Look, if something's happened to her, or she's run off like Thomas Prehn, sending those guys in will disturb and maybe destroy evidence."

"I just told you, we don't have a key."

"So let them knock it open, then we'll go in and look around."

"That's not procedure."

Hugo smiled. "Now you're starting to sound like me."

"Sorry, but these men have to go in first." She thought for a moment. "But we'll compromise." She turned to her team. "Go in and take a quick look around. Don't touch anything, don't open anything, and don't you dare break or smash anything."

The men looked at each other, then the big one with the ram nodded. "You're the boss," he said.

"*Merci*," Hugo said, but fixed the officer with a stern look. "A broken door, nothing else disturbed."

The *flic* nodded. "You can buy him a new one tomorrow."

"Maxick can do that, if she's still around," Lerens said, and looked at Hugo with a wry smile. "Want to bet she's packed up and fled?"

"I think you might win that wager, so no thanks."

"Unless she can explain her blood on that bottle, it might be her best move." Lerens looked at the big *flic*, nodded, and gave him the go-ahead. "*Allez.*"

The man set his feet, lined his battering ram up with the door handle, and gave it one hard punch, putting the weight of his entire body into it. A loud bang rattled Hugo's already-sensitive head as the jamb splintered and the door crashed open. Four armed men moved quickly into the apartment, guns at the ready, a hand on the shoulder of the man in front, a chain of security whose one job was to clear the place of any danger.

It didn't take long. After a minute, the lead officer came out of the apartment, his gun over his shoulder.

"*Tout est clair, madame.*" He looked at Hugo. "There are some linens and clothes closets we left alone, but I listened, and no signs of anyone hiding in them. And nothing knocked over or broken."

Hugo saw the twinkle in the man's eye and appreciated his sense of humor. He'd not liked being told to limit his search and was letting Hugo know it. "*Merci,*" Hugo said, "I appreciate your cooperation, really."

Lerens looked at Hugo as the rest of the intrusion team filed out of the small apartment. "Our turn." She turned to Jameson. "Wait here, please, Paul. Make sure no one comes in."

Hugo followed her inside, curious to see the home of the woman he'd come to respect. Maxick had shown herself to be smart, efficient, and obviously very kind to Helen Hancock in her time of need. Inside, he checked the back of the door and found two coats hanging there, one light and the other of a heavy wool.

To his right, the kitchen was clean and tidy, as he'd expect from Jill, likewise the living room ahead of them. Nothing obviously out of place or unduly disturbed. He and Lerens stood in the middle of the space and looked around them.

"What are you seeing?" she asked.

"No signs of a struggle, for one thing."

"It doesn't look like she fled in a hurry," Lerens offered. "Dishes are done, everything is neat and tidy."

"Someone who's used to order and neatness might instinctively leave it like this," Hugo countered. "Hang on." He went to the small, low fridge in the kitchen and opened it. "She's only been absent a couple of days, and if she's on the run we don't know when she decided to go." He closed the door. "But the fridge is well stocked."

"What would have spooked her to run?"

"That I don't know. Maybe after hitting me with the bottle she realized she'd gone too far, or left some evidence behind?"

"The latter, maybe," Lerens said. "With all due respect to your head, I think killing Baxter and Silva are a little worse."

Hugo nodded. "True enough. You check the bedroom, I'll look in the bathroom."

They split up and Hugo went into the small bathroom. Clean, tidy, with a toothbrush and toothpaste tucked into a plastic cup on the sink. He felt the bristles to see if it'd been used recently, but they were dry. A small wooden medicine cabinet hung to his right, and he opened it up. Various pots and tubes took up the shelves, along with a row of medicine bottles, all over-the-counter stuff.

"Hugo!" Lerens's voice was urgent but calm. "In here."

He went through the door into the bedroom and stopped short. To his left was Maxick's queen-size bed, slightly rumpled. Clothes, still on their hangers, were stacked on top of it. To his right was a small walk-in closet, an unusual feature for an older Paris apartment, more common in newer builds and remodels. Shoes littered the floor of the closet, and above them a thick wooden bar stretched from side to side, where her clothes used to hang.

There was a thin belt looped around the bar. The belt's other end was looped, too, around the neck of Jill Maxick, whose blank eyes bulged out at Hugo from a pale, blood-drained face, which tilted slightly to her right as if she were about to make a polite inquiry about something.

"Dammit," Hugo said. A wave of sadness hit him, followed rapidly by a feeling of exhaustion. *I'm not supposed to be doing this*, he thought. This was FBI work, tracking down killers and uncovering bodies. *I'm not supposed to be doing this anymore.*

"Looks like I would've lost that bet," Lerens said. "And I'm very sorry about that."

Hugo turned on his heel and went to the broken front door. Behind him, he heard Lerens on the phone to someone, presumably requesting the medical examiner and a forensics team. He stooped and examined the locking mechanism before returning to the bedroom.

"Find anything?" Lerens tucked her phone away.

"No. Just curious about something."

"Care to share?"

"The front door. This looks like suicide, but so did Silva's death once we found that gun with the rock attached. His still might be a suicide. But I doubt both are. I wanted to see if someone could have locked the door as they left, or whether they'd need a key."

"And?"

"Simple latch," Hugo said. "Just close the door and it locks. Doesn't tell us much at this point, but good to know."

"*Bien.* Forensics are on their way. They must be sick of us by now."

"Suicide, really?" Hugo stepped closer to Maxick. Her arms hung by her sides and her knees hovered just above the floor, her bare feet the only contact with the ground. Hugo didn't touch her, but he looked for signs of a struggle, scratches or cuts on her arms and hands. He saw nothing, just the limp, dangling limbs of a dead woman leaving no clue whether she died by her own hand, or by those of another.

Lerens seemed to sense his *douleur*. "Let's wait outside, Hugo. Let the forensics people do their thing. We can look for a suicide note on the way out."

"What are the odds of finding one of those?" he asked quietly.

"I don't know," Lerens said. "But either way I'm done making bets for today."

CHAPTER THIRTY-THREE

They pulled on surgical gloves, and, on the way out of Maxick's apartment, gave it a cursory search. Anything more thorough risked contaminating the place. Whatever was there would stay there for them to find later, but both Hugo and Camille knew that another death would have their higher-ups howling for a result, and standing by while the forensics people did their painstaking work was, well, painful.

They left the bedroom completely alone, walking through to the living room, where Hugo stood in front of a bookcase. As expected, Maxick had a complete collection of Helen Hancock's books. He felt that sadness again, this time at having to tell Helen that her friend was dead. Another friend.

Hugo picked out the last book in the series and opened it to the acknowledgments page. He smiled to himself when he saw the kind words Hancock wrote about her friend. *Many thanks to my friend and hostess, Jill Maxick, who gives me a place to stay, room to write, and the encouragement to discover ever more of Paris. Thank you for sharing this beautiful city with me.*

Apparently Hancock had forgotten to thank her for helping with research. Hugo picked up a file on the shelf below the books and leafed through it. Glancing at the photocopied pages, it looked like Maxick had done some looking into French civil law, presumably giving Hancock enough knowledge to ask sensible questions of the law firm. That made sense, considering Helen's French was good enough to get around the city but unlikely to stretch to deciphering specific and technical legal terms.

Under the legal papers were some printouts of information about exotic poisons, one of which had made it into the manuscript that Hugo had just perused.

He put the folder back and pulled out a photograph album. Maxick had scrawled the date on the inside cover, almost exactly one year previously. A lot of the photos were artistic, and really quite good, shots of Paris, in both color and in black and white. Some contained Maxick herself, and friends Hugo didn't recognize. Except one.

"Camille, check this out," he said quietly.

"What is it?"

"A photo. Several of them, in fact."

She started toward him from the kitchen. "Of what?"

"Not *what*, but *who*."

Lerens reached his side and peered at the open pages. "Are they . . . ?"

"I don't know. They certainly look like more than friends."

"Turn the page," she said.

Hugo did, and they both stared at the top picture on the right page, a color shot of two people, arm in arm and smiling at the camera on Pont des Arts, bundled up in winter coats, their eyes shining with happiness. One of those people was Jill Maxick. The other was Lionel Colbert.

"First time I've seen the guy smile," Hugo said. "And, what a surprise, another relationship hidden from us."

But it made sense. Colbert was the one covering her shift, despite not being a hotel manager. And she was the one helping him move into his new room. Lerens gave him another reason it added up.

"You know she was kind of into you, right?" she said. "I mean, it wasn't hard to see. That might explain his attitude toward you."

"No, I didn't notice that," he said. "But I suppose you're right, that might explain Colbert's attitude. Anyway, make sure to seize these albums." He held up a hand of apology. "I know, I know, I don't have to tell you."

Lerens gave him a look. "No, you don't. And I'll have the autopsy done as soon as possible, too."

"Sorry, force of habit."

"That's OK." She looked at the bookcase. "Is there anything else here that you've seen and think I should take?"

"Yes," Hugo said, tapping the folder. "This research for Helen Hancock, just in case."

"Maxick helped her do research?"

"With technical stuff written in French, yes." He turned and stared at Lerens, a thought flowering in his mind. "*Merde*, Camille, I need to get back to my office. Can Paul take me?"

"*Bien sûr.* What's going on?"

"Just an idea." Hugo held up a quieting finger. "And yes, one of those I don't want to share just yet, sorry."

"Well, as soon as you do, I'd better be the first to hear it."

"If it amounts to anything, yes, you have my word."

Lerens nodded, walked to the door, and called out. "*Jameson, vous êtes là?*"

Jameson's voice came back at them. "*Oui, je suis là.* I'm creating the crime-scene log."

"Give that to someone else. Our genius here has an idea he doesn't wish to share, and he needs you to take him back to his office."

Hugo joined them in the hallway. "Now, Camille, you know how I work."

"Doesn't mean I have to like it," she said.

"I'm ready," Jameson said. He winked at Hugo. "And I can get the information out of him on the way, if you like, boss."

"Beat it out of him?" Lerens asked.

"Ach, no. I'll drive really slowly unless and until he coughs it up."

They were all joking, of course, a dash of levity at a moment it was needed, and there was no question that Jameson would get Hugo safely to the embassy as soon as possible, but Hugo was pleased when the policeman activated the lights on his car to cut a swathe through the dawdling weekend traffic.

When Hugo got to the security offices, Emma was gone. Presumably home, but if Hugo had to guess, she'd have taken a circuitous route to delay her arrival. He woke up his computer and clicked on the e-mail she'd sent him.

Hugo, here's all I found out, no clue if it's helpful or not. If you have more questions or need different information, you can always order me back to the office, I'll forgive you . . .

Hugo shook his head and smiled. *I'm sure you would.* He kept reading.

Looks like Helen was right, her sales have been dipping in recent years, and her publisher has no idea how to handle this new scandal. My contact said she was going to get a new contract but a smaller advance, which some writers don't mind because it means they start earning royalties sooner. (If you don't know how all that works, I can explain. Either tomorrow or call my cell. Bottom line: a smaller advance can be a blow to the ego, but not necessarily to the pocketbook.) But even though it might still do so, the video has not led to an explosion in sales. As you can imagine, it's been quite the topic in the publishing world. Some people bought into the "no such thing as bad publicity" idea, but that's not been the case. Poor Helen, that could've been one silver lining for her in all of this .

Oh, and the answer to the last question you sent me is yes. It should be on the thumb drive Camille Lerens's expert gave you, I'd imagine.

Like I said, holler if you need anything else, I'm at your disposal . . . ;)

Hugo picked up his desk phone and called Ambassador Taylor. It rang five times before Taylor answered, and he was less than happy.

"Dammit, Hugo, I told you to stop working on weekends; you make the rest of us look bad."

"Lazy is as lazy does, boss. Even Emma was in here today, you know."

"I don't care, and you're not getting raises, either of you. Now, what do you need?"

"A favor. A big one."

"Get Tom to do it."

"He's out of pocket right now. Plus it's legal, so he wouldn't really be interested."

"Legal, well that's a start," Taylor said.

"Yes, literally."

"I'm not following."

"I want you to sue someone," Hugo said.

A moment of silence. "OK, so now I'm following you even less than I was before."

"It's pretty straightforward. I'll give you the name of the law firm I want you to use," Hugo said. "And then first thing tomorrow I want you to sue Helen Hancock."

CHAPTER THIRTY-FOUR

Hugo hated waiting. Technology was amazing, forensic medicine was incredible, and the officers of the French police and Brigade Criminelle were among the finest he'd ever worked with.

And yet he was still waiting. Tom, Ambassador Taylor, and Camille would be calling anytime, but until then . . . Yes, he was tired, but even so it wasn't the calm he wanted, but the storm. It came just after noon on Monday, a deluge onto the streets of Paris, heavy raindrops pounding the pavement and all but cutting off the view from his top-floor apartment. The rain made him feel even more claustrophobic, more anxious, and the weather app on his phone promising sunshine that afternoon was only a slight comfort.

Finally, at two o'clock, Camille Lerens called. He snatched up his phone, which he'd left plugged in for fear the battery might somehow drain itself.

"Camille, hey. You have news?"

"The autopsy. You want me to e-mail the report?"

"Just give me the highlights."

"*D'accord*," she said. "Let me just pull it up on my screen. OK, cause of death was combined asphyxia and venal congestion. The noose part of the belt was high up on her throat, hence asphyxia as well as the blood flow being cut off. She died quickly where we found her, Hugo, and Dr. Sprengelmeyer says everything is consistent with suicide."

"Meaning?"

"Meaning the head congestion, the petechial hemorrhages in the eyes, and the fact that he's never seen a case of murder by hanging. And if he did, he'd expect to see signs of a struggle, which he didn't."

"I'd expect to see that, too," Hugo conceded.

"The only odd thing he found were some pink fibers. There were some on the floor of the closet, and several on her forearms."

"I don't remember any pink blankets or . . . anything else pink in her apartment."

"I know," Lerens said. "She didn't seem the girly, pink-dresses kind of woman. And when we went back and looked, we didn't see anything that would have produced them."

"So where did they come from?"

"Sprengelmeyer had no idea."

Hugo thought for a moment. "You know, I might," he said. "Can you e-mail me the report?"

"What are you thinking?"

"Does it have a diagram? In fact, are there photos from the autopsy?"

"Yes to both questions," Lerens said. "Now can you tell me what you're thinking?"

Hugo checked the display of his phone when it buzzed. "Later. My boss is calling, I gotta take this."

"I'll send you the report and photos," Lerens said testily. "Then I want some answers."

"You got it." Hugo disconnected from her and connected with Ambassador Taylor. "Hey, boss."

"You want to tell me what's going on?"

"Why do people keep asking me that?"

"Because you have these hare-brained ideas that seem to come out of nowhere, and you run off after them leaving everyone else to try and catch up." Taylor sighed. "And, most annoying of all, you're usually right."

"In that case, let me guess. They wouldn't do it."

"What the . . . How did you know that?"

"What did they tell you?"

"The law firm said that they already represent her. I guess they run what they call a 'conflicts check' for every new client and every new potential defendant, so they don't end up suing someone they represent, or representing someone they're suing. All law firms do it, apparently. Anyway, when they did that, her name popped up as a client, so they can't help me sue her. Although, frankly, I still have no idea why you want me to."

"I don't."

"What?" Taylor sounded truly annoyed now. "Then why the hell would you make me go to the trouble of—?"

"Because I needed to know what you just told me," Hugo said. He was clicking on his computer, bringing up a video.

"Why?" Taylor demanded. "And what the hell is next?"

"Why will be made clear very soon. And as for what's next, well, it's me watching porn on the State Department's laptop." Hugo leaned forward to study the clip of two people having sex, his eyes not on the action but on the periphery. "Bingo," he said.

"Hugo, I'm starting to lose patience with being treated like a mushroom."

"Mushroom?"

"Being kept in the dark and fed a load of horse shit."

Hugo chuckled and sat back in his chair. "I have to think a few things through," he said. "But how about we do this old-school?"

"Do what?" Taylor said, exasperation plain in his voice.

"Well, this is all about Helen, right?"

"I don't know, is it?"

"It is, and that gives me an idea."

"Hugo, if there's a killer out there, if you know who it is, we can't be playing games. I'm serious, call Lerens and have him or her arrested. Then we can sit around while you tell us how smart you are."

"That's the point," Hugo said, smiling. "You trust me, right? And don't worry, I wouldn't suggest this if I thought there was any more danger to anyone."

"Oh, so the killer's dead, eh? Jill Maxick killed Baxter, Silva, and then herself."

"Now who's figuring it all out?" Hugo said. "Meet me at the hotel at five o'clock."

"Wait, if that's the answer, why can't you just say so?"

"Simple," Hugo said. "You missed one little piece of the puzzle."

CHAPTER THIRTY-FIVE

Hugo knew he was pushing his luck. But he also knew everyone was safe, and he really did want to do it this way. He wanted everyone in the same place so he could see their reactions, make sure he hadn't missed anything—particularly another relationship between the various parties, something that might reveal itself with a look or a shift of the body. With a suspect pool this small and with the relationships secret and intertwined, he couldn't be too careful. Plus, Camille Lerens was humoring him, and he couldn't have done this without her agreement.

They gathered in the hotel's conservatory, all eight of them: Hugo, Ambassador Taylor, Camille Lerens, Paul Jameson, Helen Hancock, Lionel Colbert, Michael Rice, and Buzzy Pottgen. Outside were four plainclothes officers, lounging in the courtyard, keeping a subtle eye on the gathering just in case. And twelve more uniformed officers were guarding the exits of the hotel, placed by Lieutenant Lerens just in case. Only with all that security had she agreed to Hugo's idea. The two cameras recording the event were also her idea, and a fitting touch after the secret recordings of Helen Hancock, Hugo thought.

He watched everyone as they took their seats, trying to read their expressions. Buzzy Pottgen was curious, her gaze flitting around the group and then lingering on Hugo, the way he was accustomed to her doing. Mike Rice was curious, too, but trying not to show it. Calm and poised, he sat down and looked at Hugo.

"Not serving us tea?" he asked.

"Maybe later," Hugo said, standing to let Helen Hancock slide past him.

"You didn't say other people would be here," she said to Hugo.

"Sorry about that," Hugo replied, and watched her settle on the sofa beside Buzzy. Jameson perched himself on the thick arm, giving Buzzy a small smile when she looked up at him.

Lionel Colbert was the last to arrive, and the least happy. He dropped down into a wicker chair and draped one leg over the arm. He glared at Hugo and then Lerens, and Hugo reminded himself that despite his tough-guy stance, they all knew about Jill Maxick's death, which meant this man had just lost someone he cared about.

When everyone was seated, Hugo began. "Thanks for coming. This is an unusual situation, but I felt like everyone deserved an explanation of what's been going on."

"If you know," Colbert said, "shouldn't you start by saying, 'You're probably wondering why I've gathered you all here . . .'?"

"Perhaps," Hugo said. "But this isn't a game. Three people are dead, and their killer needs to be brought to justice."

"Sounds like you're wanting to bring Thomas back from Germany," Colbert said.

"Hey, laddie," Jameson said quietly. "Shut yer trap and listen."

"Thomas left not because he'd done anything wrong," Hugo went on, "but because he's scared. Fortunately, there will be no more murders."

"How do you know?" Rice asked.

"Because the killer is in this room."

"What the . . ." Colbert said. "Are you fucking kidding me?"

"No," Hugo answered calmly.

Helen spoke up, and Hugo saw that she was pale, scared. "Wait, I thought Jill was the one who . . ." Her voice trailed off.

"She killed Andrew Baxter, yes. And there's a chance that she killed Ambrósio Silva, but I'm not so sure about that." Hugo's eyes roamed the group. "I was hoping the person responsible for his death would fill in that part for me." He paused for effect, and everyone looked around at each other.

Helen Hancock spoke first. "Hugo, why are you doing this?"

"I'll answer that later, I think," Hugo said. He didn't want them on guard. If he was wrong and there was another angle to this, he wanted to see it come out as he spoke. "Let's just say it seems appropriate given the setting and the people involved."

"Well, it seems cruel to me," Pottgen said. "I mean, you've put me in a room with a killer; how's that a good idea?"

"No one can hurt you, believe me," Hugo said. "You might be feeling a little uncomfortable right about now, but no one here is in any danger. And since every one of you has, at some point in this investigation, lied to me or withheld important information, I don't feel too bad about making you uncomfortable."

"How do you know we're not in danger?" Hancock asked. "You didn't frisk us or anything."

"I know because Jill Maxick was murdered. And because her murder was much more planned out than Ambrósio Silva's was. Our killer isn't the compulsive or immediately lethal type of person. No, more of a 'careful plotter.'" Hugo cast his eyes over each of the guests, Taylor, Hancock, Pottgen, Colbert, and Rice, watching carefully for any physical response to his revelations.

"Hugo, seriously, cut to the chase," Ambassador Taylor said.

"I will. Starting with Andrew Baxter's murder. He was killed because he bought the spy camera that went into Helen's room. Poor guy probably had no idea that's what it was going to be used for; he was just on a paid errand for someone who knew he needed money."

"You're saying his murder was carefully planned?" Taylor asked.

"Yes. Made to look ambiguous, though, like it could have been a crime of passion, or even a gambling-related murder."

"And Silva's murder?" Taylor asked.

"Like I said, not as well planned. Cleverly carried out, though, for sure. Again, ambiguous enough and with countermeasures to allow for some confusion on our part, right, Camille?"

"'Confusion' might be a little strong," she said. "'Uncertainty,' perhaps."

"Fair enough," Hugo said. "Uncertainty it is."

"So who killed him and why, smart guy?" Colbert snapped.

"I think Silva was killed because he found out what was going on. Maybe he wanted in, maybe he was going to tell the police, we might never know."

"And what *is* going on?" Pottgen asked. "What did Ambrósio figure out?"

"Let me get straight to the point," Hugo said. He'd noticed Lerens fidgeting, like she suddenly thought this wasn't a great idea, and he didn't want her pulling the plug or getting into trouble for it, plus, he wanted to make absolutely sure that there were no more surprise relationships that might indicate that his suspicions were misguided. "This is about money. Specifically a lawsuit that was going to be filed in the near future."

"This is about suing Helen?" Taylor ventured.

"No," Hugo said. "It's about Helen suing the hotel."

"But I'm not." All eyes swiveled to her, and she looked around. "I mean, I was thinking about it, yes, but I haven't."

"Not yet," Hugo said. "And the truth is, you were thinking about it a full year before the spy camera was put in your room, a full year before the tape appeared online. And you told Jill about your plan, because you needed her help."

"Wait," Taylor said. "You're saying Helen is . . . ?"

"Yes," Hugo said. "She's responsible for all of this, for everything that's happened—to Baxter, Silva, and Maxick." Hugo watched, scanning the group for their reactions. Surprise was the only one he saw, reassuring him that nobody else was party to this macabre plot. So he continued, "And for the sake of the legal case that will be built in the coming weeks, I suggest, Lieutenant Lerens, now would be the best time to escort Ms. Hancock to a police car and your headquarters."

Helen Hancock had turned ghost-white, and everyone in the room stared as she rose slowly to her feet. Her mouth opened and closed, but nothing came out, and it was only the quick reflexes of Lionel Colbert that stopped her from cracking her head on the tile floor when she fainted.

CHAPTER THIRTY-SIX

They gathered at the prefecture the next morning and did things properly, by the book, and Lieutenant Lerens was a lot more comfortable. Hugo was, too, in truth. He'd been grateful for the lieutenant's cooperation the previous day, but he'd also known it wasn't a game, and he didn't want to jeopardize their case. He'd not seen anything in that room to counter his theory that Hancock and Maxick had been the only ones in on the scheme, which is why he'd ended the confrontation as soon as he could. He'd always tried to help the victims of murder maintain dignity, and he was loathe to veer away from that principle. Maintain dignity, too, even for Helen Hancock, despite everything.

Hugo looked through the one-way glass at her, sitting beside her appointed lawyer at a small metal table, waiting, seemingly unperturbed now, but her fainting spell at the hotel was telling. She'd said it was the shock of a false allegation, but Hugo knew otherwise. Either she'd faked it for her own dramatic purposes, or she'd been unable to bear the idea that her callous scheme was about to put her in prison, possibly for the rest of her life.

The door behind him opened, and Camille Lerens stood there. "You have friends in high places. Plus, you're our best English speaker, so my boss says you're in. Let's go see what she has to say."

They introduced themselves to the lawyer, Charlee Brissette, who was one of the best in the city, according to Lerens. Hugo had been warned by several people not to be fooled by the attractive brunette's friendly and relaxed demeanor. And her English was impeccable.

"My client says you have made a mistake and is willing to hear you out," she said.

"Hear *us* out?" Hugo said. "I think we'd like to know what she has to say."

"About what?" Brissette said. "You have accused her of murder. She has very little to say about it, because she is innocent."

"No," Hugo said gently. "She's not."

Brissette raised a perfect eyebrow. "And what evidence do you have to support that statement? What is, as we lawyers say, your theory of the case?"

Hugo looked directly at Helen Hancock, who was staring at the table. "My theory is that due to declining book sales, a smaller advance that hurt her pride, and the chance that her French publisher had stopped paying for perks like her hotel room, Helen placed a spy camera in her room with Jill Maxick's help. She seduced Ambrósio Silva and made sure that film of them having sex made it to the Internet. She was then going to take advantage of France's very favorable privacy laws to sue a wealthy and proud hotel chain, and settle for a very large sum of money."

"Quite a theory," Brissette said.

"Quite a plan," Hugo corrected. "And it had the possible side benefit of boosting her sales, assuming the theory that 'there's no such thing as bad publicity' is true. Which hasn't proven to be the case, but it wasn't the main goal."

"My client was humiliated by that tape. To suggest that she was behind its publication is ridiculous."

"Not really," Hugo said mildly. "I didn't watch it at first. Didn't see the need. I mean, a sex tape is a sex tape, right? Except I did have to watch it eventually, once I connected the dots. And I noticed that while she was obviously naked, there are no graphic moments of her on the video. Almost like she knew it was being recorded and was preserving her modesty as best she could."

"Pure supposition," Brissette said.

"Perhaps. But what isn't pure supposition is the pair of fur-lined handcuffs visible on the tape." Helen Hancock's head snapped up, but she stayed silent, so Hugo continued. "Now, I can't prove this just yet; we'll have to wait for the forensics people to do their bit, but I remember Jill describing the video to me right after it was uploaded. She mentioned vibrators and furry handcuffs were visible, so I went back and looked at the tape, to see for myself. And, sure enough, just like most of those I've come across in my life, yours are pink. I'm betting the fibers found on Jill Maxick's body and in her closet will match those from your handcuffs."

"You can't test for that," Brissette said, but her tone was unsure.

"We'll find out, won't we?" He looked at Hancock. " How did you do it, Helen?"

"I didn't do anything," the writer said, her voice wobbling.

"Yeah, you did. Did you go over there and ask her to help with more research? Let me guess, 'Put these on for a moment so I can see how someone with handcuffs walks'? Or maybe you had her lay on the ground and told her to try to get up while wearing them? That'd be a good one, laying her on the ground, cuffed. You wouldn't have to be strong with a knee in her back, would you?"

"I didn't . . ." But her voice dropped off, like she didn't even believe herself.

"I'm guessing that's what happened. You had her put on the cuffs and lay down on the floor, and then you surprised her. Your weight on her back and a plastic bag over her head, is that it? It's amazing how quickly someone can pass out from suffocation or strangulation. And then you just moved her into the closet to stage the hanging, except it's not so much staged because that's what killed her. Inventive, I have to say."

"Why would my client kill Jill Maxick?" Brissette demanded. "That's absurd."

"For one, very simple reason. She's not good at sharing. Maybe there's more to it. It's possible that Maxick got greedy and wanted a larger slice of the pie than they had initially agreed to . . . but it comes down to the same thing: Helen wanted to keep her murderous secret to herself, and she had no desire to share the proceeds of this scheme. She doesn't like to share. She happened to mention that to me more than once, which I found interesting."

Brissette looked at him. "Why would a casual remark like that be interesting, exactly?"

"People assume it's the lies that catch people out, and sometimes it is. But I've noticed that when people are lying, trying to deceive and sell a story or an image, they rely a lot on the truth. After all, the truth is easier to remember, right? But like tics, or tells, when someone repeats something about themselves like Helen did, I try to notice. She told me twice that she doesn't share. In the moment, it didn't mean anything and so I took it to be true."

"That seems like a leap," Brissette said.

"Maybe. On the other hand, she was looking at getting millions of euros from a lawsuit; why give half to someone else? Think about it. Who was naked in front of the world? Whose plan was this? It was Helen's body online for the world to see, and her idea. I can easily see why she'd resent sharing. And not only does she lose all that money, but someone who knows she planned this is alive and kicking. Like I said, maybe Jill demanded a larger share, got greedy. Maybe she threatened to blackmail Helen for a larger share. Maybe Helen lives in an imaginary world where no one else matters, not really."

Hugo paused, and they sat in silence for a moment. Then Camille Lerens said, "Anything you want to say, Madame Hancock?"

"It's not true, any of it," she said, her voice still weak, her eyes again fixed on the table between them.

"Then explain why you have a letter from an attorney named Lisa Bowlin Hobbs who works for the international law firm of Kuhn Hobbs. In that letter, she advises you on libel, slander, and especially on issues of privacy law."

"It was research," Hancock said. Brissette put a hand on her arm.

"Yeah, I knew you'd say that. The thing is, Helen, the letter is dated about a year ago. Your manuscript makes no mention of any kind of civil law about privacy or defamation. Nothing like that."

"Stories change. Authors always go in different directions than they intended," Brissette said. "You can't seriously suggest that because my client didn't stick to her original story idea, she's guilty of murder?"

"But here's the thing. I checked, and most authors, including Helen—contrary to what she told me—turn in story ideas to their editors. That's how they get new book deals." *Thank you Emma, for your publishing contacts*, Hugo thought. "So, with her publisher's cooperation, I looked at her proposals for future stories. None of them had a story about privacy laws. Especially in France. None. And on top of that, I know this wasn't friendly research, because Kuhn Hobbs represents you. You are a current client, which I found out when I tried to have someone sue you. They wouldn't take the case; they were conflicted out. That doesn't happen with casual, friendly research. Now, I don't know if we can subpoena their correspondence with you—"

"You can't," Brissette snapped.

"I think with a warrant we can," Lerens said. "Evidence relating to the planning of a murder is unlikely to survive attorney-client privilege."

"It would," Brissette said. "If such evidence existed, which it doesn't. All I hear is guesswork."

Hugo turned to Lerens. "You have the handcuffs?"

"Yes, we do."

He turned back to Helen Hancock and her lawyer. "Good, then the forensics will give us a little more than 'guesswork.' They'll start by matching the pink fibers, and I'm pretty sure we'll find Jill's DNA on them."

Helen Hancock's head fell, and she muttered something unintelligible to herself.

Brissette looked at Hugo. "And what's your theory on why she would have killed Monsieur Silva?"

Hugo spoke to Hancock directly. "That was some clever thinking, to steal the gun. What happened, did he figure out what you were up to?"

"Address your questions and comments to me, please," Brissette said firmly.

Hugo ignored her, but when he spoke his voice was softer. "I bet that was the hardest of them, wasn't it, Helen? He could be a hothead, but you genuinely liked him. That's why you got possessive of him with Buzzy. This was more than just a fling, wasn't it? But why kill him? Did he demand a cut? Threaten to blackmail you?"

Hancock's head snapped up. "No! He's not like that!"

Hugo sat back. "No, he wasn't. He wanted you to turn yourself in, didn't he?"

It was the slightest of movements and it stayed in her eyes, nothing that the cameras would catch, but it was there: a recognition of her lover's decency, a tribute to him meant only for Hugo to see.

Charlee Brissette looked at Hancock, then at Hugo and Camille Lerens. "I think this interview is over. I need some time alone with my client."

The policewoman nodded, then stood. "This is Lieutenant Camille Lerens, terminating the interview at nine forty-three a.m."

CHAPTER THIRTY-SEVEN

"**I**'m pretty sure we don't need to be quite so formal," Hugo said. "We could do this in bed, no? Like pillow talk?"

"No, we most certainly could not." Two days later they were in his office, Claudia sitting across from him and about to switch on her recorder. "Look," she said, "you promised me an interview and the full story. I've kept my mouth shut until now, or my computer closed—whatever. Fact is, you owe me and I'm not waiting any longer."

"Fine, fine," Hugo said. He sat back in his chair and swung his feet onto the desk. "Where do we start?"

"Who did you suspect first, Jill Maxick or Helen Hancock?"

Hugo furrowed his brow. "It doesn't work like that. You journalists are so linear with your storytelling that you assume the investigative process is the same way. It's not. I don't figure out one thing and then plod along to the next clue, I just don't."

"Then tell me how it works, Mr. Patronizing."

Hugo gave her a sheepish smile. "Sorry, didn't mean to be."

"Forgiven, just don't do it again."

"Alright, I'll try." Hugo composed his thoughts. "I try to rule people out. With alibis, preferably—put them somewhere else at the time of the crime. Narrowing the pool of suspects is always the best way to go. Given the rotating staff of the Sorbonne Hotel, that was difficult in this case, with the exception of Helen being at the spa when Andrew Baxter was killed. And because of that, like the idiot I am, purely on the

271

basis of her alibi for that murder, I had ruled her out of being involved in the subsequent murders."

"Hardly surprising."

"Maybe. Anyway, later a few things made me look at her twice, a whole spaghetti of things that's hard to describe. One of those things, though, was that all of this centered around her. Which might have meant she was just the target, of course, but nobody appeared to be trying to blackmail, threaten, or plagiarize her. In the end, I simply couldn't find enough alternative connections to make her anything but a suspect."

"I don't understand. Connections?"

"Yes," Hugo said. "Between the other people. Especially between Baxter and any of the writing group, Helen included. The only link to him was that he purchased the spy camera and we found in his locker a wiped-down laptop containing surveillance videos from Hancock's room. But we knew that the laptop could have been planted, especially since the sex tape was leaked after Baxter's death. So, really, there was no definitive connection between the writers and him at all."

"I'm still not getting it . . ."

"In my mind, that lack of connection to Baxter ruled out Pottgen, Silva, and Rice, who had no reason to even know the guy," Hugo said. "And given that Helen had virtually nothing to do with Lionel Colbert or Thomas Prehn, I couldn't see them being involved."

"Leaving you with Helen Hancock herself?"

"Right. I'm doing a poor job explaining, I'm sure, but what I'm trying to say is that it became clear to me that Jill and Helen were the hubs of this particular spinning wheel. What I didn't get until later was the strength of the connection between them. It crystallized for me when I remembered the day the sex tape appeared online." Hugo shook his head as he pictured the scene. "I was at the hotel. I arrived just as Helen was storming out of Jill's office. She'd gone down to confront Jill about the tape, the spy camera, to tell her that the video was online for everyone to see."

"OK," Claudia said. "But—"

"Hang on, this is the important bit. You see, Helen stormed off, leaving Jill and me there, so of course I asked what was wrong and Jill told me. It didn't click at the time, annoyingly, but she told me what was on the tape. The details about the sex and the toys and . . . well, the details."

"Oh," Claudia said, her eyes widening. "I see what you mean."

"Right. If Helen had just told her about it that moment, if that was the first Jill knew of the sex tape, how did Jill know all of those details? She couldn't have."

"Unless she was the one who recorded it, who uploaded it."

"Exactly. Camille's forensics people are scrubbing her computer right now, so I'm betting they'll find something. But, yes, I think that's right."

"What about the second camera they found?" Claudia asked.

"A distraction, pure and simple. An attempt at a smoke screen."

"Makes sense. So what made you suspect Hancock? Jill was responsible for the distribution of the sex tape, and she pinned it on Baxter. But how did Helen become a suspect?"

"You know," Hugo said. "A lot of the time we find incriminating evidence to connect a suspect to the crime. But every now and again there's a telling lack of evidence in a case. Like I said before, a lack of a link between Helen and Baxter, but most of all a total lack of any reason for someone to spy on Helen. There was no blackmail attempt—she'd not hurt or cheated anyone. So why publish that video? And obviously it wasn't Baxter who did it; he was dead by then."

"I have no idea," Claudia said.

"I didn't either. So I thought about it from the other angle. The benefit side rather than the harm angle. And the only person I could think of who might benefit was Helen Hancock." Hugo shrugged. "Maybe Silva, too, as association with a celebrity might make it easier to land an agent, but that seemed pretty remote. He was already associated with her, was friends and lovers with her. He didn't need to do this. Which left Helen."

"Maybe," Claudia said dubiously. "But her lawyer's already playing the humiliation card for the press."

"Of course. The exact card Helen was going to play for the French courts. This country's privacy laws are very strict, and very punitive for those who violate them. Helen herself told me that suing was 'a good way to an easy buck.' Her exact words. And from her contact with the lawyer, she knew how true that was when suing a place like the Sorbonne Hotel for such an incredible violation of her privacy."

"And, this being France," Claudia added, "while it was embarrassing, it might have helped her career here because we don't care about that, about people having sex." She pulled a face. "Not like you prudish Americans."

"Hey, if you recall, I suggested we conduct this interview in bed."

"Hugo!" She reached forward and clicked off the recorder. "My editors might listen to this; be professional!"

Hugo laughed. "I'm sorry, my dear, but you deserved that."

"Maybe," Claudia said with a frown. "Now then, if I turn it back on, will you behave?"

"Yes, I promise."

She rewound the recording and stopped it just before Hugo's suggestive remark, then hit Record. She winked at him, and asked, "So what else?"

"Once the picture began to take shape, the little things started to make sense. The things that earlier had nagged at me but not loudly enough for me to focus on them. Like how Baxter had a computer only for these videos. For a man who always needed money, it made no sense for him to buy a second computer just for surveillance. And the ease of finding it, along with the books by Helen, without even a password on it? I mean, it was like a trail of very large breadcrumbs."

"Just a little too obvious?"

"In hindsight, yes. So it came down to a lack of connections and, oddly, very obvious—planted—clues. For instance, why would she drive all the way out to the funeral to meet me?"

"I have no idea."

"I think it was because she wanted to see for herself the person who'd be helping her, the person she was trying to fool."

"Right. And what about Ambrósio Silva? She had to seduce and manipulate him, too. She played both of you. But why do you think she killed him? Or did she have Jill do that?"

"I believe Helen murdered both Silva and Maxick herself. And staged both to appear as suicides. Of course, we're still waiting on forensics to confirm that she killed Maxick. As for Silva . . . that one we may never solve conclusively, unfortunately. I'm fairly sure he figured out what Helen was doing, and, if he did, he'd surely confront her." Hugo's shoulders slumped as he imagined the sad scene. "I think she stole Hunter S. Thompson's gun, then persuaded Silva to go for a walk by the river, which is where she shot him. Tying the gun to a rock and tossing it in the Seine was a nice literary trick designed to throw us off, and precisely the kind of thing a writer would come up with. Conveniently for her, Silva was an avid Holmes fan. Her distraction played to the possibility that he would commit suicide with a literary flourish like that. Furthermore, it erased any physical evidence of her involvement."

Claudia shook her head. "I still can't believe she is so cold-blooded."

"Well, I think she truly had feelings for Silva. He might have started out as a pawn, but eventually she grew to at least care for him. She didn't like sharing him with Buzzy and asked him to end that relationship. . . . Who knows? Maybe she'll confess." Hugo sighed heavily. "But that's probably unlikely. After all, if my suspicions are right and he tried to get her to come clean in the first place, look what happened to him. He took a bullet to the heart for it."

"If you're right, if Helen really did kill both Silva and Maxick, what will happen to her?"

"You'd have to ask Lieutenant Camille Lerens that question, or the examining magistrate. No doubt politics will play a role, but that's beyond me, especially right now."

"Do you feel sorry for her?" Claudia asked.

"No, not in the slightest," Hugo said. "She caused the deaths of three people, directly murdered two of them." He frowned. "I learned a long time ago that the time for sympathy is when someone's in a difficult position, as Helen was with her career, but they're trying to turn things around by working hard. Not by manipulating people. If you start treating other people as expendable, then no. No sympathy."

"But she must have felt pretty desperate," Claudia persisted.

"Desperate? Only when things started to go wrong. She absolutely was when she had to cover up her plan. Until then, she was just a famous author with a fragile ego." He waved a dismissive hand. "Sure, her career was taking a dip, but, good Lord, is that ever a reason to hurt other people? Kill them, even?"

"Maybe when you spend half your life in a fantasy world . . ."

"I think you're trying to understand Helen's motivations or mindset," Hugo said. "But it doesn't make sense to people like you and me. It never will. For Helen, her entire identity was wrapped up in being this famous, wealthy, successful author. We don't have that problem, and by ascribing reasons for her actions to her I wouldn't want you, or anyone, to somehow turn that into an excuse or justification for what she did."

"I'm not," Claudia insisted. "Like you said, I think I'm just trying to understand. Killing two people to somehow further her slightly fading book career—it doesn't make sense to me."

"You're looking at it wrong," Hugo said gently. "I don't suppose she set out to murder anyone; that was never part of her plot. In fact, when I talked with her and her students about who plotted their stories and who made it up as they went along, she said she was a plotter. But she made a point of saying that things didn't always go as planned; and, while I didn't think much of it then, maybe I should have."

"If she didn't plan this the way it ended . . ." Claudia shook her head. "It was some kind of mistake?"

"In a way. Don't get me wrong—she made conscious choices every step of the way. And every step of the way, she could have stopped this from getting worse. But I suspect a few things happened that she hadn't predicted. Maxick killing Andrew Baxter, Silva finding out about that . . . I just don't know. But this particular story—dreamed up by a writer with a vivid imagination, remember—probably just began with a spy camera and a few red faces. Followed by an increase in book sales, a slightly saucier reputation, and a lawsuit to bring in more cash."

"But when things got out of control, she continued to spin stories, to hide the truth to save herself."

"Exactly," Hugo said. "She had two ways to run. Back toward the truth, which would have been humiliating and maybe would have landed her in jail. Or away from it, which was the safer and easier path in the short term, but it meant lots of small, unanticipated steps that led to the murder of two people, and a woman increasingly desperate to save herself."

"Amazing," Claudia said. "One quite clever idea, the camera in the painting, led to a landslide."

"I wish she'd just done the tape thing," Hugo said quietly. "Paid an actor and done that as a stunt."

"Why?"

"Because despite what she told us, that videotape helped her."

"How do you know?" Claudia asked.

"A week ago, when she and I first met, she told me that it wasn't even a sure thing that her new book would be published here in France. Since then, since the tape, they've inked a deal for its publication here."

"How do you know?"

"Michael Rice told me; he met with her editor, and she was raving about Helen. And it's interesting, don't you think, that a publishing deal for that new book slipped Helen's mind whenever she was talking to me or the police?"

"That does seem odd," Claudia agreed. "If she's innocent, that is."

"Right. Also odd was the fact that Helen would not change hotels after being spied on at the Sorbonne Hotel *and* after a murder happened there. I suggested that Camille check the hotel records and see exactly how much Helen was paying for that room, and for how long."

"Why?"

"Because I'm betting it was free from the moment she got here. Hotel managers have a lot of discretion when it comes to comping rooms, especially at nice hotels like the Sorbonne, and double especially when it comes to celebrity clients."

"So there's no question in your mind that Jill Maxick was involved?" Claudia asked.

"None. I mean, quite apart from the fact that she wound up dead, it's pretty clear that she killed Baxter. And she was the one who had unlimited access to all of the rooms. She's the one who planted the first laptop in Baxter's locker and then put compromising files onto his actual laptop and hid it in Colbert's stuff. It wasn't a coincidence that she was there when Leo dropped the box and it spilled out."

"They were dating..." Claudia said.

"Which made it even easier for her to access his belongings. And why would she have the same legal research in her apartment as Helen had?"

"Yes, that *is* hard to explain otherwise."

"As his manager, she could have Baxter show up anywhere she wanted in the hotel, at any time," Hugo pointed out. "And with all my worry about connections, she's the only one. The *only* one connecting Helen and Baxter. Think about it. Why would he go buy a spy camera for anyone else? I imagine she said it was for hotel security, the poor guy."

"They used him."

"Yes, they did. Took advantage of a nice guy with a gambling problem. And, speaking of addictions, I noticed something small but interesting about Helen's drinking. You remember when we first met her?"

"At the church, yes. You thought she'd had a sip or two."

"Exactly. The first few times I met with her, she seemed to be tipsy at least. But lately she has been sober. With all that's going on, if she had a genuine drinking problem you'd have expected her to up the intake. Instead, she cut back. Why?"

"Because she needed to keep her wits about her," Claudia suggested.

"Precisely. Enough that she came up with the plan for Silva's murder—to steal the gun from the library and devise a literary distraction with a Sherlock Holmes twist." Hugo swung his legs off his desk as a figure appeared in the doorway. "Camille, come in, but beware, Mademoiselle Roux has her digital recorder on."

Lerens moved into the room, and Claudia turned, her mouth falling open. "Wait, what's going on?"

"What?" Lerens said. "You've never seen me out of uniform?"

"I've certainly never seen you in . . . is that running gear?"

"It is." Lerens turned to Hugo. "You all stretched out and ready to go?"

"Not quite," Hugo said. "Just finishing up with this pesky reporter; you know how they can be."

"You're not even dressed," Lerens said, crossing her arms. "Move it."

Hugo pointed to a bag in the corner. "All right there. Now, if Claudia will turn off the recorder and you ladies will give me some space, I can dig out the spandex."

CHAPTER THIRTY-EIGHT

They started off walking, breaking into a slow jog as they hit the Jardin des Tuileries, weaving their way past the ambling tourists and sidestepping the untethered children who chased after pigeons, and each other. They were starting to breathe a little more heavily when Hugo said, "We have to finish this run before you tell me anything?"

"I was going to run you into the ground, then make you feel better with the good news."

He glanced over. "What good news?"

"First of all, that I'm staying here. I turned down the job in Bordeaux."

Hugo felt a lightness in his step, a wash of relief. "That *is* good news."

"I like it here too much. And there's a lot of baggage waiting for me down there." She wiped a hand over her brow. "Maybe one day, but not now."

"That's great for me and the entire city of Paris. Plus, who would Tom punch if you left?"

"He'd find someone," she said with a laugh. "And in case-related good news, Helen Hancock's lawyer is preparing a proffer today."

"A proffer?"

"It's a document in which Helen Hancock fills in the blanks, provides information through her lawyer—but she doesn't sign it so we can't use it against her in court." Lerens skipped over a small dog that bounded across their path. "It'll help when it comes to sentencing; it's kind of an early admission of guilt."

"That's great news, it really is. She'll admit to everything? The legal scheme, Silva, Maxick . . . ?"

"Eventually she will, yes."

"Fantastic," Hugo said, and gave Lerens a high five.

"Anything specific you want to know?" Lerens asked.

"Yes. The hotel," Hugo said. "Did she pay for her room?"

"No, you were right. Not a penny, all comped by Maxick. How did you know?"

"I didn't. Lucky guess, is all."

"Did you figure out why Maxick hit you over the head?" Lerens asked. She took a sharp left turn, leading them onto the Allée de Diane.

"Yeah, but it's just another guess. I remembered that when Tom came to get me at the hotel, when he thought he'd seen Rick Cofer, she had followed us out of the building. He had burst into her office, and to smooth things over I briefly mentioned that he thought a bad guy from our past might be up to no good in Paris. She must have overheard the details when Tom and I were arguing on the front steps." He smiled guiltily. "I don't know. Maybe I am getting rusty like Tom says. It's possible that she tailed us to the café. When we got there and Cofer was nowhere to be found, things got a little heated between Tom and me outside. I was distracted. An easy target."

"But why hit you?"

"Like planting a second spy camera at the hotel, it was yet another distraction. The fact that she didn't *need* to attack me was the point," Hugo puffed. "You can't keep asking me questions without slowing down a little."

Beside him, Lerens laughed. "It's part of the training regime."

"Whatever. Anyway, by hitting me like that, she sowed a little more confusion and doubt. Maybe she hoped we'd start focusing on Cofer and not Baxter's murder. I guess we'll never really know. That's the frustrating thing about this case. With Baxter, Silva, and Maxick all dead, there are some details we can only speculate about. Maybe that proffer will give us some clearer answers, though. At least I hope so."

"Stretch break?" Lerens asked, and stopped beside a park bench before

Hugo could respond. She lifted a leg and rested her heel on the back of the bench, leaning forward to stretch out her hamstring. "Speaking of this Cofer, why did Tom go to Holland when he said he'd seen him here?"

"He didn't see him—he just thought he did. We both knew it. I just knew it right away. But this is about exorcising demons as much as the threat."

"What do you mean?"

"If Cofer is here in Europe, his ingress and egress point is Amsterdam. Tom knows that city; Cofer doesn't. That means Tom has a huge advantage, and you better believe he'll use every resource at his disposal to find out whether or not Cofer is coming—and, if so, when."

"You don't seem worried," she said.

"I was at first, and maybe still am in the back of my mind. But the man is playing in Tom's backyard and, of course, this is Tom we're talking about. He's dealt with people a hundred times more dangerous than Cofer since their paths crossed, which I'm guessing Cofer has no idea about."

"True. So he'll take care of it in Holland?"

"If he can," Hugo said.

Lerens smiled and switched to stretch her other hamstring. "And that's kind of the main point, isn't it?"

Hugo stood on one leg, stretching his right quad, and looked at her. "Meaning?"

"You told me what happened," she said kindly. "At least, enough that I got the gist of it all. He's taking care of it in Amsterdam because you're here in Paris; you know that, right?"

"You give him too much credit," Hugo said. "He asked me to go with him."

"Yeah, but he's taking care of it anyway, isn't he? I give him credit because sometimes he deserves it, and I think he doesn't want you involved again. He's protecting you after what happened last time."

Hugo stared at her for a moment, a small smile on his lips. "You know, that didn't occur to me."

"He's a good friend, Hugo. He can be a jerk; he will always be a jerk. But he knows what he did, and he's putting this right for you."

"As best he can."

"Precisely. That's about all you can ask of him at this point, isn't it?"

"He could have told me."

Lerens laughed. "Tom? Tell you that he's protecting you? Good one, Hugo."

Hugo nodded, and thought for a moment. "Fair enough. I guess it's OK to be a little deceptive with your friends, if it's for a good cause."

Lerens cocked her head. "I suppose, but why do you say it like that?"

"No reason. . . . But I'm glad you agree." Hugo gave Lerens a smile and put his foot on the back of the bench beside her new running shoe, leaned forward to stretch out his muscles, and quickly undid her shoelace. "Last one to the Place de la Concorde buys lunch."

Without waiting for an answer, he turned and sprinted away from her, his own brand-new sneakers spitting up gravel behind him, his arms pumping, and the warm morning air filling his lungs. A sense of exhilaration propelled him forward, as did the lieutenant's protests behind him, and he strained to put distance between them. He kept running, as fast as he could, even when his lungs started to burn and his legs began to weigh heavy. He felt confident that he could win, but more than that, thrilled that he was in Paris, living here and now running here, the sordid chapters of his recent and not-so-recent past about to be closed forever.

Thanks, Tom, he thought, *I need to appreciate you more.* He angled left, off the path and onto the soft grass, ignoring the lieutenant's renewed cries of "Cheat!" and fixed his eyes on the exit to the Place de la Concorde two hundred yards ahead. *And thanks to you, too, Camille. I'll definitely appreciate today's lunch.*

The lieutenant may have been grateful for him, too, but when she caught up to a panting and bent-over Hugo, she showed her appreciation by kicking him in the rear and promising him a meal of the most inexpensive pizza and the thinnest wine she could find.

"That's OK," Hugo said between breaths. "We're in Paris, Camille. Even the cheap pizza and rough wine here make for a fine lunch." He patted her on the back. "And you can bet I'll be ordering dessert."

ACKNOWLEDGMENTS

My cadre of loyal, super speedy, and wonderful readers: Jennifer Schubert, Nancy Matuszak, Bob Mueller, and JoAnne Bagwell. I truly appreciate your enthusiasm and your honesty. You make my books better, and I am grateful for the time and attention you give them.

Many thanks to Heather Bond at the Austin Spy Shop, for educating me as to the whats and wherefores of some very cool spy cameras and gadgets.

I'm always grateful to the professionals in my life—my agent, Ann Collette, and the amazing people at Seventh Street Books: Dan Mayer, Jill Maxick (the real one!), Jake Bonar, and possibly the best editor on the planet, Jade Zora Scibilia.

And last but first, my wonderful family who continue to support my writing endeavors and forgive my frequent disappearances to the library and coffee shops. I love you.